Tis So Sweet

Catherine Ritch Guess

Foreword by Mark L. Barden

Letters by John Glenn & Imogene Barden

CRM BOOKS

Publishing Hope for Today's Society

Inspirational Books~CDs~Children's Books

CRM BOOKS, P.O. Box 2124, Hendersonville, NC 28793

Visit our Web site at www.ciridmus.com

The Reality Fiction name and logo are registered trademarks of CRM BOOKS.

Printed in the United States of America

ISBN: 1-933341-28-9
LCCN: 2005906140

To

Mark, Barbara

and Christopher

Barden,

who truly have

become my family

Devotedly,
CR?

ACKNOWLEDGMENTS

To Lawrence E. (Larry) Barden, retired United Methodist minister of The Western North Carolina Conference and his wife, Martha; and to their children Mark Barden, Director of Mission/Outreach for The Western North Carolina Conference of The United Methodist Church, and wife Barbara, also a United Methodist Clergy, and their son Christopher; John Barden and his wife Kim; and Anna Barden, also a United Methodist Clergy

To St. Paul United Methodist Church, Goldsboro, North Carolina - which at the time of the action in *'Tis So Sweet* was known as the St. Paul Methodist Episcopal Church, South - and to Boone United Methodist Church, Boone, North Carolina

To Bishop David Kekumba Yemba of the Central Congo Area of The United Methodist Church and his wife, Henriette, and to the Reverend Doctor George Thompson, Charlotte District Superintendent of The Western North Carolina Conference of The United Methodist Church

And lastly to my mother, Corene Ritch, for being my "other eyes" at all hours to make sure this book was completed in time for the 75th wedding anniversary of the Barden's on September 9, 2005

Many thanks to all of you for your help and information, but mostly for your prayers and support for the Lift Up Mine Eyes Series based on the true story of John Glenn and Imogene Barden. Without you, *'Tis So Sweet* and the forthcoming six volumes would still be only a dream.

A Note from the Author

Being an author, besides requiring a life of dedication and commitment to one's art, has its perks in various and sundry ways. One of the ways that has recently made me realize how blessed I am that God called me into this ministry of writing after nearly thirty-five years on an organ bench happened recently on July 12th, 2005 in Denver, Colorado. I was, like many other Christian and inspirational authors, in attendance at the annual Christian Booksellers International Trade Show, along with 10,000 other people from around the globe. The wonderful part about signing books at that event each year is seeing what's new on the market, in addition to your own offerings, and meeting some dear and interesting people.

In my life, I've had many charmed and rare opportunities in which I've met some extremely notable characters (thus all the books!), but on that night – after having seen the main characters for two days throughout the course of the show – I saw the premiere screening of *End of the Spear*, a movie coming out in January 2006. The movie, a true story, is based on the book by the same title which grows out of the hugely publicized story from 1956 of the five missionaries who were killed in Ecuador exactly fifty years ago this coming January.

That in itself was quite a phenomenon for me, for I was in the midst of the final proofs of *'Tis So Sweet*, the first book in my Lift Up Mine Eyes Series based on real-life missionaries from the Belgian Congo in the 1920's – 30's. Because these two missionaries are the grandparents of one of my dearest friends, whose family I felt I knew as my own through the countless stories they'd shared with me during the past two years of research, the effect of the movie left me feeling like John Newton when he penned, "'twas blind but now I see." As I watched the showing of *End of the Spear* that evening, I saw that although it took place in a different part of the world, it dealt with missionaries who worked with natives whereby there were many, many differences – the largest one being communication.

The story I had written became suddenly real to me through the story of those five missionary families on which *End of the Spear* was based. But that was not the most intriguing factor. For the thing about that evening in Denver was not as much the movie – which I thought was incredible and, without a doubt, one of the best movies I'd ever seen – as it was the fact that I was seated right in front of the families of the survivors of those five missionaries who had been speared on January 6th of 1956, a day that we Christians celebrate as Epiphany. The irony catapulted me into life from their side.

In addition to all those family members was Mincaye, a native of the Waodani tribe who took part in the spearing of the missionaries – who is now Christian and very much involved with the spread of Christianity in his native land – and Louie Leonardo, the actor who portrays him in the film. There were also the people who have financially backed this movie, which has taken seven years to complete, the producers, engineers and marketing teams, along with booksellers, authors, recording artists and speakers from around the world who work in the field of Christian mission through their gifts and talents.

When, in the theater lobby following the private screening, I had a chance to speak at length to the children of the missionaries, particularly Steve Saint who was most instrumental in this movie and book, Mincaye and Louie Leonardo, I was struck the hardest I had ever been of how we are all in this big wide world together in the ministry of spreading the Gospel. It also struck me at the enormity of the gift that John Glenn and Imogene Barden had given in their years of service in the Belgian Congo.

And mostly, it left me feeling more humbled and blessed than I can express that God had not only allowed, but chosen, me to be a small part of that task, if no more than in telling the Barden's story. Although I've been fortunate to teach in foreign lands, the time and energy I've spent is nothing compared to the years and lives that have been given by so many in His name.

It was not until I returned home from Denver that I discovered that Elisabeth Elliot, one of the missionaries' wives from that startling episode in 1956, lived and worked in Waxhaw, North Carolina, approximately fifteen miles from where I had lived for a large portion of my life and now five minutes from the home of my sons. She is known as "Grandma Elisabeth" to one of my best friends whose parents had served as Wycliffe missionaries in later years with Mrs. Elliot. Again, I was amazed at how God had wrapped me in the fullness of such a rich heritage of so many that had served in such mighty ways.

As you read *'Tis So Sweet*, the first title in my seven volume Lift Up Mine Eyes Series, I hope that you will reflect on the lives of "Glenn and 'Gene" as they compare to your own lives, and that perhaps you will discover a way that you, like them and others who are a part of the Great Commission, can touch the lives of those around you. Please know that with the purchase of this book, a part of the proceeds goes to the John Glenn and Imogene Barden Scholarship Fund to provide financial assistance for persons from the mountains of North Carolina who are going into ministry and Christian education.

May this book, and the volumes of my Lift Up Mine Eyes Series that follow, be for you a most blessed read and may you come to know and love the Barden's as much as I have.

- - CR?

Foreword

As I write these words sitting at the old portable writing desk that belonged to my dear and devoted grandfather, memories from the past... his past... seem to flow from its deep recesses and into my soul. Memories from a lonesome Methodist missionary deep in the heart of Africa searching his heart for the one true love that patiently awaited his return to the United States.

From this desk beginning in 1926, my grandfather, John Glenn Barden, a missionary having just arrived in the Belgian Congo (now Democratic Republic of Congo), began and nurtured an amazing relationship by corresponding with a special friend, Imogene ('Gene) Barrett, whom he had left behind in Goldsboro, North Carolina. By today's lifestyle, it was an unlikely way to begin a lasting and loving relationship that would lead to 56 years of marriage and an incredible journey through life. But the letters they left behind reveal a love transcendent of close physical proximity that could travel and endure through time and space

Typically, it would take three months for a letter to travel from the Methodist mission station at Wembo Nyama to a post office in eastern North Carolina. And it would take another three months for a response to arrive back at the mission station. When the mail would arrive once a week, Glenn eagerly yearned for a letter to be in the mailbag from 'Gene. Despite the distance, two young souls were brought together in such a way, that when Glenn returned home in 1930, he married the love of his life and devoted the rest of his days to her.

From the little Methodist Church in Stantonsburg, North Carolina where my grandparents were married on September 9, 1930, the groom and his new bride left their beloved homeland to minister together as missionaries among the Otetela people in central Congo. During their tenure, they would both teach and learn from a remarkable people who endeared themselves to the Barden family through generations even to this day.

I traveled with my father to his birthplace in Wembo Nyama in 1998. From the time the mission pilot welcomed him home as the small plane touched down on a landing strip, to the throng of excited villagers who had prepared a welcome fit for royalty, the memories of my grandparents came to life before me in a way that could never have been conveyed solely through their writings or stories. I experienced life much like they experienced it in the 1930s in central Africa. I smelled the smells of sweet flowers, heard the songs of the birds, saw the grand vista of the savannah below Wembo Nyama, felt the velvety dew on the jungle foliage and tasted the native foods. Life in the Congo took on a new meaning for me.

When I returned home, I read the letters that provide the basis for this novel. Once again new life sprang forth from the pages. With fascination, I read the accounts of missionary life in Africa and saw how the love between two young persons who barely knew one another grew with each letter written.

I knew that one day their story must be told for it is one of true devotion that would inspire the hearts of both those who knew my grandparents and readers who would meet them for the first time by reading the letters.

In this book of reality fiction, Catherine Ritch Guess genuinely captures the essence of my grandparents through the characters of Glenn and 'Gene Edgerton. Most of the events are based on something that actually happened. Others are purely fiction. Some are a mixture of both. It will remain a mystery, known only to the author, as to what is real and what is not!

This story is not so much a historical account of my grandparents' lives but rather a story of a love that blossomed despite the fact that a great ocean and thousands of miles separated them. Their love transcended the months between letters and replies. It grew stronger with each carefully chosen word. Their love for each other was far more than an emotion; it was truly a life-long devotion to one another.

Years after their marriage and hundreds of letters, the complimentary closing at the end of each of their letters was "Devotedly." That is how I remember my grandparents: two persons who were totally devoted to one another. Despite illnesses, hard times, uncertain futures and the typical trials and tribulations of life that can strain a marriage, they remained devoted to one another unlike any other couple I've known. Their love for each other taught me that a deeper form of love could be found in true devotion to one's spouse.

May the love of my grandparents leap from these pages to touch your heart with the same warmth and devotion that gave them a remarkable life together.

Mark L. Barden
September 9, 2005
On the 75th anniversary of the marriage of Dr. John Glenn Barden and Imogene Barrett Barden

Tis So Sweet

Friday morning

Dear Jim,

First of all we thank you for your telegram and how very much I appreciated it. It was so very very thoughtful of you to send it, especially as I did not get to see you again. I did hate to come away without just one more word for with you. But we can't always have just exactly what we want—

a very good time—I got on my sailing the first of second day out and haven't from seasick at all. I'm so thankful because those who were looks so miserably un-comfortable. It wasn't in an awful feeling however. I may get it good case of it on this second lap of the voyage or before I reach my destination, but I hope am pray that I shall not.

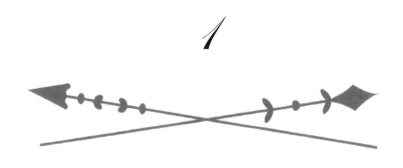

On Board S. S. Belgenland
Friday night, June 4ᵗʰ, 1926

Dear 'Gene,

First let me thank you for your telegram and tell you how very much I appreciated it. It was so very, very thoughtful of you to send it, especially as I did not get to see you again. I did hate to come away without just one more word with you. But we can't always have just exactly what we want all the time. It will be such a long time, though, before I shall see your cunning smile again.

Of course you have heard all about the departure and all that took place at the train that night. It was so thoughtful of them to write me those fine letters. They did me so much good after I got out to sea and read them.

The weather has been stormy practically the entire

voyage and we have yet to have our first fair sunset. But I wish you could have seen the one this evening. The sun was entirely hidden by clouds, but near the horizon the rays had broken through and looked like a huge fan with the outer edge dipped into the water. Here and there across the sky the dark clouds were tinted with pink. I wish you could have been here to enjoy it with me.

In spite of all the stormy weather, I've had a very good time. I got on my sea legs the first or second day out and haven't been seasick at all. I'm so thankful because those who were look so miserably uncomfortable. It must be an awful feeling. However, I may get a good case of it on the second lap of the voyage or before I reach my destination, but I hope and pray that I shall not.

'Gene, I'm very sorry that I did not have an opportunity of coming to know you better. I was favored with seeing you only a few times, but they were most pleasant indeed. I think the young people of St. Paul Methodist Church are so very fortunate to have you come and live and work among them.

It surely has seemed good to have almost nothing to do on board. To eat, sleep, read, write or play at one's desire is quite different from a fixed schedule of steady work. I surely have done my share of all of it and I'm just feeling great.

I'm traveling with Mr. and Mrs. Wm. DeRuiter who are going to the same station as I am. I did not know about them until I reached New York City. They have been married but a month and at times I almost wish that I had a bride along. We shall meet Bro. and Mrs. Stiltz in Antwerp when we land there Monday.

You have seen, I'm sure, the short letter I wrote Brother Daniel about my ordination. It was such an impressive moment to me. Bishop Cannon ordained both DeRuiter and me. The only witnesses were Mrs. DeRuiter and Dr. Sheffey who came up to give us a final send-off with Bishop Cannon. But there in Room 1056 of the Prince George Hotel, God was so very present that one could feel the very nearness of Him. And when Bishop Cannon placed his hands on my head and ordained and commissioned us, it seemed that our Father placed His hands on my head also. Oh that I may be given the grace to live up to all the responsibilities which come with being a minister of God. I hope that in whatever I may do God may have a hand and direct me. I know He has called me to go, and I have the faith that "I shall abide under the shadow of the Almighty."

This is my first voyage across the Atlantic, and although storms have beset our path, I have not been afraid. I did have the faith that God would guide us safely through – "Tis so sweet to trust in Jesus."

I have made many acquaintances since coming on board and they have made my passage pleasant. I have been interested too in observing the different types of people who are traveling. I have met a very interesting young man who has been an employee of the British government and located in Singapore with work also in the island of Borneo. He has told me so very many interesting things about the life and *natives out there. Their life is more primitive than that of the natives in the Congo. I just know my work is going to be great.*

Now be sure to pray for me and write whenever you can.

A friend in His Service,
Glenn

John Glenn Edgerton was the epitome of a true southern gentleman. Called "Glenn," his mild-mannered demeanor was backed by a no-nonsense way of living. He was a tall man with bright red hair and a carefully groomed mustache that gave him the appearance of the fine young man he was. His gentle blue gray eyes expressed both a seriousness of spirit and a caring attitude. Glenn was extraordinarily precise and attentive to every detail of the way he looked. It was extremely important to him that he both looked and lived the life of a proper gentleman.

Now, as he sat at the small wooden counter in his second-class room on the second evening of his trans-Atlantic voyage, he read over the letter he had just composed to make sure it was befitting of his high standards and mannerisms. He wanted to make sure that it showed his pleasure at receiving a telegram, especially from someone who also was acting in God's service and could have somewhat of an understanding of what he was setting out to do. But at the same time, Glenn didn't want to sound overly friendly, as he was aware of her known courtship with Sonny Ledford, a young fellow and a dear friend from his hometown.

Eugenia May Bennett, who was known as 'Gene and had signed her telegram to him as such, had been recently hired by his home church of Saint Paul Methodist in Goldsboro, North Carolina, as the Assistant to the Pastor. Although she was to work primarily with the children and youth of the church, she also served as the secretary, which meant that on the evening of Glenn's departure, she was called away to be a substitute delegate for a district meeting.

The secretarial position meant that she was probably the one to have opened his letter informing the St. Paul congregation about his ordination, which prompted her to send the congratulatory telegram that doubled as an apology for having to rush from his farewell celebration at the train station. Not to mention that she felt badly that Glenn knew she had been transported to the district meeting, for which she was responsible for taking notes, by way of Mr. Ledford.

Glenn had been ecstatic that his church had the foresight to recognize the need for someone to work with the children and youth. His heart also felt the desire to work with the children and youth, but with those in a foreign land. That was what made the telegram so special for it came from someone who was of the same heart and mind as he, someone who understood his call into the ministry. He had been in charge of the boys at the church prior to his departure so he felt most confident that 'Gene would find someone equally as interested in their well-being as he had been to work with them.

He read over the telegram again to make sure that he had addressed all of 'Gene's comments and to get a feel of what he felt comfortable sharing with her. Glenn thought about whether to add his surname to the signature, but then decided that she would surely know from whom it was sent. *Besides*, he concluded, *if she went to the trouble of sending the telegram, she knows me well enough to be on a first-name basis.*

The letters from his congregation were beside his right hand. Glenn momentarily left the letter he'd written to 'Gene as he read through all of them again. He liked the letters; he could already tell that they were a sense of comfort to him in this voyage that would take four days from New York to Southampton, England. From there he would travel to Antwerp, Belgium and on to the winding way that led to Wembo Nyama in the Belgian Congo of Africa. Images of faces from home, most of them faces he had known since his first recollections of a church family, came to him as he read the complimentary closing and signature at the bottom of each letter.

No, the surname won't be necessary, he definitely decided.

As he went back on deck to enjoy the night sky, Glenn said a prayer of thankfulness that a goodly number of the members of St. Paul Methodist Church had shown up at the train station for his departure, each one of them bearing a letter of well wishes for his voyage. They had given him a royal send-off full of pride for their "son" who had accepted a call to be a missionary in the Belgian Congo of Africa. *And how kind indeed it was for Miss Bennett to send a telegram since she was unable to stay for the train's departure. Thank you, God, for sending such a fine young woman to St. Paul to carry on Your work.*

Glenn looked up at the stars against the velvet black sky. *How humbling it is to know that you'll be missed and that so many are praying for your journey.*

That thought took him back to his years of growing up on the Sunnybrook Farm back in Goldsboro. The white farmhouse was a beautiful Victorian-style with a wrap-around porch that was perfect for sitting on in the evenings. After the death of his mother, Papa had remarried, and his family of three siblings had grown to nine over the years. Since he was one of the first set of children, it seemed that a great deal of the work fell on him, so in that respect, he didn't fear the difficulties of the tasks that would be thrown at him at the mission.

He was aware that the boarding situation would be a far cry from the large farmhouse, and even the second-class room on the ship, but that was of no consequence to the young missionary. Glenn was not expecting an easy task; that had been a part of the commitment in accepting his call.

His biggest concern was the language barrier and his ability to work through traditions and prejudices, but again, he had faith that God would be with him in all of his adjustments and endeavors. Various passages of scripture ran through his head, many of them the same ones he had used in the teaching of his boys' class back at St. Paul. He focused on the power of the moment from his ordination in that New York hotel room and asked that God allow that same fervor to follow him in all of his steps forward.

There was no doubt that he would miss his family and his friends, and most of all those boys to whom he had become a mentor. *But they, like me, will find the change to be a blessed one.*

Glenn closed his eyes as he held onto the rail of the deck and let his body feel the lilt of the water's wake as he hummed *'Tis So Sweet to Trust in Jesus.*

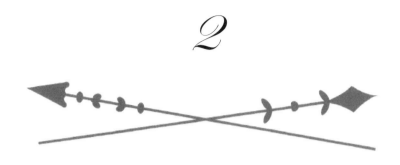

2

"Lydia Mason, I hope this home proves to be everything you've ever dreamed of." Ward Mason, who had carried his wife of twenty-seven years across the threshold, put her down so that she could stand up, but continued to hold onto her as he planted a kiss firmly on her lips. "And more!" he added, kissing her again with a love that had truly grown sweeter with each day of their marriage, even through all the struggles and disagreements, which had been relatively few.

"Oh, Ward, do you have any idea how long I've dreamed of this home?"

"As a matter of fact, I do. It was since the day that we were married. I know how much your own little nest meant to you, but it seemed so impractical with the moves incurred by my teaching jobs. The faculty apartments on the various campuses served us well during those years, but now that I've been named Professor of Education at Appalachian State University, we should be settled here for as long as you wish. I know it's not exactly the white picket fence style that you dreamed about, but . . . ,"

"It's perfect," Lydia interrupted. "I knew from the day we saw it sitting atop this hill that it was the house for us. There's such a charm about it. I'm thrilled that you wanted this one, too."

"What more could I want? It's within walking distance of my office, it's convenient to shopping and restaurants, the view is great, and it came furnished. It was a most practical and logical choice. I only hope that you'll love it just as much a year from now as you do this minute."

"I don't think there's any doubt of that," she smiled. "Come outside with me. I want to show you what I found this morning while you were getting settled into your office."

Ward followed Lydia out to the corner of the front yard. He took his hands and pulled away the weeds from around a large overgrown rhododendron bush where she pointed, revealing an old wooden sign that had a faded painting and green letters, barely still readable, with the words "The Rhododendron."

"The people who used to live here must have named the place. I know a lot of the mountain vacation homes had names, but this was a year-round residence."

"Well, it certainly is fitting," he acknowledged, pointing to all the rhododendrons in the yard hidden in the shade of the overgrown trees. "How would you like it if I took this sign and gave it a fresh face?"

"I'd love that, but how are you going to find time to do that with classes starting in a couple of days and all the meetings you have?"

"For you, I'll make time. I've promised you this home for a long time, twenty-seven years to be exact, and I want it to be perfect for you."

His warm hazel eyes stared down into the rich brown eyes of his wife. Ward's light brown hair was just beginning to show flecks of gray trying to peek out around the edges. His average height and lean shape, kept through years of living within walking distance of his jobs, showed that he tried to take good care of himself. He had a face that spoke comfort, not only to his wife, but to all the students to whom he had taught, making him much more of a mentor rather than simply a teacher. It was that quality which served as the foremost of his attributes that caused him to be chosen over the numerous other applicants vying for his new position.

Their marriage had begun with Lydia planning to be a stay-at-home mom. That was her one ambition in life. However, nature did not allow for her dream to be a reality. Because she'd not planned to be a part of the work force, she didn't go to college after her high school graduation. Instead, she got a job at the corner drug store on Main Street of her small town where she continued to work and save until Ward's graduation.

They had been high school sweethearts, but had not actually begun to date until the prom of their junior year. Ward was so timid that it took him that long to build the courage to ask Lydia out, even though he had been enamored with the richness of her sable brown hair and dark eyes from the first day of tenth grade when they sat across the aisle from each other in biology class. Until that sophomore year, he had hated assigned seats.

However, once he looked into those endearing eyes, he prayed that the biology teacher was not one of those instructors that changed seating assignments every three or four weeks.

It was that day of the frog dissecting episode when his heart knew that Lydia was the girl for him. He wanted to provide and care for her for the rest of his life. Her 5'5" height seemed the perfect compliment for her to gaze into his eyes, which she did that day as she softly whispered, "I don't think I can do this."

After that, they walked together to most of their classes, they met at the ball games and sat together and even held hands occasionally, but Ward was so shy that he'd clam up every time he tried to ask her out. In fact, Lydia had broached the subject of the prom by asking him if he were going. Instead of him asking her to go, his response, was "Yes, with you." He'd fumbled over his words once they were out, as she tried not to giggle uncontrollably, and then added, "that is, if you're not going with anyone else."

She answered with, "Ward Mason, I thought you'd never ask. I bought my dress days ago."

Such began a relationship that had made them nearly inseparable. Even so, there was nothing spectacular about their marriage – at least if you asked Lydia. It certainly was not a marriage of convenience. The inability, which at first seemed horrific, to have children had served to bring them closer together since there were never little ones bidding for their time. But, in Lydia's mind, there was no "flame" that burned wildly between them. It was, sadly, what she feared too many people in her age bracket had come to know as "comfortable."

She was definitely in a comfort zone. There was no way that Ward would leave her, even though he was in contact with younger and attractive women day in and day out. *He'd never muster up the courage to ask anyone else out*, she reasoned when he first began his teaching career. Lydia never gave him cause to want to leave her, nor had he with her. They had truly grown together, yet she wondered secretly if there wasn't something missing.

The subject had never been discussed for she didn't want Ward to think she was unhappy; she wasn't that at all. It was simply that she wanted a little something more, although she was not sure herself what that was. And she didn't dare mention her concern, which in itself was far too strong a word for what she sensed, to anyone else for everyone connected to them saw Mr. and Mrs. Ward Mason as the perfect couple.

Except that we don't have our own little abode, she'd think every time someone mentioned their envious situation.

Ward had never asked Lydia to wait for him while he went away to work on his undergraduate degree. But then, there was a bond, something akin to an unspoken trust between them that made him understand that she would be there the day he finished, which she was. Neither of them seemed to understand that what they possessed with each other was, in reality, a very rare gift indeed.

He thought of her while he was away at college and tried to write to her at least once a week; he looked forward to her letters in return. Ward was typically able to get home once a month, when they'd go to a movie or have dinner at one of the local dives.

It wasn't until Ward's senior year, when graduation was in sight, that he surprised Lydia by coming home unexpectedly one weekend and took her to the fancy steak house - to which neither they nor their families had ever been - and popped the question.

Lydia, who gladly accepted, had begun to wonder if that question, like the one of the prom, was also going to have to be generated by her own devises. They left the wedding date open for Ward wanted to be sure he had a job and could take care of a wife. Her career of working outside the home did not begin until he re-entered an institution of higher learning to earn a Master's and then his Ph.D. That was when she became a teacher's aid.

The work never bothered her for it gave her the children to love that she had never been able to call her own. Plus she was so elated to see how sincerely Ward appreciated her efforts in helping him to secure a better job that she not once begrudged becoming a part of the work force.

Now, as she watched him retreat, aged sign in hand, to the garage, those years became precious memories as she fell in love with him all over again. The tenderness in his eyes was the very same as it was that day in sophomore biology class.

The Rhododendron sat atop a hill on Howard Street in Boone, North Carolina, adjacent to Appalachian State University – ASU, once known as Appalachian State Teacher's College. It was a white two-story house with forest green shutters that had been vacant for some time, causing it to need the special attention of someone who could love and nurture it. Lydia had seen the underlying beauty in it immediately, while Ward had seen the practicality of it. Both of them agreed that it was a most suitable house for them.

It had a steep set of steps coming up from the sidewalk, and a sharply inclined driveway that led to a garage attached to the back of the house. At one time, there had been a structure of four apartments next to the house, but they had been torn down in years past leaving a comfortably terraced yard for benches, flower gardens and a hammock.

Nestled in the midst of the Appalachian Mountains, Boone was a college town that had, especially in the past four decades, grown vastly past overflowing. Nearby ski lodges added to the crowds that swarmed to the area during the winter months, and attractions such as the outdoor drama, *Horn in the West*, depicting Daniel Boone's life during the Revolutionary War, and cooler climates brought tourists throughout the summers. The autumns were some of the most spectacular in the country, promising an annual array of colorful leaves in every direction. Added to the tradition of incredibly delicious food served family style at Daniel Boone Inn, which sat practically beside The Rhododendron, there was never a time when streets weren't full of traffic and life did not abound.

That had been one of the drawing factors for Ward and Lydia Mason when he applied for the recent opening of Professor of Education. Besides the fact that the school was a fine institution in many areas of study, the couple, never being able to have children of their own, loved the college atmosphere. Lydia had attributed that to the fact that, for most students, adolescent and young adult years typically brought clashes with parents, but she and Ward could show love and compassion for them because it was much easier when you didn't have to live with them or pay their tuition bills.

She had continued to work as a teacher's aid until the move to Boone. That had been a satisfying job in that it gave Lydia so much interaction with children. And without children of her own, she felt that she was better able to give love and acceptance to some children who didn't get it at home. Her attitude became an inspiration to all the elementary students and other teachers. "I may be the only smile these children see every day," she'd offered as an acceptance for a special award she received when she left her job after Ward landed the position at ASU.

Now, she felt a burning desire to be a positive influence on the life of some college student who needed that same kind of love and acceptance. "Children never outgrow that need, no matter how old they are," she'd told the principal at the school when she left.

"Lydia Ward, you see and hear things in situations like I've never seen in another teacher," the principal had responded. "You certainly have a knack for seeing past the outer layer, for discovering what makes one tick, for sensing what's on the inside. Know that you'll be missed, but that we all wish you well in your journey."

Those words were special to her. They became etched in her heart.

3

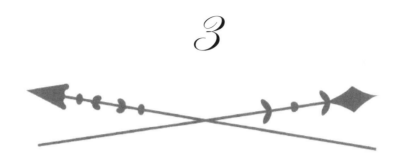

Eugenia May Bennett sat at her desk and looked at the letter that the postman had just delivered to her. The same letter that had been undeliverable to Rev. John Glenn Edgerton on board the S. S. Belgenland. It sat on her desk at the St. Paul Methodist Church, where she was unable to take her eyes off of it.

"Unable," she said aloud as she looked gloomly down at the envelope that bore the words UNABLE TO DELIVER in bright blue letters with NOT ON BOARD over to the side.

There were several dates ranging from June 5th through August 28th, stamped on the envelope for the letter that had been written on May 28th, 1926.

"Why?" she asked. "And I had even been so precise as to handwrite the letter two times and then type it so that there would be no mistakes. I wanted him to see how efficient I could be, perhaps for later reference."

'Gene, as she was called, had been careful to type explicit

instructions on the front of the envelope to make sure that if the S. S. Belgenland had sailed and missed the letter, it would be waiting for Rev. Edgerton when he arrived in Antwerp on his way to Africa. "Please forward if necessary to Methodist Mission, M.E. Church, South, Antwerp, Belgium," she read aloud.

All they had to do was follow the directions I gave them and it would be in his possession right now. Now he doesn't even know that I wrote him a letter.

She opened her center desk drawer and pulled out the postcard that she had hidden underneath several other items. "At least he got the telegram that I sent him in New York before the departure of the ship," 'Gene resolved as she read his message of appreciation on the back of the card. She flipped it over to see the colorful picture of Hotel Seville that was across Fifth Avenue from the Marble Collegiate Church and beside The Little Church Around the Corner.

A smile broke through the forlorn sense of regret that was written all over her face as she gazed at the two sanctuaries on the front of the card. "Little?" 'Gene snickered. "Compared to St. Paul, it looks like a European cathedral."

The laughter stopped. "We may be small, but there can't be any more spirit than we have here. And there's not a church anywhere that could be more proud or supportive of one of their own going out into the world in the role of a missionary."

Rev. J. M. Daniel walked into the office and looked around. "I thought I heard you talking to someone."

'Gene was trying to think of an excuse for why she was raving to herself when the "Preacher in Charge" saw the letter laying on her desk.

"I see that Glenn didn't get your letter."

"No, he didn't." She gave a sigh that said more than any words she could have offered. "I felt badly in that as my position as Assistant to the Pastor, I was unable to be there on that Tuesday when we sent Rev. Edgerton off. I didn't even have a letter in the stack that went to the train station for the surprise "send-off" that the church gave him."

"I'm sure that this is totally work related and that there is no personal interest in Glenn whatsoever."

A hint of a blush shaded 'Gene's face as Rev. Daniel smiled and walked back toward his office. "You know, if I wouldn't have had to go on the search again to find an assistant for St. Paul, I'd have been most delighted to have allowed Glenn to borrow you for a few weeks as his personal secretary. But I'm afraid you would not have returned and we'd be without again."

She heard the preacher's door shut and immediately took the letter opener inside her drawer and carefully slit underneath the edge of the envelope's tab. "All those letters he got and not one is from me." 'Gene's whisper sounded more like an audible pout.

"How am I to explain why I didn't write sooner when it will take another three months for a letter to get to him?" She pulled the paper out of the envelope and unfolded it, again using great care not to mess it up. *Who knows? I might want to resend this one with a note of explanation of why he didn't get it earlier. I wouldn't want him to lose interest.*

'Gene looked down at the impressive church letterhead

that bore her name at the top. *At least I don't have to worry about him finding someone else over there.* She tried to convince herself that three and a half years was not such a long time.

Rev. Daniel came back out of his office, causing her to quickly place the letter under a stack of papers. In his hand he carried a letter and a photo of a very attractive young woman who stood poised in a nurse's uniform. "It appears that one of my colleagues has just said good-bye to his daughter, a Miss Armstrong, who has also left to go to the Congo. Why don't you send this photo to Glenn with a note telling him to keep an eye out for her? Who knows, perhaps they'll run into each other at annual meetings while out there?"

One glance at the picture told 'Gene that she'd rather *not* send it to Glenn. *What was that I just said about him meeting someone else while there?* Suddenly the fact that there were nurses and other teachers, single women, who had also followed their call to Africa became very real to her.

That does it, she decided as she watched Rev. Daniel again retreat to his office. *This letter is going out with another one to let him know that we haven't forgotten him here at St. Paul. I have to make sure that he doesn't forgot about the ones he left behind.*

'Gene pulled the letter back out from under the papers where she had stuffed it and began to read, dictating the next one in her mind as she went.

St. Paul Methodist Episcopal Church, South

200 JOHN STREET, SOUTH

GOLDSBORO, N. C.

REV. J. M. DANIEL
PREACHER IN CHARGE
204 JOHN STREET, SOUTH

M. J. BEST
CHAIRMAN OF BOARD
MISS IMOGENE BARRETT
ASSISTANT TO PASTOR

May 28, 1926.

Dear Glenn:-

I am so sorry that I did not see you again before you
left, but at the last minute I found it almost necessary to
go to the District Conference at Ocracoke as a substitute
delegate. I thought of you Tuesday night when you were leaving
the "Old North State" to be gone for three and a half years,
and was sorry that I could not be one of the many who gave
you such a royal "send-off". I didn't even have a letter in
the lot that was so beautifully bound with Buttie's possessions!
However, this is not intended to be one of the farewell letters.

I am sending you a clipping from Wednesday's "News and
Observer". Probably your family or some friend has sent you
one already, - if so, pardon this. Am sure you saw the write-up
in the local papers Saturday and Sunday.

You did not leave a list of the _____ ____
periodicals you want sent to you. Y_____ so that
the subscriptions can be sent _____ be
interested in clippings, _____ be
glad to include them_____ ____res
of yours, the _____ hem
to you, kee_____
I would_____

UNABLE TO DELIVER

NOT ON BOARD M. M. CO.

Rev. John Glenn Barden
New York City
S. S. _____   Red Star Line

AUG 28 1926

Please forward if necessary, M. E. ___ Mission,
Antwerp, Belgium

_____ of one of
_____ impressive to all
_____ so insignificant and
_____ of difference in the sac-
_____ es in comparing the work of each
_____ though I couldn't go to Africa as
_____ nce) or your private secretary, I am happy
_____ Goldsboro and maybe I will surprise everybody
_____ really do something worth while.

May 28, 1926

Dear Glenn,

     I am so sorry that I did not see you again before you left, but at the last minute I found it necessary to go to the District Conference at Ocracoke as a substitute delegate. I thought of you Tuesday night when you were leaving the "Old North State" to be gone for three and a half years, and was sorry that I could not be one of the many who gave you such a royal "send-off". I didn't even have a letter in the lot that was so beautifully bound with Sonny's possessions! However, this is not intended to be one of the farewell letters.

     I am sending you a clipping from Wednesday's "News and Observer". Probably your family or some friend has sent you one already - if so, pardon this. Am sure you saw the write-up in the local papers Saturday and Sunday.

     You did not leave a list of the magazines and other periodicals you want sent to you. You might send the list so that the subscriptions can be sent in immediately. If you should be interested in clippings, etc., I am sure the Leaguers would be glad to include them in letters. By the way, I have two pictures of yours, the two you gave me for the press. Shall I send them to you, keep them, or what? I can't possibly think of a soul I would like to have them. Let me know.

     I received your card this morning and was really surprised to hear from you so soon. I greatly appreciated it. However, our church in this little city hopes to keep in constant touch with you and your work while you are away for

I believe the people of this community rightfully expect great things of you with your qualifications and sunny disposition. I think you have proved to us in many ways that you are thoroughly capable of handling the forces of the great task that has been assigned to you in stimulating, nourishing, and elevating the real Christian life of each individual with whom you come in contact in your educational work.

The farewell service and later the departure of one of the choicest young men from among us was very impressive to all who attended. It made me, personally, feel so _insignificant_ and _unimportant_ to think of the degrees of difference in the sacrifices, difficulties, and efforts in comparing the work of each of us. But never mind! Even though I couldn't go to Africa as your assistant (hindrance) or your private secretary, I am happy in my work over in Goldsboro and maybe I will surprise everybody some day and really do something worthwhile.

If at any time you need the help of the young people of our church just let us know and I am sure the call will be answered. We are just hoping that the best of your past will be the worst of your future, and that the very best of everything will come to you.

With kindest regards, and very best wishes for a long life of service, I am

Very sincerely,
Eugenia May Bennett

Eugenia May Bennett, 'Gene to all her friends and family, often teasingly referred to herself as "well-padded." Although she inherited her father's stocky build, she still exuded a naturally classic sense of beauty. Her chestnut brown hair graced her round face that featured a cute pug nose. With skin as smooth as silk, the red rouge on her cheeks made them seem like rose petals. The lipstick she often wore made her already ruby red lips glisten like jewels, especially when she gave a broad smile or hearty laugh. The sparkle in her brown eyes added an aura of excitement and a bit of mischievousness to her radiant face.

To everyone who knew her, 'Gene was "quite a gal." She had an outgoing personality that could bring sunshine into anybody's day.

A well-educated woman for her era, she had recently completed her degree at Trinity College in Durham, North Carolina. Its name had changed at the beginning of her last year to Duke University, making her a member of the first graduating class of the prestigious private school of higher learning.

Her degree was in English with a double minor in education and religious education. Now that she was out of school, she returned to her Oak Forest Plantation home near Farmville, North Carolina, a small town in the eastern part of the state, to find her way in life.

Both of 'Gene's parents had died when she was only a

young girl. After that time, her Uncle John, a prominent doctor in nearby Greenville, and his wife Anna, accepted responsibility of running the family farm – in addition to continuing the medical practice – thereby moving to Oak Forest Plantation with their own children where they could raise both families. They made sure that 'Gene, as well as her brother and two sisters had a fine life, later sending all of them to college insuring them of a bright future.

Unlike her siblings, 'Gene wanted to work in a church setting. To look at the picture from her senior yearbook, it would be difficult to see that here was a woman whose life revolved around her church. Her love of music and the arts had gotten her a gig in a dance band, playing the piano, while she was still a college student. That was how she earned her extra dollars for spending money. On Sundays, she would be at the chapel services enthralled by the sounds of the huge pipe organ and the glorious hymns and music of the masters.

Her short bobbed hairstyle and designer clothes made it hard to differentiate between whether Miss Eugenia May Bennett was a full-fledged "flapper" of the Roaring Twenties, or simply a product of her era. Whichever was the case, she was a tease to the hilt and enjoyed life and all it had to offer immensely. She was a far cry from the typical female student of Christian education who, sometimes quite erroneously, had been stereotyped as quite plump and certainly "frumpy."

There was no lack of laughter where she was concerned, yet her heart was as pure and full of love for humankind as any in the hallowed walls of the noted Methodist-related university. 'Gene took her work most seriously and had a heart for all of the church's children and youth - and later with school students - many of whom had not been afforded the same luxuries of life as she had. Teaching came naturally to her and in that realm, she saw it her bounden duty to go beyond the textbook, or the Sunday School lesson guide, and also give her pupils a knowledge of manners and to instill a sense of confidence that would allow them to find their stations in life – no matter their backgrounds.

After her college graduation, 'Gene heard through the *North Carolina Christian Advocate* – a newspaper for all the Methodist churches and organizations of both the North Carolina and the Western North Carolina Conferences – about a job opening in Goldsboro, a town approximately thirty miles southwest of Farmville – for a position of Assistant to the Pastor. She was quick to apply for it since it was in her same North Carolina Conference and was not too far away from home. It would allow her to be close enough to do graduate work at Carolina, should she decide to do so, at some point down the road.

Even in light of her abundant lifestyle and the fact that she adored her Uncle John and that she had grown up in a large two-story plantation house, white with majestic columns, she was anxious to get out into the "big wide world" and find her own way.

She knew that would mean a significant difference in the pampered lifestyle to which she had become accustomed. *But dorm life has surely prepared me for a lower station in life than that of Oak Forest Plantation.*

'Gene had enough common sense to know that life was

not all peaches and cream. *And silver, china and fine linens!* she'd laugh to herself every time she pondered moving out on her own and facing the real world. In spite of the life she'd lived with her brother, two sisters and Uncle John and Aunt Anna, she was a ball of spunk that was ready to face any dilemma that life threw at her.

One of 'Gene's favorite activities was her participation in the Women's Society of Christian Service — WSCS for short — an organization of women who fervently met and prayed for the missionaries around the world. They did various projects to support the missions in their own communities, as well as in foreign lands. The thing that she loved most was learning about the various individuals who had committed themselves to training and then actually pursued a life of spreading the Gospel on uncharted soil. To her, that was indeed a most highly respected and revered adventure.

"There's a letter for you here, 'Gene," called Prissy. "It's postmarked from Goldsboro."

'Gene came flitting down the stairs from her room where she was catching up on writing letters to her school friends, many of them who were already finding employment in teaching fields and others who were becoming engaged or getting married. She thanked her older sister and took the letter, ripping it open.

"Dear Miss Bennett," she read, "our committee at St. Paul Methodist Church in Goldsboro, North Carolina, has looked at your application and resume and would like to speak with you in two weeks. We would like to consider you further for our new position of Assistant to the Pastor.

"Would it be possible for you to arrange to be here for the service on the first Sunday in Febuary and meet with our committee following worship? One of our members, Mrs. Beulah G. Effingham has volunteered to have us to her house for lunch.

Sincerely,

Mr. J.M. Daniel, Preacher in Charge

St. Paul Methodist Episcopal Church, South

Goldsboro, North Carolina"

"Good morning, brothers and sisters. We would like to introduce to you Miss Eugenia May Bennett whom we have just hired as our new Assistant to the Pastor. Her position will include working with our children and youth, and teaching the older girls' class on Sunday mornings. She will be working with all of our teachers of the various ages to make sure that our programs continue to grow and be an active part of our community here at Goldsboro.

Her office hours will be three days a week so that she may have the other two days in the office to plan for her education duties. Please join me in welcoming her following the service as we have lemonade and cookies on the lawn."

Rev. Daniel looked out into the congregation and extended a hand to one of his parishioners, indicating for him to come forward. "This is truly a day of celebration in the life of St. Paul Methodist Church. The angels must surely be looking down on us today."

He stood with the young man who had joined him at the podium and placed a supportive hand on his shoulder. "I'd like to recognize Mr. John Glenn Edgerton this morning. Glenn, as we call him here, has just this week been accepted as a foreign missionary by our board in New York City. He will be leaving four weeks from this coming Tuesday on a train for New York City, where he will be ordained by Bishop James Cannon. Following that, he will set sail for Wembo Nyama, one of our Methodist mission stations in the Belgian Congo of Africa."

Sudden gasps were heard throughout the small congregation. Some of the men broke out into a round of "Amen's" while the women whispered about how proud they were that one of their own favorite sons had been called into the world of mission. They would begin planning a farewell party for him the minute the Benediction had been pronounced. Mrs. Beulah G. Effingham was already mentally wording the article that she would send to the *North Carolina Christian Advocate* to let the rest of the Methodists around the state know what they had produced at St. Paul - with her leadership, of course - "a foreign missionary to spread the Gospel of our Lord and Saviour Jesus Christ around the world."

Sonny Ledford couldn't help but feel a bit envious that his

"shining star" position had just been taken over by Glenn Edgerton. Not only that, but now this friend of his, a childhood playmate, would be traveling to the ends of the earth via trains and ships and surely meeting all kinds of people. *And just think of all the available young women he will see in New York City, not to mention sailing to Southampton, England.* His mind was already hard at work thinking of how he could reclaim his position as the favorite son at St. Paul in four weeks once Glenn was gone. Sonny was sure his Aunt Beulah would see that happened.

Miss Eugenia May Bennett closely observed the young man standing at the podium, whom she considered to be four or five years her senior. *He looks like any other graduate of Carolina.* She overheard some of the whispers on the row behind her about how "this will surely be a change from his nice big house at Sunnybrook Farm."

"I do hope he can stand the heat. He looks so fair," came another comment from behind her.

"Dear me, he'll surely catch some foreign disease and die over there."

"Oh, won't our Women's Society will be the envy of the Conference?"

"Isn't this exciting? I've always wondered what life would be like as a missionary."

The comments buzzed up one row and down the other until Rev. Daniel began the Morning Prayer.

And in the far reaches of 'Gene's mind, she was lifting her own personal prayer. *Dear God, this man looks so young and naïve. But surely you see him as fiercely strong. Be with him and his family as he prepares to leave all of his known comforts, and be with him in the years ahead that he may always seek Your guidance. Keep him from harm and bring him back safely.*

She couldn't help but follow him with her eyes, as he walked humbly back to his pew, and wonder what it must feel like to have God place that kind of responsibility and confidence on one's shoulders.

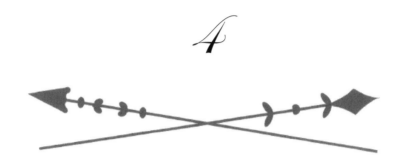

Lydia ran her fingers over the desk, the object that had first caught her eye when they entered this house with the realtor. It sat in the far back corner of the room that Lydia had referred to as "The Museum." She appropriately called it such for it was filled with masks, spears, boxes and all sorts of "things" that were now covered in inches of dust.

When the realtor saw her disheartened stare at all the "pieces" in the room, he quickly commented, "I know it's in bad disarray now, but someone with a good eye could do wonders with it. I'm sure that we can even have all this junk thrown out before closing if you're interested in the house."

What he didn't notice, as he led the prospective couple through the rest of the house, was the wink that Ward had given Lydia, for he knew that her eye had already surveyed all the possibilities, both for the interior and the exterior of the house. He could see the gears of her mind busily at work envisioning the finished product.

Ward knew Lydia's creative abilities to take anything and turn it into something beautiful. It was a gift she'd had since he first met her, but one that had gotten laid to rest during her years of teaching. "This house is filled with treasures," he could imagine running through her head as she winced when the realtor said the word, "junk." Her disenchantment had come from the inches of dust that had accumulated rather than the collection of "things." Just like the years when she'd first worked at the little corner drugstore, she was always finding an ingenious way to take the items that didn't sell or had become damaged and create works of art that quickly left the building. *With a good price on them.*

Lydia, being the sharp person she was, had known not to let the realtor see how much she loved the house. Her coolness had helped in the negotiations of the price, but there had been no doubt in her mind, from the moment she first stepped in the front door, that Howard Street in Boone would be her new address.

Now that she was actually living in the house, having un-packed most of the boxes that they had brought with them, Lydia took her time going from room to room making mental lists of priorities. The furniture was an eclectic mix, the stuffed chairs and sofa appearing to have been left over from the forties, and the bedroom suite from earlier than that. Although the pieces were old, they were in great condition. Where they were worn, it was obvious that they had been loved.

During the process of "arranging and rearranging," Lydia was repeatedly drawn to the desk, which was in the large room that she had chosen to work in last. There was some unknown magnetism about the small, dark brown, somewhat primitive in style, piece of furniture that would not let her get too far away from it for very long. There was something about it that struck her - physically and emotionally - like it was literally calling to her to reach out and touch it.

Finally, she stopped everything she was doing and ventured into "the museum" to take a closer look at what seemed to be the equivalent of "Pandora's box." After several attempts to open it, she discovered that both of the drawers were locked. She searched for the keys, but to no avail. It wasn't long before every drawer in the house had been searched in Lydia's effort to find a way into the desk.

Now, as she ran her fingers across its surface again, it seemed there was a beating in the distance. It was a dull distant sound that she heard each time before when she'd strode past it, but now it was growing louder and louder.

Lydia dismissed it as her anxiety of not being able to see inside the drawers.

The inlaid wood told her that this was not a cheap piece of furniture. Although there were several interesting accent pieces throughout the house, most of them wooden, this was the one that held her attention.

She made several passes into the kitchen, where she worked on shelving the cabinets or arranging items to make them easily accessible. Then she tried rearranging, for the hundredth time it seemed, the furniture in some of the other rooms.

For a week, this became a daily routine. Each time, Lydia wound up back at the desk, usually seated in front of it in a small wooden chair that wasn't at all comfortable. Every day, she would run her fingers over the entire exterior surface as if through her touch, she would discover a way to get inside it.

Finally, at the end of the week and the increased pounding she heard as she walked past it, she could no longer stand the unknown. She went to the basement to find Ward's toolbox and borrowed his hacksaw.

Guilt of breaking into it riddled her every step as she went back to the ground level of the house, but Lydia ignored it. It was not nearly so bothersome as the desire to release whatever was inside the desk, calling to be found, to be heard.

The principal's words drifted into her thoughts. *Is there really something inside that wants to be seen? To be heard? Is the principal right in his assessment?*

She didn't have much longer to wait before finding her answers to those questions for Lydia took the blade off the hacksaw and, putting it between the drawer and the lip of the desk, carefully sawed back and forth trying to avoid scratching the wood. Her efforts shortly paid off as the blade give way, after managing to cut through the locks that kept her from opening the drawers.

Lydia closed her eyes and imagined what she might find inside. *What if there's nothing there? Perhaps it had just gotten stuck from lack of use. What if there's jewelry, or old coins?*

Again she sensed the beating of a drum. *It must be the pounding of my heart in eager anticipation.*

She opened her eyes and weighed the decision of whether to jerk the drawers open or whether she was invading the secrets that laid buried within.

"It's my house. We are paying for it. Whatever is inside belongs to me now," she said boldly as she slowly opened the drawer and cautiously felt inside.

Paper?

Lydia pulled out a packet of letters, bound together by a green ribbon. She reached back a second and third time, only to retrieve the same thing, only these bundles were held together by a pink and a blue ribbon, respectively. There was one more bundle, tied with a white ribbon, that had been pushed to the very back of the drawer.

She opened the other drawer to discover a pair of glasses, probably that belonged to a man, and a dainty white linen handkerchief. *Most definitely a lady's.*

"Agh!" she screamed aloud as she pulled out a pair of teeth. "And God only knows who these dentures belonged to!"

Lydia couldn't help but chuckle as she looked at the stacks of letters. "Guess I can really sink my teeth into these," she muttered, bursting into a full-fledged laugh.

Not exactly what I would have presumed to be locked away as if they were highly valuable. It was hardly worth going to the effort of sawing the desk open.

She looked at the letters as she started to reach them back into their place of safekeeping. That's when the postmarks caught her eye.

Congo Belge?

Lydia began to thumb through each of the stacks, noting that every single postmark revealed that the letters had come from Africa, some postmarked again in Europe.

Maybe there's something to these after all. She took the linen handkerchief and used it to put the teeth back in the drawer. *I have to show these to Ward before I throw them away. He'd never believe me otherwise.*

She left the letters on the top of the desk. *They can at least wait until after lunch. They're not that important.*

Union Mission House,
Kinshasa, Congo Belge,
Sunday night - Aug. 15th.

Dear Gene,

Since arriving in Congo, practically all of my letters have been written on the typewriter, and it is only on special occasions such as this one that I take the time to allow my thoughts to transcribe themselves on paper with pen and ink.

For some peculiar and unknown reason for the past few days something has been moving me to write to you again before I reach Tumbo Nyama. I don't understand it

5

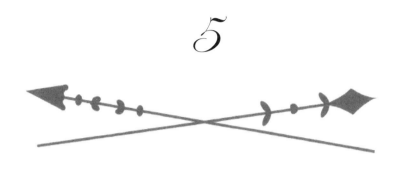

Dear 'Gene,

Since arriving in Congo, practically all of my letters have been written on the typewriter and it is only on special occasions such as this one that I take the time to allow my thoughts to transcribe themselves on paper with pen and ink.

For some peculiar and unknown reason for the past few days something has been moving me to write to you again before I reach Wembo Nyama. I don't understand it exactly but nevertheless I am heeding that impulse.

Won't you pardon me if I am perfectly frank? You see a man in Congo who isn't expecting an answer for many weeks needs to be frank. Now just what I'm going to be frank about I hardly know, but perhaps you had rather that I just remain John Glenn Edgerton.

The first thing that I want to know is have you plighted your love and heart to Sonny Ledford? I know that this is a very personal question but I do want to know. You remember the last night we went riding, you sang, "I'll be loving you always." Since that time I have often wondered just how much of it you really meant, if any. Now did you actually mean it, or were you just singing because it was a melody that lends itself to song? Please, won't you tell me? I <u>must</u> know.

Thus far I have had a very pleasant time in Africa. Of course, I haven't yet left the place where there are a lot of white people. I don't know very many people here outside the missionary circles but at the same time I see them every day and know that they are here.

Sonny is one of the finest fellows I have ever known. In fact, he is one of the best friends I have in the world. I know he would make a very fine companion for you because where love is, nothing else matters. I would do nothing to break friendship if I could prevent it. But, 'Gene, won't you answer the question I have asked?

I shall be looking forward to a letter from you by the return mail. Now don't disappoint me, will you?

The very best wishes be yours,
Glenn

It was with much prayer and trepidation that Glenn sealed the envelope and laid the letter on his writing desk to await tomorrow's weekly mail pickup. He did not wish to be too forward, yet, at the same time, there was something in 'Gene's voice that last Sunday afternoon – two days before his departure - when she'd sung those words to the highly popular song, *I'll Be Loving You Always*, that told him that it was more than simply a tune running through her mind by chance. He was sure that she had played the song many times over with the dance band while in college, so perhaps it stayed frequently on her mind as a particularly favorite selection. *After all, it is a beautiful melody with equally touching words.*

There was also something about the spark in her eye that told him that she enjoyed his company. So much so that he found it difficult not to spend the entire time, that he needed to be preparing and packing for his upcoming departure, riding about the countryside with her and talking about their work and the many things in which they shared a common interest.

Lastly, Glenn had seen the look in Sonny Ledford's eyes when he'd spied the two of them together. Sonny was a dear friend, one he'd known his entire young life and one who would surely be a faithful and loving husband. He was an active participant in St. Paul Church and, in fact, had been the one responsible for planning the dear letters of farewell from his home congregation and binding them all together in a book, which was presented to Glenn at the train station on the Tuesday of his departure. However, his education had ended with high school, which was of no discredit. It was simply that 'Gene had completed a degree at Trinity College — which became Duke University her final year, making her a prestigious member of it's first graduating class. Glenn wondered how that education would fare with a local home-grown business. *Would it be a source of clash down the road? Would someone who had made the commitment to a life of Christian service be content to live her life as the local businessman's housewife?*

As he licked the envelope, Glenn was sure that these questions which were bouncing around in his head were surely the same ones bouncing around in 'Gene's. That was the concluding point that made it possible for him to confidently tap the envelope as he laid it on the desk, ready to be stamped and sent.

My dear Sonny, I'm not out to interfere with your love life. Simply to disavow any problems that may surface later should this be for you a mere case of infatuation with the "new girl in town."

Glenn felt certain that God knew the intent of his heart, so he lost no more thought on the matter as he went back to the work of the African mission.

Oh, dear me! Lydia exclaimed as her eyes skimmed over the page. She went back to the beginning of the letter and read it aloud not wanting to miss anything.

A love triangle? She looked at the pieces of the puzzle, which were the postmark, the address, the writer, the receiver, Sonny Ledford, North Carolina, Africa, 1926, a Mission House, a popular song and "a special occasion."

The historical romance novel that she'd purchased during the morning hours at the Skyland Bookstore in Blowing Rock had just been pre-empted for a promising "juicy detective novel."

Lydia dug through the desk drawers again – watching out for the teeth – and then thumbed through the four stacks in search of a letter postmarked prior to the one that she'd just read. Forty-five minutes later she'd discovered the prologue to what was to become a living, breathing story of redemption, victory and love.

6

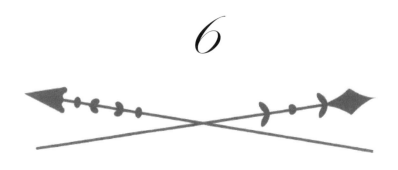

St. Paul Methodist Episcopal Church, South

Eugenia May Bennett, Assistant to Pastor

September 15, 1926

My dear Glenn,

 I've thought of you many times and have really felt negligent for not having written you the church, city and county news before this. However, I'll put off doing so for a few more days until I have plenty of time to write a long letter.

 Is it really true that you haven't heard from me at all? <u>*Certainly*</u> *- for the only letter I've written you came back. It got to New York too late. However, I wrote it just as soon as I could after I returned from Ocracoke. I'm <u>mighty</u> glad you got the telegram before you left. I've hesitated to send* this letter on but after holding it for nearly a month I've decided to send it on. It was written so long ago I've almost forgotten the content but, anyway, I'm sending it on just to prove to you I did write.

I've been right busy since my vacation and guess I'll be more so from now until Conference November 10th (in Durham). School has begun, the tobacco markets have opened; consequently, we have lots of strangers in town. Then too we are busy in Sunday School with Promotion Day, Rally Day, and Children's Week. I've begun <u>teaching</u> mission study classes both in the Senior League and the Junior Missions Society. For the past two weeks the Leaguers have been practicing a pageant called "What Is Worth While?" to be given Sunday night at the Union Epworth League Meeting to be held at St. Paul. The pageant is very simple, written by Miss Eugenia May Bennett (yours truly), do you know her? I do hope it will be put across all right for it is my first attempt at staging anything original. Will write you about that later.

Mr. Daniel comes in every few days and says, "'Gene, we must write to Glenn!" I don't believe he has done so yet but he thinks about you and speaks of you often. It was on the first Sunday in July when your picture was presented to the congregation. Col. John D. Langston, in almost <u>immortal</u> words, accepted it in behalf of the stewards of the church. Mr. Daniel spoke very beautifully of you, so did Col. Langston; in fact, the entire service was very impressive. I have a copy of their "brief remarks" and I'm sure you would be interested in knowing just what they said.

I have received both letters you have written me. One written June 4ᵗʰ On Board; the other written June 16ᵗʰ, in Belgium. I must tell you how much I appreciated the compliment in your first letter. I've read the letter dozens of times and each time I enjoy it more. It is truly a beautiful letter and I have thought each time of how happy you must be in your work doing, with all the strength you have, what you know God has given you the strength to do. It must be so wonderful to be a real foreign missionary! We are all looking forward to your coming home for I know you'll have some rich experiences to relate — even though I may not be in Goldsboro to welcome you home.

The boys and girls appreciate hearing from you. Of course we all exchange news each time and it is wonderful to me to see that you write each person <u>entirely</u> different letters. You are certainly remembered by the Leaguers. Also the Missionary Society. 'Twas only last Monday that Mrs. Davis read a letter that had been received from you.

I will write you again in a few days when I can write without being constantly interrupted and with less haste. With sincere good wishes for your happiness and success, I am

Your Friend
'Gene B.

What compliment? What is she reading over and over? Why didn't she send the letter right away that came back? Maybe it got stuck back in her drawer between interruptions and she forgot about it.

Lydia saw that the next letter came from Congo, Africa dated . . . *January 26ᵗʰ, 1927. What happened to 1926? He just left New York!*

METHODIST EPISCOPAL CONGO MISSION
DEPARTMENT OF EDUCATION

Wembo Nyama
Wednesday night, Jan. 26ᵗʰ, 1927

My dear 'Gene,

Your letter of December 4ᵗʰ arrived tonight along with several others among which were the ones from the members of your mission study class. I surely did appreciate those letters from those dear little girls and shall write to them immediately. I shall not attempt to tell you how much I did appreciate your letter and I don't know how to describe my feelings when I read it. I re-read it for the third time before I could replace it in its envelope and then I had to read it again when I sat down here to write.

I don't know just now what I shall say and there is no

telling what I may find that I have written before I bring this letter to a close.

No, I wasn't disappointed because you have not answered my questions earlier, but I must admit that I was beginning to get a bit anxious and wondering just when I would hear from you. But somehow I just felt that you would be writing to me. And tonight when I had read your letter I was seized with an intuition that I must write to you immediately. I don't know just why it came, but anyway I am acting upon it.

I appreciate very much indeed your confidence in me and for the frankness with which you spoke. However, I do so wish that you had expressed some of those things rather than leaving me to surmise them. I wish – oh I wish so much that I knew you better! Now let's have a real talk, want to?

Perhaps you meant for me to read a lot of things between the lines, but you must not think hard of me if I tell you that many of those intervening spaces were clothed in a mystery which I was unable to pierce to any degree of satisfaction. Will you pardon me again if I am so bold as to ask a few other questions?

It is about Sonny. It made me feel almost as though I were looking at him when you were describing some of his qualities and you yourself admit that he has many excellent ones. Please don't misunderstand anything I say, because I would not have you think that I am trying to take his place in your heart.

But, 'Gene, are you absolutely sure that you really

and truly love him, or is it that you love him but at the same time know there is someone else whom you will learn to love more than you do him now? I could not understand what you had in mind when you said, "there are so many things that must be taken into consideration and that _really_ matter" (other than love). 'Gene, do you mean the work which you feel that you must do, the comparison of the education of each of you, possibilities for Sonny's future in the business world, or is it that you feel you two would never be supremely happy should you marry? Please don't think I'm asking these questions just because I just want to be asking them.

Now that they have been asked you don't _have_ to answer them unless you so desire, but I would like for you to, if you feel free to do so. I may ask a few others and I am sure that you'll understand that all of this is confidential between you and me.

You spoke something about "years after I have left this wee city" meaning that you are intending to depart from Goldsboro some time in the future. Where are you going, and in what capacity? You said you would write me, if I am interested (and I certainly am) of any recent development.

'Gene, frankly, would you be interested in doing foreign mission work? If so, what field would you like to go to? Perhaps a more important question would be, what are your deepest desires for your life? I am sure that you are not so different from all that host of wonderful girls who think the building of a Christian home is one of the highest ideals a girl may have. But 'Gene, where do you wish to build that home and with whom? You perhaps have long ago settled these questions, recently in a very definite way, but perhaps, too, you may not be averse to giving me an answer. Does the work in Africa appeal to you at all?

'Gene, I do appreciate your prayers and all those that are being rained to the throne of Grace in my behalf. Somehow when anyone tells me he or she is praying for me the chords about my heart begin to quiver and vibrate, and I want to become more worthy in His sight. I could not be able to do the work out here were it not for the strength given me from on high in answer to those fervent prayers that are being uttered in my behalf. I feel and know that the people of St. Paul are constantly in my prayer, and I am confident Jesus will bless that church in the work she has undertaken.

I am not telling you anything about my work in this letter because I am sending one to the Sunday School in the same mail. But I must say that I am wonderfully happy in my work out here and God has wonderfully blessed me with health and friends thus far. Remember me most kindly to Mr. Daniel and Mr. Jerome and all our best of friends.

Awaiting your next letter, I am
Your sincere friend,
Glenn E.

P.S. In compliance with your desire I am burning your letter and I would like for you to do the same with this one.
G.

He's already had Christmas? Lydia deduced from the letter. *What happened to September, October, November and December?*

She studied the postmarks on the letters. *The first one was written from on board the ship in June, the second one was dated August 15ᵗʰ - before he'd even reached his assigned station - and this third one is* . . . Lydia leafed back to the first page. *January 26ᵗʰ?*

That's slower than a mule train. At this rate, this courtship is never going to get off the ground.

Lydia thought back to those years in history. *What was going on in the world at that time?* She tossed the letters back in the desk drawer and headed to the huge reference department of the ASU Library. During Ward's first day of moving, he had checked out the brand new five-story library, with which he was most impressed, and she had gotten the opportunity to meet Olivia Parsons, one of the library's reference specialists, who also told her about Skyland Books & Chickory Suite Coffee in Blowing Rock where she'd gone to purchase the romantic novel.

"You're welcome to come and use our reference department anytime you'd like," Olivia informed her.

At the time, Lydia had no idea of needing the reference department. Now, she found herself zipping, like all the thousands of students on campus, to the huge vault of information to find out what life was like back in 1927 and to see why it was taking so long for Glenn to get his letters. She was a bit unsure why all of this interest, but it was like she was now on her own mission field — *one to learn all I can about Glenn and 'Gene and their work.* She grinned precariously. *Not to mention their love triangle!*

7

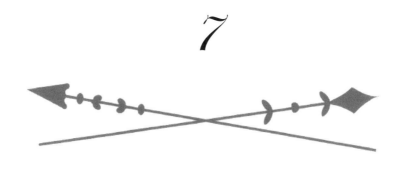

Aha! We've advanced to personal stationery imprinted Eugenia May Bennett, Goldsboro, North Carolina, rather than the St. Paul Church letterhead. *Either we've taken a much more personal interest in the addressee of the letter, or we didn't want our words to be seen by someone who might come into the church office. Or both! Is Sonny lurking in the wings waiting to see if someone else is in the picture? Is Mrs. Beulah using her self-acclaimed position to play matchmaker?*

Lydia had taken her long-distance detective journey very seriously and was trying to think of all the possible variables in the situation. She read between the lines of 'Gene's letter trying to unearth any clue that might let her know what was happening in the community of Goldsboro and what waves of emotion were crossing the waters from Africa.

April 22, 1927

My dear Glenn;

Your letter came just one month ago and already I have read it so many times! I've tried so hard to get just the thoughts you intended, but I am uncertain as to the conclusion I might attain.

I realize thoroughly your position and your actual condition of loneliness and my whole heart goes out to you during these months while you are separated from your loved ones. I just know you are the bravest and most courageous person in all the world to give your whole life unselfishly to service, and particularly the strength and glory of young manhood to the building of a civilization in a non-Christian land.

But Glenn – I wonder if you realized just what you wrote me? Yes, I believe that at the time it was written probably you felt that you, at some time, might care for me. No, I am not averse to giving you an answer to any of these questions you have asked but do you really think it would be fair both to you and me? I feel that we hardly know each other well enough to consider deeply such questions. However, I deeply and sincerely appreciate your frankness and <u>extreme</u> <u>confidence</u> in writing me thusly. If you were to write me again <u>now</u>, would you write with the same vision as you formerly wrote? We never know what attitudes will develop and what actions will take place. Probably you will meet and learn to love some girl while on your journey. I am still old-fashioned enough to believe in falling in love! Now, I'm sure you know Miss Armstrong! I just wonder if this is a possibility of you falling in love with her? Please pardon this thought – but I've wondered often about this. I know; 'ere this, you are forced to believe I have no confidence whatsoever in you. But Glenn – I *do*! But I am willing – oh so willing for you to do just what you feel and know is best for you to do. I think it takes time for such vital points to be worked out and I, personally, feel that I am still young enough to look forward to this glorious time when these determining matters can be considered more seriously.

I have kept your questions in confidence but oh! how it hurts! I had never dreamed that you would open your heart to me and be so frank in expressing yourself. Your four points or I should say <u>reasons</u> were extremely well thought out and I am still glad to find that you really know me well enough to interpret my lines that evidently <u>were</u> <u>not</u> "clothed in mystery."

I just must be fair in the game. I cannot play a double role. "Sonny" just wonders and wonders what I will eventually do. As I have said, it will only take time. I am sure you must know I admire you a great deal for I have expressed myself so already so many times. But I am afraid that both of us would be acting very unwisely should we plan ahead and make known to each other our deepest desires. But Glenn, you'll never know how I felt as I read with utter delight – yet sacredness – the last few questions in your letter. Please, may I answer that I have not decided "decently and in a very definitely" way the matters your spoke so beautifully of, for as yet I think I have never loved any man deeply enough to consider seriously those things which should be the deepest desire of every normal woman.

I am glad that you are well and happy in your work. I, too, am very happy, and I do feel that I have a work to which I am willing to give my very best. When I reflect upon the privileges that have been mine a deep gratitude fills my heart and with it a keen desire to be more worthy of the trust. I have no idea what my plan might evolve into for the future but I do want to have the satisfaction and contentment of knowing that my life will have been spent in worthwhile service. It is true that even in my small brand of the task at times it may seem dismal and gloomy, but somehow it has proved to me that it is the best way in which I can serve. After all, to be happy in life is to search and find the little nook our Creator has prepared for us, and fill it to the best of one's ability. For the two years I have been in this work, I have discovered with most profound gratitude an expansion and development of my own spiritual and mental faculties, which has made my own life richer, stronger, and happier.

Assuring you of my kindest regards and constant thoughts, I am

Just

'Gene

Lydia noticed as she folded the letter to fit it back into the envelope that "Keep – 1927" had been scribbled on the back of the last page so that it showed when one opened the envelope's flap. She felt a shudder run through her as she realized the depth of the thought and the seed of love that was being planted through the words that she had just read. There was such a purity, and "sacredness" 'Gene had called it, about this letter - *not just this letter, but all of Glenn's letters*, she reasoned - and the thread of care and devotion that was being woven between the passing of the letters across the giant mass of water that separated the two.

She felt an increasing wave of power surging inside her, causing her to barely withhold herself from standing up and screaming to the top of her lungs. Lydia had no idea what caused that desire to yell, but she considered that if the emotions wrought from these letters were this strong for her, what must they have felt like for the sender and receiver of these?

Once she had gotten past her initial reaction of the letter, she wondered whether 'Gene was truly concerned about Miss Armstrong, or whether her words were simply a ploy to detour Glenn's plight of love from going in that direction. *Is it not remarkable that two people travel to the other side of the world, only to meet up once they get there?*

Reality of the spiritual world hit her. *Possibly not remarkable. Maybe miraculous.* Now the words of 'Gene's letter seemed to ring loud and clear with apprehensions of what might progress in the small remote village of Wembo Nyama between two "called" individuals.

For the first time, Lydia sensed a real concern for 'Gene. *Perhaps she's wondering if they are "called" to more than their work.*

The next letter in the bundle immediately appeared to have been penned by 'Gene as an afterthought to the one she had just read. By the second page, she was pondering what thoughts were being created in Glenn's mind as he read the words from thousands of miles away.

Goldsboro, North Carolina
June 18, 1927

My dear Glenn,

Your letter written Wednesday P.M. January 26th was received in March. I must say I was glad to hear from you, as I always am (for I look forward to your letters). I feel that I am due you an apology, though, for waiting so long to mail the letter I wrote you on April 22. Yes, I did try to write an answer and did not totally ignore and neglect writing you. I mailed the letter in May and guess 'ere this it is well on the way to you. I beg of you to accept it for what it is worth to you and pardon any thoughts that I have perhaps expressed too frankly.

Somehow, I just couldn't burn your letter as you requested but you may be sure it is safe!

At this time I am sending you a clipping from May's (1927) "Epworth Era."

So many things have happened since I last wrote to you – I hardly know where to begin.

First of all, I must tell you that we had a great revival service in May. Mr. Stanburg, from Edenton Street was with us. Mr. Finlay and Mr. Frederick led the singing. At the same time Mr. Stanburg was here, Peels and H.M. North were holding meetings in Rocky Mount and Beaufort.

I, myself, have been busy running around to various Conferences and at the same time holding St. Paul on the corner. Since April I've been to Rocky Mount to the Sunday School Conference, to Sanford to the Woman's Missionary Society Conference, to Newport to District Conference, and to the League Institute. Now I am planning to go to Louisburg to the Epworth League Conference.

Also, I have been to Raleigh to hear the renowned soprano Amelita Galli-Cursi, (with Sonny and Mrs. Beulah), to New Bern to spend just one day fishing, and chatting with my own dear Uncle William. I wanted to go to Duke to the May Day exercises for one of my very good friends was the May Queen. But alas! the Preacher went fishing and when he goes – I stay. I am very <u>busily</u> and <u>happily</u> engaged at present in a Church Vacation School that is being promoted under my leadership. It is free for boys and girls 4 – 14 years *of age and continues each morning 9:00 – 12:00 except Saturday and Sunday mornings, throughout the month of June. I have a faculty of 20 volunteer helpers who have certainly been most faithful. The attendance is excellent. One day we had 279 present. Isn't that just glorious? Yes, and I was so happy!*

We still have no signs of a new Sunday School building. Mr. Daniel has written you the condition of things in this part of the country, I am sure. Yes, our people are despondent. But in spite of that I am so happy to tell you that they have not fallen down on their mission pledges to our Special! Please let me tell you that just this week I received checks for $50.00, $35.00 and $25.00 for the Glenn Edgerton Mission Fund. (I am the Treasurer.) It seems that if I can't be your Secretary in the Foreign Land, I can be your Treasurer at home. I do want to assure you of the fact that you, your ambitious aspirations and ideals are sincerely appreciated by the people of Saint Paul Church and every message that comes from you just reaches every one of them. You are a real hero to our children and they just want to name every organization for you. In fact, one of the groups of the Bright Jewels, of which James & Fred Smith are members, have named themselves the "Glenn Edgerton Boy's Band."

I wonder if you have received any of the magazines? I've sent the subscriptions long ago but I never heard again, but I do hope you have received them all right. If there is anything we can send you to make you more comfortable or your work easier please advise us.

Your letter containing your impression and description of the first Easter in the Congo was beautiful. It was a
glorious day here, too. I arose at 5:30 and played the chimes.
At 6:00 A.M. a beautiful Sunrise Service was held. The other
regular services were conducted during the day and in the
evenings the <u>Vested</u> <u>Choir</u> rendered "The First Easter" - a
beautiful and magnificent cantata. I say magnificent because
of the marvelous orchestra accompaniment with the piano
and organ.

I am glad to tell you that I have recently been re-
elected for another year as Pastor's Assistant at Saint Paul.
I accepted. I do wish I had someone to advise me what to do.
I have wanted to go back to the Conservatory for pipe organ
and piano and I know if I stay away another year, it will be
harder than ever to go back. However, I feel, as I have written you, that probably this is the capacity in which I can
best serve. I love my church, and my people here, and would
be very slow to consider a change. I have had two excellent
places offered this summer but somehow I feel that less than
two years spent in a town means very little.

I must close for it is early Saturday morning and I
have lots of work to do, such as mimeographing my bulletin,
writing notices for the papers, making department programs,
etc. I really should have typed this letter but I had no idea it
would be so lengthy. Pardon? Won't you?

Please remember that you are constantly on the minds
and hearts of our people and that I too am praying that you

may be kept strong and happy so that you can do great good in His name.

Assuring you of my sincere appreciation of your kind letters, and with best wishes, I am

Just

'Gene

Lydia used the art of basic psychology of "Fickle Women 101" as she tried to decipher whether 'Gene was trying to make sure she didn't push Glenn to far away by the comments of her April 22nd letter, but at the same time, make sure he didn't wander too far away since Sonny was still in the frontline of action on the home front.

She looked down at the letter's postmark again. *June 18, 1927? And how long does this relationship continue,* she pondered, thumbing through the letters of all four bundles. Lydia dared not look at the last one, or even the postmarked date on the envelope, for that would be like reading the last page of a book first.

With a huge sigh, she placed the letters back in their safe spot of hiding. *Safeguarded by the teeth!* she laughed, as she closed the drawer and walked downtown to the infamous Boone Drug Store on West King Street - the place that reminded her of her post-high school job - that was quickly becoming their favorite hang-out, to meet Ward for lunch.

8

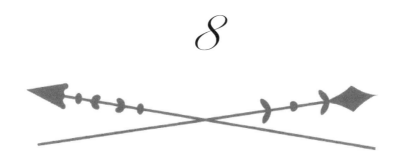

DEPARTMENT OF EDUCATION REPORT
Wembo Nyama, Congo Belge
Aug. 3, 1927

The opening month of a new quarter is always more crowded that the closing month of the old quarter, and July has been no exception. In fact, it has been about the most crowded month that I have ever had and certainly the most so since I have been on the mission field. Anyone who is inexperienced at bookkeeping, or rather shall I say, anyone who is learning and trying to balance his or her first set of books, will understand something of what I have had on my hands during the past month. But I have gone at it cheerfully because I knew that I could do only so much and give any time at all to my other work. I have done what I could and the remainder is waiting until I can tackle it.

I have had my first experience in teaching a Sunday

School class out here. I used to think that I had the ability to express my ideas fairly well in English, but I have a very difficult and different problem when I try to put these same ideas into Otetela. It is difficult enough when one has a command of the language and a large vocabulary such as mine. But it is a real experience, and one which I enjoy very much and one which I think will prove to be very valuable to me in the future. I only hope that in the process I can here and there drop a word that may mean something to my boys.

You perhaps would have laughed had you dropped down on the station here on Saturday evening two weeks ago, and seen me at the hospital . . .

Glenn was hastily studying the lesson he had prepared for the Sunday School for his boys the next morning. He was trying, with great difficulty, to put together the words he knew in the native Otetela language that would speak of Jesus' love for them through the particular New Testament story.

"Kitoko," called one of the boys, speaking the man's name in Otetela. "Owanji Kitoko," he yelled again, this time in excited desperation.

Hearing all the commotion, Glenn looked out his door.

The boy pointed toward the mission's hospital facility where Glenn then saw and heard a great deal of clamor.

Owanji Kitoko - "Friend Glenn," as the boy had called him - rushed toward the hospital, meeting Mr. Anker, another of the missionaries from the station.

"Mr. Edgerton, Mr. Anker," yelled Miss Armstrong, the nurse. "I need your help! Throw on the doctor's aprons hanging on the wall and get over here."

Both men did as they were told, having no clue what was going on except for the fact that their doctor had gone to help out at another station for a few days. Glenn looked toward the table and became immediately nauseous.

"Don't even think about being sick," commanded Miss Armstrong. "I need all your attention on helping me with this man. He has a horrible second-degree burn. The man with him explained that the man was out with his two children and was burning off the place for the garden for his next season's crops. Apparently the fire surrounded the man before he realized he was in danger. He tried to run through the flames, they said, but fell. The children ran for help, but when help came, he was still lying there."

Glenn began to pray over the man and over Miss Armstrong, as well as himself and Mr. Anker, and the boys who had just run through the door to assist them.

"I've never administered ether before, Miss Armstrong," he warned. "This is the first time I've even been in a room where it was being given a patient."

"Do exactly what I tell you. Mr. Anker will help you. We have to get him some relief for the pain so that we can even dress the burn."

The two men listened carefully, doing everything they were instructed, until the man was sedated to the point that they could even work with him.

"This is going to be much harder than necessary, which is already a toilsome task, because the natives have covered him in mud and dirt and anything else they could find to keep off the air. We're going to have to remove all of that as gently as possible before we can even attempt to put on the dressing."

The three of them, with the help of hospital boys who had to follow by example instead of words, worked way into the night, as natives stood outside the hospital and watched – the ones of them knowing Jesus praying – while the team of workers hastily, but calmly, went about the charge of caring for the man.

"Even under the most favorable conditions and with all the latest equipment and electric lights," explained Miss Armstrong, "this would be a terribly difficult procedure. But with only these lanterns held by our boys, this will take hours."

After all of the mud and dirt and other debris had finally been removed and the three adults were able to begin applying the dressing, Miss Armstrong looked briefly at the two men helping her. "I know this is out of your realm of expertise, but I truly thank you for all your courageous efforts. This is a hardship even for me, and I've seen some dreadful and appalling cases out here."

"Think nothing of it," replied Glenn. "One can never know what they might encounter on the mission field. I'm sure I speak for Mr. Anker, too, when I say that we are only too willing to do what we can in order to help those people among whom we work, serve and love. One can never tell what opportunity is going to offer itself that will lead to an opening for the teaching of a lesson about Jesus Christ."

"Precisely," nodded Mr. Anker as they continued to work with the man. "God will give us whatever we need to carry us through this situation."

No one spoke again until finally all of the burns on the man's body had been dressed. Even under the influence of ether, the pain had to have been horrific judging from his moans as the two men tried to get him from the hospital table to a bed.

The following afternoon, after Sunday School, Glenn and Mr. Anker returned to the hospital where once again their services were needed to assist Miss Armstrong with the changing of the dressings.

"I'm afraid we're going to have to give him ether again," warned the nurse. "Even with that, the pain is so intense and with what we'll have to do to help him, it must be nearly unbearable for him. I so wish there were more that we could do to help."

The two men again put on the doctor's aprons and went to the task at hand. Still, the procedure took nearly three hours just to change his dressings. While he was still under the ether's influence they were able to get him back to his room.

"Gentlemen," Miss Armstrong began, "I'm not sure how much longer our patient will live. We've done all we can do and

I'm amazed that he's lived this long. I need you to pray for him and for his family and for all of these friends who are gathered here with him."

Both Glenn and Mr. Anker understood what she meant as they somberly retreated back to their huts in prayer.

It was about nine o'clock that evening when Glenn heard the wailings that were so peculiar of those in mourning coming from the hospital. He bowed his head and began to pray for the people "with whom he worked, served and loved." Soon a messenger came from the hospital to say that the man had passed across the river.

Glenn's head fell to his chest in sorrow for the man's two children and other family members and friends. *Lord, give us a way to teach about You through this experience.*

We have had an epidemic of sickness in the village during the past month. At one time there were as many as forty of my Mission Boys out of eighty who were sick. School was closed for a whole week. It was something like influenza. I was so impressed as I made the rounds in caring for them. Of course the nurse would visit them too, but there were so many sick in the village, as well, that she was fortunate to get to see them once during the day. No matter what kind of medicine I wanted to give them they would take it without

a word of protest, and no matter what I told them to do they would try their best to do it. Some of them cried to go home, but I would not let them go. Regardless of the distance when one of the natives here becomes sick he wants to go home. But they gradually improved, and now they seem to be well and happy again.

There is quite a difference in the boys who have been in school at the mission for a few years and those who have never been in close contact with it. They do not trust in "fetishes" to make them well again when sickness comes. They know the worth of a Christian doctor or nurse. But greatest of all they come to know Jesus Christ who is able to heal both their sick bodies and sick souls. At all times we strive to keep Jesus and his teaching before them.

Lydia held the mission report that had been written by Glenn and thought about what a hardship it must have been to try to teach the natives that God was with the man who died. *And the boys who want to go home when they're sick, that's exactly how it is with people here in America. Human nature,* she reasoned. *I guess there are no barriers in that.*

His message through the report spoke loudly to her as it brought out a point that she had never considered before. *How do you tell people that God loves them, or that He cares for a loved one when that loved one "passes across the river?"*

She began to see that not only was she reading the history of a foreign missionary, or the beautiful legacy and love of a dedicated and devoted couple, she was learning about life's lessons in a way she had not previously known. *Glenn's teachings are still at work*, she smiled as she put the report back in the stack of letters and moved to the next one, anxious to find its hidden message.

Fleeting thoughts of Glenn, 'Gene and Miss Armstrong - that had followed Lydia to bed the evening before, and taken her on a missionary journey all her own as she dreamed of the plight of serving others in a foreign land - fled with the appearance of the next letter in the second stack of letters. *I don't recognize this handwriting*, she observed. Lydia struggled to read the postmark until she finally gave up and flipped the envelope to see if the back gave her any information.

"B. Arthur Tisson." The letters underneath the name were so elaborate in the Old English typeset that she still was unable to read what they said. She gently reached into the envelope, that was threatening to tear into two pieces at the slightest touch, and pulled out several pieces of letterhead that also bore the same unreadable letters as on the back of the envelope.

"c/o Mr. Graybill, Amer. Pres. Mission, Peking, China. May 14th, 1927 . . ."

Lydia jumped up from the chair and rushed to the kitchen to pour another cup of coffee. It was unusual for her to go beyond one cup each morning, but the adrenalin rush that jolted her entire body at the sight of the origination of this letter called for something more and she wasn't quite ready for lemonade or soda. She rushed back to the chair, *and the letter*, as hastily as she had rushed to the kitchen and sat back in 'Gene's chair to see the Light at work in another part of the world. *With a letter that's particularly perfect for this morning's read.*

How exciting! She was nearly beside herself as she wished that Ward could have been home to share the impending disclosure with her. As she skimmed over the body of the letter, Lydia noticed that the handwriting was one of the most beautiful, *and easiest to read*, she had ever seen. *Totally unlike the Old English that's on the envelope and letterhead.* She marveled at how the writing look perfectly like what had been in the writing samplers that had been used to teach cursive writing when she had been in the second grade all those many years ago. *And to think that the hand behind this fine penmanship is in China*, she chuckled thinking of how many people in America had handwritings that were incapable of being read.

c/o Mr. ~~E.C.~~ Gleysteen,
Amer. Pres. Mission,
Peking, China.
May 14th, 1927.

Dear John,

I have been holding off my answer to your fine, long letter of December 19th until I might have something definite to tell you about what I will be doing in the China of the future. For the present China is in chaos, and for many of us China missionaries our future work is hanging in the balance. Now when I am at last constrained to write you fearing longer delay, my circumstances are more uncertain than they have ever been before. Just now for many (if not most) of the Christian workers in China it is a case of wait — wait with what patience we can on the side-lines, while we see the game often going hard against us, and the fruit of decades of Christian labor being given over to destruction. Of course, we know that material destruction of buildings or personal property is really nought, or even the apparent falling into nothingness of Christian organizations and personnel built up with so much toil. All genuine efforts for Christ — and genuine successes — are of themselves independent of material bandages. The harvest comes of itself with the sowing of the seed. But despite one's assurance of this, one must grieve when the compound that we have grown to love, with its familiar school, and hospital, and church buildings, is laid waste. Especially for the older missionaries who have given so much of thought, and labor, and incessant planning to these things, their loss comes as a heavy grief. For we younger ones, with less of our hearts' blood and toil in them, the burden is far easier to bear.

And, of course, looking at the missionary enterprise in China in the large, under a sort of eternity,

Dear John,

    I have been holding off on my answer to your fine, long letter of December 19^{*th*} *until I might have something definite to tell you about what I will be doing in China in the future. For the present China is in chaos, and for many of us China missionaries our future work is hanging in the balance. Now when I am last constrained to write you fearing longer delay, my circumstances are more uncertain than they have ever been before. Just now for many (if not most) of the Christian workers in China it is a case of wait – wait with what patience we can on the side-lines, while we see the game often going hard against us, and the fruit of decades of Christian labor being given over to destruction. Of course, we know that material destruction of buildings or personal property is really naught, or even the apparent falling into nothingness of Christian organizations and personnel built up with so much toil. All genuine efforts for Christ – and genuine successes – are of themselves independent of material bandages. The harvest comes of itself with the sowing of the seed. But despite one's assurance of this, one must grieve when the compound that we have grown to love, with its familiar school, and hospital, and church buildings, is laid waste. Especially for the older missionaries who have given so much of thought, and labor, and incessant planning to these things, their loss comes as a heavy grief. For the younger ones, with less of our hearts' blood and toil in them, the burden is far easier to bear. And, of course, looking at the missionary enterprise in China in the large, under a sort of eternity, the* recompenses for the losses even at this early date begin to show themselves. We have doubtless depended too largely upon the streams of money that have flowed so largely from the lands of the West to China. We have perhaps spent our money too largely and munificently in buildings to house our fundamental labors of preaching, teaching, and healing. Our organizations here have been directed perhaps too largely toward the largest amount of work possible to be accomplished, <u>counting on the foreigner to supply the moneys and maintain the standards</u>, forgetting to adjust a load to the struggling Chinese Church with the extreme poverty of its members and the extreme lack of education and training among them. In short, we developed a Juggernaut that crushes them under its weight when the foreigner leaves, and leaves them helpless to carry on the work.

Of course, this is not true in every case (especially the larger centers), but by and large it is a fair criticism and a straight lesson. And we must remember that the foreign missionaries have often had to leave their Chinese fellow workers just when the accumulated fever of civil war and militarism begins to rage the fiercest. In spite of all handicaps much of our work is being shouldered and carried on by the Chinese Church, especially on the evangelistic side. The technical training required along medical and educational lines makes these branches more difficult for our Chinese to cope with.

As we look at China missions of the future even at this early day it seems inevitable that there will be fewer *foreigners and less foreign money engages. Perhaps this past year has seen the peak of Western moneys and men engaged in bringing Christ to China. The Chinese themselves must now more and more shoulder the burden, and this brings in its train the much closer and speedier arrival of our mission-ary ideal the world around – a self-governing, self-support-ing, and self-propagating Christian Church. Who of us can say this is not a blessing? For doubtless in many cases we Westerners were holding on to the reins of authority when with larger effort they might have been turned over to our Chinese fellow workers.*

To come down to me personally, it seems almost im-possible to convey to you what our group at Hwai Yuan has gone through these last few months. You have no doubt heard echoes at least of what has been done in China by the Kuomintary (People's Party, springing from Sun Yat-Sen's principles for the still unfulfilled China Revolution begun in 1911 when the Manchers were dethroned.) in the past year. For indeed, it is less than twelve months ago since these Southern armies under their amazing leader Chiang Kai-shek began their march from Canton northwards, until to-day it is only the few militarist war-lords of a few North China provinces that bar their way to a complete conquest of China. Two things have made this possible: (1) an unstinted almost fanatical nationalistic enthusiasm of the People's Party members (comparable to that which swept all Europe before the French revolutionary armies); (2) unstinted sup-plies of money, men, and technical military advisers, as well as war munitions, from Soviet Russia. These two things have made the Kuomintang military successes possible.

Along with these advances has gone widespread rioting, destruction (especially of foreign and Christian ownings), and general lawlessness. Much of this is the inevitable concomitant of a revolution, with armed forces rampant. But much has been carefully fostered by Russian Communists, and a very active minority of Chinese Communists. To this group belongs the responsibility for the Hankow riotings, as well as the murders of foreign men and violations of foreign women at Nanking the last of March, 1927. Unfortunately, this group temporarily controlled the Kuomintang during these last eventful months. It cannot be too strongly emphasized that the mass of the Chinese people have no anti-foreign, anti-Christian hatred, beyond the natural aggrieved feeling that the Western Powers have been and are still trespassing on Chinese national sovereignty in the matters of Customs control, concession areas held by armed foreign troops, and extraterritoriality privileges. In spite of this, the mass of the Chinese people are friendly toward Westerners. Britain, perhaps, bears a larger onus of Chinese hatred than properly belongs to her.

What is the present political situation? China is roughly divided by the Yangtze into a South and North – a South controlled by a Kuomintang – Communist regime flushed with its successes, a North controlled by unscrupulous, greedy militarist war-lords, from whom China has gained, but who can gain nothing. (Yet, the Southern group has wantonly offended the Western Powers, while the Northerners sedulously protect foreigners – that is why I am peacefully residing in Peking just now).

But what is the hope we have of the Kuomintang? Just this – that it will unite and rule China. The role of a prophet is hard in China, so bear with me if my interpretations of current events at this point are contradicted by later occurrences. It seems as though Communism is not natural to China and will surely go – if indeed, it has not already gone in large measure. I am one of those who have faith in Chiang Kai-shek. This commander-in-chief has now definitely repudiated the Russian-Chinese Communist group at Hankow, and established what he calls the true Kuomintang government at Nanking. This splits the Southerners into two rival camps, and much jockeying of rival generals now goes on south of the Yangtze impossible to interpret, but which I prophesy will end in the downfall of the Hankow Russian-Chinese Communist clique. With that will go the greatest danger to China's future peaceful relations with Western Powers.

Despite this Southern split, within the last week an active Southern offense both from Nanking and Hankow has begun its trek northwards. Most observers here believe this offensive will land the Southerners in Peking before the summer is over. The Northern war-lords (Chang Tso-lin, Chang Chung-ch'ang, etc.) are threatened by Feng Yu-hsiang on their Western flank as well as by the direct frontal Southern attack – _and they are not liked by the people here_. With the *capture of Peking the Southerners will control the Eighteen Provinces (Chang Tso-lin will probably be driven back into his three Manchurian provinces from which he came). Then will come the real test of the Kuomintang. Will they be able to unite, pacify, and constructively rule their domain? If they can, China will enter a new era (of complete Western Power withdrawal and full Chinese sovereignty, which the Powers are only too ready to grant a stable China gov't.), and so will the Christian enterprise in China. If not – more years of chaos.*

But where does Hwai Yuan fit into this? Well, we were about 100 miles north of Nanking. All thru the winter our work went on under the shadow of Southern advance. We caught our breath when in Hunan (which happened to be a province containing half the Communists in all China), Christian missionary work was ruthlessly destroyed (including the large Yale-in-China medical and educational work at Ch'angsha), foreigners as well as Chinese Christians being forced to leave the province. Then came Hankow, and Britain turned over her concession there to this Communist group. This apparently whetted their appetites, until at the capture of Nanking a Communist-led army ran wild, killing Faiths' father, five or six other foreigners, and violating foreign women (which the Foreign Powers have sedulously suppressed, so that no one knows the number). When Nanking fell to this mob of ruffians, we at Hwai Yuan were cut off, the battle-line being between us and Nanking. For ten days we had absolutely no news, knowing nothing of the Nanking horrors. Then advices from our Council (of our Presbyterian work in China) ordered us to leave Hwai Yuan. This we disregarded, as it told little of Nanking and we did not appreciate the gravity of the situation. Just then, trains were not running north, anyway – they were all being used by fleeing Northern troops. A few days more and a consul letter from Peking Legation ordered us out. (Previous to this, however, we had sent mothers and children to Peking). Still we would not leave our work, which we were still prosecuting among a friendly country-side. Then the American consul at Tsinanfu sent a man down to get us out of Anhwei from the path of warfare. From him we first learned the terrible events of Nanking. Hurriedly we arranged committees of Chinese to assume charge of the work, paid advance salaries to our workers, and left with only a trunk each (much more than many people in other places took). We traveled north for two days in a box-car (which the special passes of the man sent down for us enabled us to get), a mixed party of men, women, and children, Chinese and foreign. We left behind us only the Men's Hospital and the Boy's School running in a reduced scale.

Since our evacuation on April 4th, our buildings have been occupied again and again by lawless soldiers as the Chinese there have written us. Schools and churches, and foreigners' residences (often with the furnishings of many years' savings from our missionary salaries), have been wantonly looted.

What are we planning to do? Those near furlough, or

in need of health leave, have been sent to America. The others of us are scattered from Shanghai to Korea all thru North China. This group constitutes the Presbyterian Emergency Reserve Force, and we are laying plans to return to our places of work as soon as conditions allow. First, the Chinese must fight this war out, which, as I say, may be over this summer, perhaps not for years. Other Missions in China are meeting the situation in a similar ways – some Canadian groups are sending almost all their missionaries back to Canada, but most of the Boards are keeping as many as possible here hoping for a speedy resumption of the interrupted work. Consular advice (of all nations) has called practically all foreigners out of the interior to places near the seacoast.

These months of forced inactivity at least offers us a chance of studying the language at more leisure, and from this point of view this time is not a dead loss. From all indications I have four full, uninterrupted months of language study ahead of me. I have been offered a position in the English Department of Peking University this coming fall, and will probably be teaching here if I am not able to return to my station at Hwai Yuan in Anhwei at that time.

As I re-read your letter, I am touched by your warm expression of friendship, and appreciate it and am thankful for it. I'm an undemonstrative cuss myself, but I'm sure you realize how strongly I reciprocate your friendship. If I seemed a bit "blue" in my last letter, the events of this year have shook me out of it, and that's that. I enjoyed the description of your first African itinerating trip very much; I don't see how you can say you failed to get the color of it in. It's all there, and I envy your home church and folks - such vivid descriptions of your surroundings and work. Everything seems fresh, and new, and simple; I don't think you face quite the problem we do here of fitting ourselves into a keen nationalistic self-consciousness that makes the Chinese (especially students) extremely wary of committing themselves to us unreservedly. Of course, in one way the overcoming of such a difficulty is the problem of the missionary worker in any land. Again, the educated Chinese (non-Christian) have a strong feeling for the centuries of cultural life behind them, and are ready to resent any violation of it, even tho they will as readily admit our superiority in the material side of life. I've come to see and feel that Christ must fulfill and prefect their own inherent Chinese aspirations, not utterly stamp out and eradicate their ideas and ways that easily seem strange and unaccountable to us as Westerners.

You'll be interested to hear that Kilpatrick has been visiting China, coming from India. Lately he has been giving a series of lectures in Peking. He lived with us here at Language School for several days, and one evening when I asked him led a discussion group here on education in its relation to the missionary enterprise. The group was composed almost entirely of missionaries, and you can imagine what a grand time we had of it to get his viewpoint on the problems pressing us. He particularly scored us for our compulsory Bible classes and chapel services. I was glad to see that he seconded my previously formed opinion as to the real constructive elements in the Kuomintang, when it does not run wild. The Kuomintang are strongly nationalistic, and Western privileges must go by the board wherever they come into control. As a matter of fact, we were hoping to be by when the Kuomintang came into power at Hwai Yuan, and were preparing to meet the requirements of their Educational Board. These comprised a majority Chinese Board of Directors (which we were electing), a Chinese principal (our vice-principal was preparing to assume this responsibility we had been trying to give him for several years), and voluntary chapel and Bible classes (which we were also willing to grant upon initiation by our Chinese Christian faculty-members. As it is, the turmoil that forced our leaving prevented us from welcoming in the Kuomintang. If they can only clean house and found a stable government in China, the sovereign rights they are dead set on regaining will be turned over to them soon enough by the Western Powers, I now feel convinced.

I don't know just how you ought to address me your answer to this letter. Perhaps c/o <u>China Council, American Presbyterian Mission, Shanghai, Forward</u> will be the safest of all.

And now, good-bye, old pal, until your next letter. Best wishes to you in all that you do. God help you always.

As ever,

Art

Lydia sat stunned. She felt as though she were reading through some history textbook, yet she could not put down the words of the letter. Art's portrayal of what the Chinese missionaries were enduring seemed all too realistic in the living room of The Rhododendron. *Especially in the wake of the dreams of the evening before.*

Is Glenn in danger? Does he feel swept up, with uncertainty prevailing?

She laid the letters together inside the desk drawer, not binding them together, so that she could again return to them in a few moments. *But for this moment, I have to take a break.* The connection she had felt through Art's letter had worn on her physical being, as well as her mental capacities. Lydia pieced out, much like one would do with a quilt, some general qualities and ideals that she sensed a missionary should have. Then she laid out the many issues they would have to face, and tried to see the whole picture, making it into a thing of beauty in spite of all the hard efforts to make it into a lovely thing where all the pieces come together to make "One Whole."

Lydia feared that she was not made of the ilk of what it would take to do missionary service. *But that doesn't make me a bad person*, she assured herself. She focused back on the letter from 'Gene that had stated "probably this is the best capacity in which I can best serve."

Does that make each and everyone of us a missionary? Lydia questioned. She had once heard a minister long ago challenge that everyone was a disciple, a follower of Jesus. At the time it didn't really register and she had no idea how she remembered it just now. Her mind searched for answers to some in-depth subjects for a few minutes as she thought of her role – someone who could send cards to those in faraway places away from friends and families. Someone to make phone calls to the lonely. Someone to pick up prescriptions for the elderly who were homebound.

Before she had even picked up a pencil and begun to write, Lydia had filled an entire sheet of paper with ways for which she possessed the capacity to serve. *Beautiful ways. Meaningful ways.*

And now what do I do with them?

9

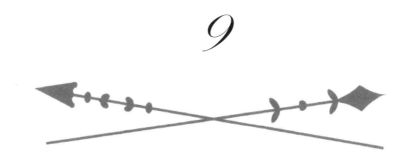

My dear 'Gene,

It is late afternoon and only a few minutes before time for tennis, but time for writing is so short that I have to write "by spells" and use little bits of time here and there. We had a nice rain this afternoon just about the end of the rest hour. It has been quite cool and cloudy since then. It is about the end of the dry season. Each day now we are looking for rain and the natives say that the rains are near.

Tomorrow will be the end of this school term and then there will be a vacation of two weeks. During this time I am hoping to catch up with the work on the books in the office and get my reports to the Board of Missions for last quarter. They should have gotten off much earlier but I have too many other duties to take care of to get them done on time. Now if I just had someone to help me, — but there's no use talking about that because there is no one near enough to lend a helping hand. But perhaps some day, — but that is a closed door and what it may hold for me behind it, I know not.

I am due to go on an itinerating trip during the next two weeks but I shall not be able to go. I have made but one itinerary this year and it looks as though that will be the last one before the close of the year. I regret it so much because I was hoping that I should have the opportunity of seeing all the schools in Wembo Nyama District within the year and thus have a basis for planning my work for the new year. But perhaps when the opportunity does come I shall be better prepared and more capable of really helping the teachers in the school.

I am becoming more interested in the work every day and only wish that I was able to be about a half-dozen persons at once. There is so much to be done and such a real opportunity of helping these people. Really I have become very much attached to them. I never stop to think of the difference in their color and mine, and think of them as boys and girls possessing lovable qualities and possibilities for development as I used to do in America.

Just after I wrote the last letter to you I received a letter from a pal of mine , Art, in China. He and I were in school together in New York City and I thought so much of him. He sailed for China in Aug. of 1923. In his letter he told me about some of the experiences which he and other of my missionary friends, and the majority of the missionaries there, have been experiencing during the past year. It makes one's heart strings ache to hear of what has happened. One of my very dear friends, Dr. John E. Williams was assassinated during the Nanking incident. I suppose you read of it months ago in the papers. But he had great faith and hope in the China people and that is what is going to count.

The mail is late this week. We always become somewhat anxious when it doesn't come on time. It is due on Wednesday afternoons or evenings. Even though there is none for us we are wanting to know that too. Getting the mail is quite an event in our lives when it comes but once a week. I don't know what it may contain this time but I would enjoy another letter from 'Gene.

The majority of the young people will have returned to college by the time you receive this letter. But practically all of our "advanced" age will remain. Remember me to all our friends.

Most sincerely,
Glenn

"What can we help you find today?" Olivia asked Lydia, sure that the letters had brought her on another quest.

"Nanking, China. Somewhere in the vicinity of 1926 and 1927 should work. There was an incident . . . or several," she remembered from the letter about 'the experiences of the past year,' "in which a missionary was assassinated. I want to look and see if I can find anything about what was going on at that time, and maybe even about a Dr. John E. Williams."

Olivia directed the patron to an area of books. "You know, most of the encyclopedias are online now. Are you familiar with how to use them?"

"Yes," Lydia nodded. "Being married to a professor of education does have a couple of advantages." She laughed jokingly. "Or at least one."

Olivia enjoyed the cheerful spirit of the woman in front of her who was quickly becoming a friend.

"Even as a teacher's aid in elementary school, we had to show the children how to find things on the computer. Many of them in the area where I taught did not have computers at home. Their only opportunity to use them was at school during class hours."

As Lydia delved through the indexes of the volumes, Olivia volunteered to help her.

"Thank you for your assistance. I'm surprised you have time to take a break from your work to help me with my own little personal project."

It was then that Olivia offered an understanding smile. "My father was killed in the war overseas. I never knew him; I was one of the many war orphans."

Lydia dropped the book she was holding to the floor. "I'm so sorry. I had no idea." She fumbled to pick the book up and straighten out its pages. "I hope this is not a hurtful thing for you that I came in looking for this incident."

"No," Olivia revealed. "It gives me an opportunity to use my own experience to help others. I was blessed to have had the chance to go to France and see exactly where my father's plane was shot down. He was a pilot."

The surprised patron stood looking at the librarian trying to find some appropriate response. "You seem to be totally at peace with this."

"It was a strange experience. There were times of hurt, and anger and bitterness. I was horribly angry that I never knew my father. I was glad that I never knew him so that I didn't see what I had missed out on. I was hurt because the children around me had fathers to play and do things with them. I was bitter that my father was killed in trying to protect his country. My emotions ran the entire gamut of contrasting feelings."

Olivia sat in one of the nearby chairs, inviting Lydia to do the same. "I'm not exactly sure how old I was before I worked it out in my mind that my father gave the greatest gift that he could give. He knew when he went into service that he was defending his country. He was standing up for something he believed in. He laid his life on the line for that . . . and lost it." She gave a deep sigh. "But in giving his, he saved the lives of countless others and gave me a life of freedom."

Lydia heard each word of each sentence and realized how

similar they were to what Glenn was doing in Congo, and even more so, how similar they were to the Christ whom Glenn had dedicated his life to telling about in Africa. She began to wonder about the dangers of Africa and the numerous risks of life involved with Glenn being there.

"Thank you, Olivia," she acknowledged, putting the book back on the shelf from where she had found it. "You've given me all the information about this incident that I needed."

A confused look came over the librarian's face. "But you haven't even seen anything about Nanking yet."

"What I was searching for went far beyond an incident in Nanking. You helped me to see that through your story."

Olivia nodded graciously, still not sure how she had helped.

"And for the record," Lydia assured, "the story and your attitude about your experience are more of a help to people than you know." She turned to go toward the elevator. "See you next time."

10

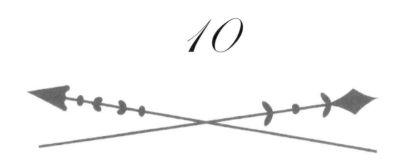

"You've gotten quite involved in those letters, haven't you?" Ward observed as he walked into the living room and took a seat on the sofa beside his wife.

"Moving here has been the greatest education I've ever had," she disclosed.

He laughed. "What makes you say that?"

"I've been to the library twice since I've started reading these letters."

"Really?" he asked, somewhat shocked. "I've never known you to spend a great deal of time in libraries. You seem to enjoy the bookstores where you can hide away in a little corner and feel like you've gone to another world."

"That "little corner" is what I've found in this house. Or rather, in this desk I should say."

A puzzled look still covered Ward's face.

"When I read these letters, it really does take me away to

another corner of the world. I'm finding out things about people and places . . . ,"

She paused, wondering how comfortable she felt about broaching this subject with him. "Ward, do you love me?"

"Of course I love you. What kind of question is that?"

"I mean, do you *really* love me?" she inquired further.

"Yes, I love you. You know that I love you."

Lydia took a deep breath before she ventured forward with the conversation. "I know we've never really talked about this much, so I guess I'm not sure what you'll think of me for feeling this way . . ." She looked into his eyes, the warm hazel color and the intenseness of them giving her the confidence to move ahead, "I'm finding out a lot about Jesus and what it truly means to be a Christian through these letters."

"You had so much difficulty sharing that with me?" he asked, still unsure of her hesitance.

"Some people think you've gone overboard if you spend too much time talking about faith or church or Jesus. I know we've attended church in the past, especially after your brother's heart attack, but we never made it a real part of our lives. We've never read the Bible together or discussed it's principles. I guess I just wasn't sure where you stood with all of that."

Ward gave Lydia a hug. "This really is important to you, isn't it?"

"Yes," she nodded, a tear forming in her eye. "It really is. Do you mind if we have this discussion?"

"Not at all, dearest," he said as he gave her a harder hug of support. "Not if it means this much to you."

Lydia sat looking at him, waiting for him to make further comment before she said any more.

"I believe everyone has some form of faith," he expressed. "To some people, that form is no faith. Or so they say. I frankly find it hard to go through something with a loved one, like I did with my older brother, when you don't call on some One or some Thing to help you deal with the pain it produces. Whether we want to believe in a power greater than ourselves or not, I do believe it's there. Past that, I'm not really sure what I believe. I, like you, went to church with my parents as a child, but we didn't' say much about it past walking through the back door on Sunday after the service. It was an act we did because most everyone else, at least those who wanted to be accepted in the community, did. Times have changed since then and the tides have turned. Church is no longer important to many people, and in fact, the majority of people have no idea what it is all about."

Lydia, whose zeal and confidence had grown with his words challenged, "Do *we* know what it is all about?"

Ward was certainly not ready for that question and did not have an immediate answer. There was total silence for a few minutes as he searched himself for an answer to that question.

"It's a strange thing," he finally spoke, "but with all of the other education I've gotten over the years, that's one thing they don't teach you. Having gone to a state-supported institution, I never got much of a background in religion other than with the Holy Wars, which I couldn't quite grasp as being very religious. Your question has made me face a decision that I've never had to face before. It's like, 'are we or aren't we?'"

He jumped up from the sofa and headed briskly toward his office.

"Where are you going?" Lydia quizzed, fearful that she'd gone too far with their discussion.

"To find a Bible. I know I must have one in my bookcase somewhere." With that response, he wheeled around. "I guess that in itself says that we aren't too serious about our faith if we don't even know whether we own a Bible and if we do, where it is . . . huh?" He turned back to his path and came back shortly, blowing on a bound book and dusting it off with his hand.

"Do you have any idea how long it's been since I've opened this book?" he said, rather ominously.

"Much longer than it's been since I sat down with my last twenty novels," she answered.

Both of them felt the presence of shame in the room that had shrouded around them as he sat back on the sofa. "Isn't this odd?" Ward questioned. "I have a doctorate. I'm a professor of an educational department that sends students out to instruct and mentor children all over the world. I never get lost, even without the aid of a map." This time it was he who took the deep breath. "But I feel as if I don't even know where to begin."

Lydia placed her hand on his knee, offering him the same support he had given to her minutes earlier. "Why don't we pray about what God would have us to read?"

Ward took another long slow breath as he looked at her, this time his questioning eyes drawing comfort and strength from the richness of her brown eyes as they silently bowed.

"I do know enough to know what a concordance is," he

stated. "Shall we simply look for a passage about Jesus and love?"

"That sounds like a super starting point to me," said Lydia, who saw this as the beginning of a new and wondrous adventure.

"I hope I can recall the order of the different books from my college lit class."

"There is a Table of Contents at the beginning with the order of them."

"I know, but that seems so wrong."

"Which is more wrong," posed Lydia, "seeming wrong or continuing to be wrong?"

"You're right," he said. "I do not want to be looking in the Contents. Neither do I want to reference something. If God is all we say He is, we should be able to open this book and find the words He wants us to see and hear." Ward looked at Lydia for approval.

She nodded her head in agreement.

Ward held the Bible in his left hand and with his right, opened the book to a page and put his finger where he chose to begin. "So when they had dined, Jesus saith to Simon Peter, 'Simon, son of Jonas, lovest thou me more than these?' He saith unto him, 'Yea, Lord; thou knowest that I love thee.' He saith unto him, 'Feed my lambs.'

"'He saith to him again the second time, 'Simon, son of Jonas, lovest thou me?' He saith unto him, 'Yea, Lord; thou knowest that I love thee.' He saith unto him, 'Feed my sheep.'

"'He saith unto him the third time, 'Simon, son of Jonas, lovest thou me?' Peter was grieved because he said unto him the third time, 'Lovest thou me?' And he said unto him, 'Lord, thou knowest that I love thee.' Jesus saith unto him, 'Feed my sheep.'"

"Well," he said, seeing that Lydia was as shocked as he that the conversation between Jesus and Peter was practically identical to the one they had just shared, "I think there we have our answer." He closed the Bible. "It didn't take a rocket scientist, did it?"

Lydia simply nodded her head. She was so startled that she was still trying to catch hold of her feelings.

"Why don't you decide which church you would like to attend this coming Sunday and find out what time the service is?" he suggested.

"That I can gladly do," she accepted as she leaned over and kissed him on the cheek. "Thank you, Ward." Lydia gazed deep into those hazel eyes that had given her comfort on countless occasions since that day with the frog. "I don't even really understand why I'm thanking you, but I know that I feel more gratitude toward you right this minute than I have in a very long time."

She got up and moved toward the kitchen. "I guess it's about time I feed this person for whom I feel so much gratitude."

"Lydia," Ward said simply as he grabbed her hand and pulled her back enough so that she could see his face, "I really *do* love you."

11

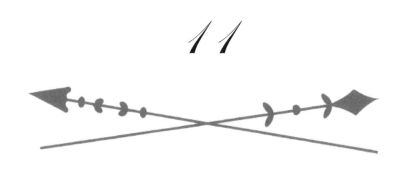

Lydia heard the sound of a car stop at the curb in front of the house. Moving from the kitchen, where she was hard at work baking Moravian cookies using her grandmother's recipe, she stepped toward the front door.

She didn't recognize the man who got out of the blue car. *Some college parent must have gotten the wrong address for his child's apartment. Or could be some seasonal renter with the wrong address.*

Along with the recipe, her grandmother had also taught Lydia to offer something to every guest who ever knocked at her door. *Too bad the cookies aren't baked. He could be the first recipient of my freshly baked sweets in my own new home.* She thought of the store-bought varieties in the cupboard. *Ah, least ways it won't be a wasted trip.*

Lydia opened the front door as he walked up the sidewalk from the steps that led from the curb. "Good afternoon. May I help you?"

"I hope so," he answered, breathing heavily. "I'd forgotten how steep those steps were."

"So you've been here before?"

"Yes, many times. My grandparents used to live here." He caught another breath. "My family and I were going home after a last-minute summer vacation and I had hoped to show my wife and son this place. Do you mind if we walk around the yard for a minute while I share stories of my ancestors with them?"

Lydia looked out to the car and waved at the other two passengers. "Was your grandfather by chance John Glenn Edgerton?"

"Yes…," he began to explain but was cut off in midstream

"Was he really a missionary in Africa?"

"He most certainly was. How did you know that?" Then the man figured she had heard tales of his grandparents from her neighbors.

"I was so intrigued by an old wooden desk, which happened to be locked, sitting in the back corner of the long side room that I sawed through the lock. Inside I found some letters which I'm afraid I've been reading. I apologize if I…,"

This time it was the man who cut Lydia off in midstream. "You mean Grandfather's old desk? That was his writing desk from Africa."

"Then you must come in and have a look at it. Why don't you go and get your family? I'm in the process of making some freshly baked cookies, and by the time you get through walking around the place and come back in, I'll have some ready for you."

"Thank you." The man patted his stomach. "I don't miss

too many chances to eat." He started to turn around, then looked back at her and held out his hand. "Phillip Edgerton. Pleased to meet you."

"My name's Lydia Mason. Maybe you can clear up some questions I have about your grandparents. There are some things in that desk I'm sure you'd love to see. Take your time wandering around outside, and when you're ready to come in, tap on the door. I'll be listening."

She walked back to the kitchen, delighted that she would have someone to share her cookies with when they came out of the oven, and rushed to have them ready in time for her visitors. Lydia was still rolling out dough for a second batch when she heard a light rap on the front door.

"Come on in," she yelled.

Phillip held the door for his wife and son. "Mrs. Mason, this is my wife, Francie, and my son, David."

She wiped the flour on her hand onto her apron, and held out her hand. "Pleased to meet you. And please, call me Lydia."

"We don't mean to be a bother," offered Francie.

"Why, you're no bother. No bother at all. This is only our third week here and I was making cookies to pass around the neighborhood this week. Thought it might be a good way to meet our neighbors."

"Shouldn't that be the other way around?" Francie asked. "It seems that they should be baking the cookies to welcome you to the neighborhood."

"I'm sure there's no rule that says that in the Boone town laws. Besides, this is the very first house that my husband and I have ever owned and I wanted to do something special."

"I'd say that's pretty special," blared David. "I wish I was your neighbor if you're going to be making homemade cookies."

All of the adults laughed at the child's frankness.

"There's also a Sunday evening ice cream supper at the Boone United Methodist Church this weekend and I planned to make some extras to take for that."

"You're Methodist?" asked David.

"Well, not really. We just moved here and thought we'd give that church a try. I guess partly because of your grandfather's letters," Lydia directed to Phillip. "I called them to inquire about the time of their Morning Worship and found out about the evening event. It seemed a nice way to meet some of the people in the area. Besides," she snickered sheepishly, "my husband, Ward, and I read in the Bible last night where Jesus instructed Simon Peter to, 'feed my sheep.' I figured that would be a good way to start."

Phillip gave a huge laugh, joined by his wife.

"Are you also Methodist?" Lydia asked of them.

"Yes, ma'am, we sure are," Phillip answered. "As a matter of fact, both my wife and I are United Methodist clergy from Charlotte."

"How about that? Guess you took up in your grandfather's footsteps, huh?" The hostess gave a small chuckle. "How about your dad? Is he a minister, too?"

"Yes. He's retired now. But Francie and I make the third generation of Edgerton's who are a Pastor/Christian Educator combination."

"Boy, I feel privileged now. As my grandmother said when

she used to invite the preacher over for Sunday dinner, 'No chance of the devil getting in this house today, is there?'" She chuckled again. "Won't you sit back and visit for a while?"

Lydia looked over to David. "I have a batch of Moravian cookies in the oven right now. They're made from my grandmother's old recipe. Would you like to help me cut out the shapes for the next batch?"

The boy glanced toward his mother, making sure it was all right. A nod of Francie's head gave him the permission he needed. "Sure." He followed Lydia into the kitchen as Phillip looked from side to side, taking in the walls and all the memories that they held.

"David loves Moravian cookies," Phillip volunteered from the living room. "My dad makes them each Christmas. It's my grandmother's old recipe, too. He would make them for her since the denseness of the dough made them so hard to roll out. She had a hard time getting the dough just right, so he'd roll it out paper thin and make them just for her. It was a treat she looked forward to every year."

"Of course everyone else was only too anxious to help her eat them," interjected Francie.

"You ever help him cut them out?" Lydia asked David.

"No, ma'am."

"Well, next time you see him, you can surprise him by offering to help him make some cookies. There's nothing to it. You just have to put a little elbow grease into it," she winked. Lydia washed her hands and left the water running for David to do the same. "My grandmother always said the most important ingredient was love."

Love? Feed my sheep? The scriptural passage from the evening before rushed through her mind. "That's odd."

"What?" asked David.

"Oh, nothing," she dismissed. "Just a sudden thought from last night ran through my head. I guess I must have been thinking aloud."

Lydia turned back to Phillip and Francie. "Make yourself at home. I'll have this first batch of cookies out in a couple of minutes and the next ones in."

Phillip walked over to the writing desk and ran his hand across the top.

Seeing him eyeing the piece of furniture, Lydia called out from the kitchen, "I found that when I first entered this house with the realtor. It was covered in dust and one of the legs was broken." She saw the combination of both appreciation and curiosity on the visitor's face.

"Go ahead and open the drawers. It's all right. I haven't changed a thing in it."

"Do you know these drawers stayed locked for forty years? The whole time I knew Grandfather, the drawers were locked."

"I had to saw the locks open one day a couple of weeks ago because it got the best of me. It was like every time I came near it, I heard a sound, like someone beating a drum." One day, I sat down at it, and it was like the beat became a part of me. It had the same rhythm as the pulse of my heart. I knew this piece of furniture had been an integral part of someone's life."

"You could say that again. This was like his lifeline. It is where he wrote, and opened and read all of his letters when he was in the Congo. It was his connection to his home and the loved ones he had left. It was also the place where all his lessons and communications with the Bishop and the Missions Board were written."

Lydia followed David back into the living room where he sat a tray of cookies on the coffee table. She carried a platter of glasses, milk, tea and lemonade.

"I feel that I know your grandparents personally. I guess I shouldn't have, but I found their letters to each other in that desk, and I had to read them. I wanted to know all about them."

"They were quite an interesting couple. As different as day and night, but they sure did love each other."

Lydia, anxious to hear the rest of the story, stepped back into the kitchen and pulled another batch of cookies from the oven and placed the last ones in.

"My grandfather played the lap organ, and my grandmother played the piano and the organ. She had wanted to go back to the conservatory to take lessons on a pipe organ, but the opportunity for a teaching job came open and she decided to take that instead. It was a terribly difficult decision for her from what I understand."

"One of the letters mentioned that she played in a dance band. Back in the twenties?"

"Oh, yes!" Phillip confirmed. "If it had not been for the fact that her Uncle William, who was a prominent Methodist clergyperson, had a lot of pull that got her and her siblings into Trinity – later Duke University – I do believe she might have been quite a flapper."

"'Gene sounds most interesting from the letters." Lydia secretly wondered if Phillip had ever heard of Sonny and that part of the story.

"Oh, she was. Both her parents died when she was very young so she, the two sisters and brother were taken in and raised by their Uncle John who was a doctor. During his career he worked hard to make sure that all four of them earned degrees. Uncle Buddy became a doctor, the two sisters were both old maid teachers, and Grandmother, well Grandmother . . . ,"

"Don't tell me!" screamed Lydia. "I want to find out from the letters. This has been a most intriguing story to me and I want to find it out in your Grandfather's words." She quickly rushed back to get the last batch of cookies from the oven.

Phillip laughed. "Then that you shall." He moved back to the desk, where he'd been previously interrupted by the call of warm Moravian cookies.

"Did you look inside?"

"No, not yet." He rubbed his hand across it again. "I'm not so sure that would be right. I mean, if Grandfather would never permit it . . . ,"

Lydia walked to the desk, opened the drawer with the letters and handed them to Phillip. "There now, you still didn't cross that boundary set by your grandfather."

He laughed as he looked at the four stacks of letters she handed him. On the top was a handmade Christmas card, with pastel original artwork and a poetic greeting.

"Hey, look at this!" Phillip called to his wife and son. "I

recognize this card from my grandmother's stories. I never saw it, but she often relived that Christmas when it arrived, right before she was to go to a church social and children's pageant. She'd discreetly beam as she said, 'This came just as I was about to leave to do the pageant at St. Paul. It lifted my spirits so high that I thought my heart would nearly pop if I became any more filled with the spirit of the holiday. I was to be Sonny's date for the social following the pageant, but my thoughts were in Africa with your grandfather.'

"We'd always laugh after we'd get out of the house, for it was clearly apparent that my grandmother had already fallen 'head over heels in love' with my grandfather. My brother and I would have to sneak outside before we burst into laughter. Now when we get together for family gatherings, it's always a topic of conversation as we routinely revert back to the love that was created through that courtship of letters."

Phillip looked back at Lydia. "I hope I didn't spoil the story for you," he apologized.

"No, not at all. It appears that all the letters are from him." *So he* does *know all about Sonny.*

"That's because . . . ," Phillip caught himself before he let the proverbial "cat out of the bag."

"Would you like to have these?" Lydia asked. Her face spoke what she was unable to verbally express, which was that the letters had become a genuine part of her daily existence, yet she wanted a treasure so precious to belong to a family member of the Edgerton's, which she felt was the rightly thing to do.

Even without her unconscious expression of love for the

letters, Phillip had already made his decision. "No, Lydia, you are a dear sweet soul for making that offer, but these belong with Grandfather's writing desk, where they were all either written or read, and the desk belongs here in The Rhododendron."

"So you did call it "The Rhododendron" all those years ago?"

"Oh, yes. Grandfather gloated every time he told the story of Grandmother stepping out of the car when they first came to Boone. He'd been hired as Professor of Education, and given that the institution's title at that time was the Appalachian State Teacher's College, he felt quite sure that his job was secure."

"Wait a minute!" Lydia interrupted abruptly. "Your grandfather was hired as Professor of Education at Appalachian?"

"Yes, he was. He taught at Duke University for a while after he finally returned from the Congo the last time, and then taught for a period at Presbyterian College in Clinton, South Carolina. But when he acquired the job here, they bought The Rhododendron and he stayed in that position for over twenty years, from 1944 - 1967."

"That's exactly why we're here," she proclaimed. "Ward was just named Professor of Education."

"That's amazing," noted Francie.

"Please continue with your story," coaxed Lydia. "I was simply not expecting that."

"One of the prerequisites for the home that Glenn would buy for his 'dear 'Gene' was that it sit to where she could see the gorgeous scenery from her loom room, which included an entire row of rhododendrons across the front. The only one left in the front, I see, is the one in the corner."

"That's where we found the sign bearing the name of the house. It had become overgrown in the shrub, so Ward took it and repainted it."

"It looks just like it used to out there. You tell Ward that Grandmother Edgerton would have been proud. Oops!" he stopped. "I'm afraid I'm going on again and telling too much."

"No, this is fine. I'm enjoying the tales immensely. It's just that I don't want to know what happened up until they moved here. Please, do continue."

"Okay, if you insist. You see," Phillip explained, "my grandparents got into weaving at some juncture of their marriage. I guess it began as a way to pass the time, but it became another source of a way in which their love grew by doing something together. They used the far end room of this house as their 'loom room.' It was always interesting to my brother and sister and me to see what latest project they had going when we came to visit.

"Grandmother was exceptionally good when it came to crafty things. She had a very creative mind, so she could take an idea and turn it into a real work of art. Like her quilts, for example, they typically had all the squares, or whatever pattern she used, pieced together by different stitching designs. Designs that she'd create so that there was a new one for each piece of fabric. She was quite the homemaker for someone who'd . . . ,"

He stopped suddenly. "I'd better not tell you that part yet."

She smiled.

Phillip thought for a minute. He realized that Lydia had no background on his grandparents other than these letters that had been locked away for two generations. They might have given her a tremendous insight on the hearts, souls and beliefs of these two individuals, but they did nothing for the visual imagery.

"I have an idea," stated Phillip. "There are some things that I'd like for you to see. They are things that were once in this house, mostly wall hangings, pictures and such as that. There's even a whole box of old home movies." His enthusiastic voice lost a bit of its spark as he added, "And a video of them at their 56th anniversary. That was only two weeks before Grandfather died. But they are all things that would allow you to see, *really* see, my grandparents. When you've finished reading all of the letters, why don't you let us bring them back here for you?"

"That sounds like a great idea," agreed Francie. "I'm sure you'd enjoy them."

"I don't know," Lydia hesitated. "I would love that and I surely appreciate your offer, but that sounds like a lot of trouble."

"Oh, no," voiced David. "It's no trouble at all. Will you still have cookies?"

Lydia was so excited by the offer that she could hardly contain herself. From out of nowhere had appeared this family, this connection to the couple who had become a strengthening obsession for her, who could also build her knowledge of Glenn and 'Gene. "That sounds wonderful! But are you sure that isn't asking too much? I mean, after all, it isn't exactly across the street from Charlotte."

"Lydia, you must understand. My family is a tremendous source of pride for me. I'm very proud of my grandparents and their service . . . ,"

He broke off the sentence again, heeding her wish to read the letters. "I feel that it was my love and respect for their backgrounds that gave me such a heart for missions." Phillip turned again to Francie, who concluded his thought for him.

"Phillip is the director of Mission and Outreach for our Western North Carolina Conference of The United Methodist Church. He is greatly involved with mission projects all over the world. It is inherently in his heart and in his blood."

Lydia smiled as she looked at the woman who sat in "Grandmother's chair," as Phillip had informed her that it was. "And what about you?" she asked Francie. "Like his Grandfather Edgerton, Phillip chose a wife who had given her life to servanthood?"

A pinkish blush brushed across Francie's face.

"I'm afraid so," rescued Phillip with his answer. "Francie's the Minister of Christian Education at Myers Park United Methodist Church in Charlotte."

"Is that the impressive stone sanctuary that sits in the fork of the road in Charlotte near the big hospital? The one with the colossal stained glass window that looks like it came out of a cathedral in Europe?"

"That sounds a lot like it," affirmed Francie. "We're only a few blocks from the Carolinas Medical Center, which used to be called the Charlotte Memorial Hospital."

"That's it! That's the one!" exclaimed Lydia, now even more excited. "Ward had a brother who was in that hospital with a heart attack years ago. He had the most wonderful doctors." The woman's eyes were ablaze with recognition. "We made a wrong turn out of the hospital and instead of going back toward the freeway, we wound up at that intersection. I'll never forget it for there was a man standing there, right in the crux of all that traffic, slinging something that looked like a dishrag and directing traffic. All I could think about was that scene from the movie about General Patton, which was new back then, where Patton got out of his jeep and directed the tanks and various military vehicles through an impassible traffic jam."

"You're absolutely correct," admitted Francie. "That would have been Hugh McManaway. I never actually saw him, but he was such a fixture in that area for so many years that nearby "friends" raised the money and erected a bronze statue at that same intersection in front of the church.

"He was actually a member of Myers Park Presbyterian Church next door to us, but everyone in the community knew him. Hugh would stand out there sometimes and play his violin or fiddle - some instrument. And even in the rain, he'd be out there in a hat, I guess it was one of those waterproof things, and sling that dishrag or towel – whatever it was – at the passing motorists to direct them through the intersection."

"Yes, he did that for years," continued Phillip. "He became an icon to Myers Park. That's why the statue. The dates on it read 1913 - 1989, and I'm sure he spent a goodly number of those years standing in that intersection."

"I see," nodded Lydia with great interest. "There was also a restaurant there on the corner. Seems like it was next to an A&P or some chain grocery store."

"You're right again." This time it was Phillip who gave

the explanation. "It was called the Townhouse Restaurant. It was there for at least three generations, I think. Both the locals and the business people of the area loved it. I remember going once years ago with my father. You could go in there and get an elegant meal, with linen table clothes and silver, for a decent price. It was pretty upscale. In fact, I've heard it said that Hugh's mother and father, who was a doctor, made arrangements for Hugh to eat all his meals there after their deaths. He was mentally handicapped, but was a viable part of the community. His parents apparently wanted to make sure he could stay in the area that was home to him. There was no doubt that the neighbors would all make sure he was well cared for. As Francie said, he was noted throughout the entire community."

Francie nodded. "I think it says a lot for an area that's known as 'the elite' section of a large city like Charlotte, where most of the residents have come from long lines of family fortunes, for the people to not only accept someone like Hugh McManaway, but to so proudly call him 'their own.'"

"I think you're exactly right," agreed Lydia. "What a beautifully touching story." She gave a tender smile. "The thing I most remember about that restaurant, 'The Townhouse' as you called it, is that we sat at a spot where that stained glass window was our view. I'll never forget it, for Ward called my attention to it.

"'Look at that,' he said. 'It's an image of Jesus holding out his hands to those in need of his love and acceptance.' While I looked at the window, he went on, 'It was no accident that I took that wrong turn. I needed to see this picture of Christ today. I needed to feel him wrap his loving arms around me.'

"Ward never admitted it, nor did I ever ask, but I feel certain that he made a pact with God that day at lunch. You see, we never went to church before that. It wasn't that we were opposed to church, but it didn't seem to be a necessary part of our existence. After that day, we began to visit the churches in our area until we found one that felt right for us. I truly do believe that Ward vowed to give his life to God if God would spare his brother. The brother was spared, and we became pseudo-active in the life of that congregation. That is, until we moved here."

"Are you a church member anywhere?" Francie inquired.

"No." Lydia bowed her head, seeking the courage to explain, and then looked back at the couple. "You see, even though we *went* to church then, we weren't really *into* the church. It was more of a social thing. Once we moved to another location for Ward to teach, it kind of got lost in the shuffle." A hint of a smile brushed across her face. "It wasn't until I read the letters that I had a desire to go back to church." The smile broadened. "In fact, last night is the first time in all our years together that Ward and I actually sat down and read the Bible together. It was truly amazing how the verses we read seemed to precisely fit with the topic we were discussing."

"Did you think that was by accident?" asked Phillip.

"Oh, no," she quickly responded. "I'm sure that Ward and I both sensed that it was by design, and not by our own. But after that, we decided that maybe it was time to put church back in our lives. That's why I called Boone United Methodist this morning. It was because of your Grandfather Edgerton's association with the Methodist mission."

"How interesting!" noted Phillip. "That's the same church my grandparents attended. In fact, Grandfather was instrumental in making sure the church installed a new pipe organ after the sanctuary burned down some years ago. Then when the church moved to another location, the pipe organ was not a matter of contention. The congregation simply took it for granted that a pipe organ would be a part of the furnishings. They not only moved the one that Grandfather insisted upon, but added to it for their new facility."

"Oh, it's a beautiful sanctuary and organ!" exclaimed Lydia.

"Indeed it is. That old location is also where both of their funerals were held," he added.

"Isn't it most odd that there are so many ties between us?" Lydia speculated aloud. "We happen to buy the same house as one of the former professors of Education, we visit the same church where he was a member, his grandson shows up on our doorstep, whose wife is a minister at the only church we know in Charlotte, and that's because it was a source of hope to us. Life really is uncanny, isn't it?"

"I think what my grandfather would say is that 'life is full of relationships.'"

"That's a lovely saying. Yes, I suspect from the letters I've read that you're right," agreed Lydia.

12

It was Friday, the last morning before the weekend when Ward would be home. Lydia could hardly wait for him to leave for the office so that she could settle down with the letters. The minute he stepped out the door, she pulled out the next one in the stack to note that it had been typed on official letterhead of the African Mission Office.

Could this stationery be new for Mr. Edgerton?

Lydia suspected that if the African mission was coming along in the world, it was largely in part of Glenn's efforts and love for the people and his work.

Or should I have said "His work?" she rationalized as she poured herself a morning cup of coffee and sat at the writing desk with the stack of letters, now a daily habit.

She began to think over her habits. Perhaps because she'd spent her working days as a teacher's assistant and hadn't the time previously, she'd never been much into daily routines. But during these last few days she had become accustomed to a daily morning ritual for the weekdays. A ritual that included a letter or two, followed by prayer, and which was accompanied by a cup of caffeine. Lydia wasn't into the flavored coffees. She was content with the regular blend that she'd had as a teen at home, mixed with enough cream to give it a blonde touch of color.

As she sat reading this morning's "official letter," she wondered what Glenn drank in Africa to begin his mornings. Then she wondered how 'Gene started out her days. She realized that through the letters, she had also become more satisfied with the simple things in her life, things that still to much of the world were considered a luxury.

Lydia's mind recalled a recent survey on poverty that she'd come across in a magazine while waiting at the doctor's office with Ward during his physical for ASU's insurance. She'd had no idea that the rate of homeless and uneducated people was still so astoundingly high. It had been a reality that she'd found most disturbing and alarming.

For all those years, she'd longed for a dream home, *any home that had Ward's and her name on the bottom line*. That had seemed a lifelong goal that most Americans had obtained at an early age. *Or so I thought*, she remembered from the day she saw the article with the statistics. Now as she sat at the window that overlooked the mountaintop, she thanked God for giving her such a wondrous and rich blessing.

The regime of letters had also brought about the added reading of a daily devotional, something that had in the past been foreign to her. With that came the addition of Ward's Bible so that she could read the passages recommended in the devotional and get the "full effect," she'd called it when she told Ward about it on those days when he'd come home and asked what she'd done during the day. He no longer asked, for he knew she'd become a person of strict habit.

She'd raved so much about the letters that she had even convinced Ward to join her on the past two Saturdays as she read them. *Will tomorrow make it three in a row?* Lydia wondered as she untied the thin pink ribbon that held the current batch of letters from which she was reading.

Now if I can just convince him to join Boone United Methodist with me on Sunday. She conceived that her longings had become prayers, which she consciously began to say at the end of her readings. The prayers always ended with the words, "And Lord, let me learn about You through the dedication and commitment of Glenn Edgerton. May his life's work never be diminished, and please show me a way to keep it alive for others."

As Lydia uttered the final phrase this morning, she felt that she had been given an answer from God for the first time in her life. She no longer felt the need to persuade Ward to join the church with her on Sunday, for she felt that God was taking care of that in her husband's heart.

"Oh, thank you, God!" she screamed aloud, not realizing what she'd done until after the words escaped her mouth. For the first time in her life, Lydia felt that she had been an active participant in a blessing. "Oh, thank you, God," she uttered again, this time much softer, as she brushed the tear from her eye and opened the envelope to read today's lesson in the letters.

Wembo Nyama, Congo Belge

August 20, 1927

Again it is Saturday night and the end of another week. How time does fly! Days become weeks and weeks become months before our very eyes and yet we realize it not until they have passed into that eternity from whence recall is impossible. How it behooves us to make the most of every opportunity for telling the story of Jesus and for bringing light where all is darkness. I took very seriously for myself the lesson which one of our native preachers was making much of in his sermon to the children a few Sundays ago. "You have heard the story, and now it is up to you to go and tell others."

A few nights ago, about three o'clock A.M., I heard moanings coming from the village which I immediately recognized as those of people weeping for one who had just passed away. The next morning upon inquiry I learned that the person who had died was one of the best men in our village. He had been sick for many days and all that could be done for him was powerless to ward off the death angel which had been hovering around the door of his life.

And well they might mourn because he was one of the most outstanding Christians of our village. Not only were the natives sorrowful but also the missionaries. However the latter were better able to control their grief whereas the natives gave full vent to all their emotions. Some of them moaned and groaned with all their might and at times screamed at the tops of their voices. After much persuasion they were better able to control themselves.

On the second morning he was buried. As the small procession wended its way toward the cemetery it was headed by four men carrying the corpse on their shoulders. Behind them came the friends and mourners. Some were carrying a few of his belongings which it is their custom to deposit in and on the grave. Last came the widow moaning and weeping.

He was bourne to the newly made grave where the service was conducted. Hymns were sung while the casket was being lowered into the last resting place for the body. Then the mat, or bed, of the deceased was lowered into the grave, after it had first been pierced in two or three places so that it would never be of any further service. One of the missionaries gave a few words of tribute. All on the station who were able to go were present. Then the grave was filled. A few more hymns were sung. There were only two shovels, but everyone present helped in the filling of the grave. Those who had no shovels used their hands, both men and women and even the widow. After it was finished, a few trinkets which numbered his earthly possessions were placed on top of the grave. Most of them were first rendered useless. It was useless to do this because the majority of the natives would not have dared remove any of them.

The people then returned to the village. This time they went silently, not mourning as when they came. It is the custom for his friends to do no work for several days, only sit about the place and mourn silently. In some villages the mourning lasts for a month and even several months. In one place that I know of the mourning lasts for an entire year. The effect of extended mourning is not good for them. All of them wear on their bodies signs of mourning. Some of them are only painted on, others are made of a kind of grass. These they wear until they become so frayed that they fall off. When the last signs will have disappeared the period of mourning will have ended.

Those who have become Christians do not have such extended periods of mourning, nor do they indulge in many of the heathen rights which often accompany them. They are comforted because they know that Jesus has taught that those who trust in Him and strive to do His will shall have eternal life. They say that they know that their friends are waiting for them in the "city in the sky." "Blessed are they that mourn for they shall be comforted."

Before the coming of the missionaries it was the custom of the people to bury their dead beneath the floors of their houses. Others buried them in the rear of the houses. This is still the custom with those who are not Christians or who do not live in mission villages. There are several reasons for this. One is to protect the last resting place of the body from the inroads of wild animals such as the hyena from digging into the grave and mutilating the body. Another reason is that they can be near the body throughout the entire period of mourning.

In many places the period of mourning toward the end is marked by feasting. Oft times feasting is indulged in off and on during that time depending upon the number of relatives and their wealth. It is an easy time especially for the men because they do no work. The women prepare all the food. It is brought to them so all that they have to do is to eat.

It is very hard to get these people to give up any of their old customs. This is not hard to understand when we think how people in enlightened countries are enslaved by customs. We do not attempt to get them to give up all of their customs. Many of them are very good as we try to encourage them in keeping them and in forming others like them. It is almost an impossibility to persuade them to renounce all their evil customs at once, and it takes a long time and lots of patience to bring them to see so clearly which is the right road of life that they are willing to forsake their old lives for it.

The letter ended abruptly. It was only when Lydia looked inside the envelope to make sure that she hadn't missed a page that she discovered that this was the letter to the Sunday School of St. Paul Methodist Church of which Glenn had mentioned in an earlier letter.

She took a guess that the rest of the letter had been copied or pasted to the minutes of the church – by 'Gene – but for whatever reason, she was indeed enlightened by the message of the letter. *It seems that each of these letters contains a lesson for me,* Lydia surmised as she placed the official stationary back in the envelope and reached for another letter.

Ah! she sighed. *I see the difference now. This letter, typed on plain paper, was to his "sincere friend, 'Gene." That's why the official letterhead on the other one. I see that Glenn doesn't consider his writings to Miss Eugenia May Bennett official business!*

She took a sip of the coffee, which was now the perfect temperature for her, and settled back in the chair that she had a couple of weeks ago learned was the one that belonged to Mrs. Edgerton.

Tuesday morning
August 23, 1927

My dear 'Gene,

I hope that you will pardon the use of the typewriter this morning, as I want to get a letter off to you in this mail. It is true the mail will not leave until Friday, but I never can tell just what is going to turn up at the last minute to keep me from writing a letter. I wished to get one off to you in the mail last week but so very many things happened during the last two or three days previous to the departure of the mail that I did not have the opportunity to write to you.

It is useless for me to say that I was not very happy to receive your letter, because I was very, very happy indeed. It did me so much good to hear from you again. When your last letter came I wondered just a little bit about how long it would be before I could expect another one from you. I am very glad that you did not wait so long to mail this last one. I hope there are several more on the way to me. You know, I somehow feel that we are going to be real good friends.

Mental telepathy must have been in operation in the vicinity of you and Mr. Daniel when you were writing to me because in the very same mail with yours came a letter from him, too. He wrote me such a fine letter and I enjoyed every bit of it. I surely do treasure him as a friend.

Well of all things! You are keeping that letter which I asked you to destroy. However, if you care to do so, you may follow your own inclinations. I thought that perhaps you would never care to see it again and so that is why I suggested that you dispose of it in that way. Just as you like about it will be satisfactory with me. Keep it safe as you are doing with our little secret.

It was a treat to have all the news about all the things that have been happening in and about Goldsboro. Sometimes I have so little news from there that I wonder if I live there, or used to live there, at all. Even though I am this far away, I like to have the news of the happenings. I so appreciate hearing about what you are planning and doing, and in fact all about everything.

And so you think that you can't be my secretary in the foreign field, do you? That's a good one, I think. However, I am indeed very proud to know that my church has such an efficient treasure in the homeland. I am coming more and more to the conclusion that I need both a secretary and treasurer out here. Mr. Daniel suggested that if such was the case that all I would have to do would be to send him a wireless stating who I wanted and that he would send "her" out. But I know better than that because where two are concerned, certainly two must and will have a voice. Isn't that true? I did not quite understand from that statement about secretaries and treasurers whether you had in mind ever considering such a position or not. They keep telling me out here that I need other positions filled also, but I have not yet decided about that for myself.

I suppose you think that I am a very silly person indeed from the forerunning paragraph and perhaps you have come to the proper conclusion. Sometimes I wonder myself just whether I am not very much so. I would not be at all surprised if that be not true. Now, would you? Perhaps if you knew me better you would say that I am exactly right, but I shall leave that entirely for you to say.

Well, I must stop for this time. Kind regards to all our friends. May God bless and keep you.

Your sincere friend,
Glenn

Mr. Daniel, the minister, knows of Glenn's fondness for 'Gene, too? If he knows, I wonder how many other people know? Perhaps she's nothing more than a big flirt who wishes to make Sonny jealous because another man is showing interest in her. Or perhaps she's like most other women who become heartily interested in the "new man on the block."

A sudden thought of discovery — *a clue in my detective novel*, she snickered — ran through Lydia's mind. *If Mr. Daniel is a minister, who happens to know 'Gene's Uncle William, who also happens to be the Presiding Elder of his area, that would mean that Uncle William is Mr. Daniel's immediate superior. It would also mean that Mr. Daniel would probably much rather see his new Assistant romantically involved with a missionary than a businessman.*

Lydia laughed aloud. *Or it may simply mean that he's well pleased with his new secretary/educator and wants to keep her for a long time. If she marries Sonny, he will not want her to work. If she's interested in Glenn, she's not going to be leaving for a while.*

The laughter stopped with the sincere realization of the more probable answer. *Or most likely Mr. Daniel was experienced enough as a minister to recognize true love when he saw it.*

She put the letter back in the envelope, satisfied with her conclusion.

As Lydia replaced the stacks of letters in the desk drawer, she reflected back to her prayer, her answer and the sensation of being a part of her first miracle. *Or at least the first one I recognized.* She wondered what God would do to get Ward's attention in a way that would make him want to be a *real* active member of a church. She also wondered how long it took for prayers to be answered, especially when one had already heard God's will for the answer of that prayer.

13

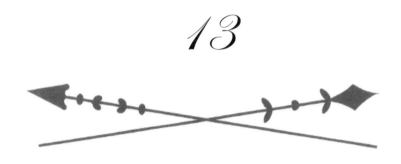

Wembo Nyama
Sept. 4, 1927

Dear 'Gene,

Again it is Sunday morning, and a beautiful one at that. We are all very happy this morning because of the arrival of a new party of missionaries yesterday. I must tell you all about it because it is quite an incident in our lives when new missionaries arrive.

Yesterday morning about 2:30 the sentry came over and called me. (That is an unearthly hour to be disturbed, isn't it?) I could not imagine what the trouble was, and about half awake I asked him several questions about who was sick, etc., but I finally understood him to say that he had a letter for me. So I crawled out of bed and read it. It was a note from the Captain of the steamer, who is here at this time, saying that the steamer, which we have been awaiting for some time had arrived at Kabengele. I wrote a note saying that I would get up and go over on the truck early to get the party.

I went back to bed and instead of going back to sleep as I thought that I could do, I began to think of all the things that I would have to do that morning early before I could get away. I finally decided that I could not go back to sleep, and so I sent them a note and told them that if they would fix a little breakfast for me I would go as soon as I could get ready. They did and so I got the truck ready, ate breakfast and finally got away about 5:30.

It took me about four hours to drive the forty miles there. Upon my arrival I met Dr. and Mrs. Lewis, who were returning missionaries and for whom we have been looking, Dr. Janet Miller, and Miss Bryant. We have been looking for all of them and we were very happy that they had arrived. Well we loaded up the truck and got away in about another hour and started on the return trip.

The trip was very lovely and as it was somewhat cloudy it was not at all unpleasant traveling in the middle of the day except when we stopped. The truck ran fine all the way and I surprised everybody by getting back to the mission about the middle of the afternoon. I was somewhat tired after such a long drive and having gotten up so early in the morning. I rested well last night and feel none the worse this morning from such a hasty trip.

We surely have had a lot of excitement on the field

for the past month. Some people may think that life out here is very droll and that nothing ever happens to cause excitement but I can assure you that such is not the case. I would tell you all about it but is all local and you would not be able to appreciate all the spirit of it unless you knew the circumstances, etc.

There was a very sad incident connected with the arrival of the new party. They left Antwerp about four months ago and of course had had no mail since that time as they had expected to come on immediately to Wembo Nyama. In the course of time many letters had arrived. I took them over with me yesterday morning and gave them to the different ones. Miss Bryant had just loads of letters, but the first one that she opened and the first line that she read told her that her father died a few days after she had sailed from Antwerp. It almost broke her heart even though he has been ill for some time, and she knew that death might come at any time. She could not finish the letter nor open any of the others until after she had arrived here.

It is very hard but that is a thing that those of us who come out here have in a way to go through even before we sail from the fair shores of America. It is a thing that we know must come sometime whether we are here or there and we have to be ready to bear the news of it when it arrives. Before we come out (I know I did and I am sure that the others did too) we have to see our loved ones dead as well as alive. It is only when facing such an experience and having passed through it that one can freely say, "Here am I, Lord, send me to Congo."

Spring has just arrived here. By that I mean the rains and the new life in all vegetation. But by the time that this letter will have reached you it will be late fall there and the days will have begun to get cool and frost will be in the air. It's a grand feeling isn't it?

Mail time is very interesting at times. I am often impressed by the many different parts of the world from which my letters come. In the mail last week I had news from friends in different parts of the United States, China, Japan and Siam. I at times wish that I could grow a pair of wings and drop in for a friendly chat with these friends. Some of these times when I am going home on furlough I am going by India, Siam, Japan, China and the Philippines for a visit with my friends. I think that it would be a most illuminating trip.

I am hoping that the next mail and many thereafter will bring me letters from you.

It is time to close as it's time for me to get ready for the Junior church service. I am glad that I have Mrs. Lewis to give the talk this morning because I know that she will have something good for them and then too it has given me the opportunity of writing to you.

With the best of wishes to all my friends, and a prayer that God may bless you in the work which you are doing, I must "ring off" until the next time.

Very sincerely,
Glenn

P.S. I bought a snakeskin, python, the other day. It measures 11 feet, 1 inch long and the snake was killed near Wembo Nyama.

Isn't that just like a man? mused Lydia. *You want a young lady to come and share in your life in a foreign country and you bribe her with thoughts of a python eleven feet long? And don't forget the one extra inch. That makes it even more special! Oh, that I had a man to love me enough to endear me with a snake's skin!* she ironically teased.

"Lydia, can I get you out of those letters? If so, I'd like to talk to you about something before we go to church this morning," Ward called as he went outside to capture the essence of a work-free day and get a sense of the temperature.

What? I thought he'd told me last night he'd decided to stay home this morning.

Ward walked back in the front door holding his arm up in the air with something dangling from it. "Look what I found out in the street this morning." He held up a snake's skin. "It would appear we've had a small friend hanging out around here."

Lydia got a puzzled look on her face as she gazed down at the envelope of the letter she'd just read.

"Are you alright? I didn't mean to frighten you so," Ward said throwing the skin back out the front door and into the yard.

"No, no, you didn't at all." She looked at Ward in a way

that appeared she was gazing past him and into another time completely. "Do you remember when you said that turn down the wrong street, the one that led you to the stained glass window in Charlotte, wasn't a wrong turn at all?"

He nodded as he sat down in the chair that had belonged to Dr. Edgerton. "Yes, I remember that window and that day very well. It was the day that my brother finally took a turn for the better and the road to recovery after that heart attack when we thought we had lost him."

"Remind me to tell you after church today about a similar experience that I had recently."

"I will," he replied, wondering what had so consumed her, but more eager to speak to her before they left for church. "Lydia, I've been thinking . . . no, it's more like I have a feeling . . . like a premonition or something."

Her brown eyes, that had momentarily been in a daze became set on his face as she watched him search for words - something that he rarely did.

"We've visited the church here for a couple of Sundays now and we've sat together and read a short scriptural passage each evening before going to bed. It seems that we're making a valid attempt at "playing" Christians. For some reason that won't seem to leave me alone, I have this underlying feeling that if we're going to 'talk the talk,' we're going to have to 'walk the walk,' as the trite expression goes."

"I'm not quite sure that I understand what you're saying," Lydia responded, knowing that God and her prayer from two days earlier were both involved – or accomplices – in Ward's words.

"I never really committed myself to God after that day in Charlotte like I promised. I went to church and I went through the motions." He squinted his eyes, still obviously in turmoil over the words that weren't coming easily. "But I didn't really get anything out of it."

She looked into his face and realized how true the statement about two people living together so long that they began to think alike actually was, for she knew exactly what was on his mind, his exact words that he was struggling so hard to find.

"Is it because you didn't put anything into it?" she asked caringly.

"That's the point I was trying to make exactly," he beamed, proud that he'd successfully formulated the thought into words.

"And now your point is?" she led him into the next part of the statement.

Still pleased with himself and the way he was taking charge of this conversation, Ward smiled, "It appears to me that if we're going to be active participants who give as much as we receive, if not more, we can't do it from the outside looking in."

Lydia looked at him, fully expecting his next words.

"I believe that we should become members of the family of Boone United Methodist Church."

She could believe her ears, but what she couldn't believe was the expediency with which her prayer was answered. *Or what happened to cause it.* Lydia was overjoyed that God had allowed her to experience both a miracle and a blessing firsthand and recognize it.

As she went upstairs to get dressed for worship, *and to*

receive a huge new family, the snake's skin slithered through her thoughts. Not one to have been an analyst before, she intended to question the minister on the symbolism of the snake – *or asp*. *Perhaps the fact that it left its skin and traveled elsewhere meant that "the asp" knew that there was no room for him in this house.*

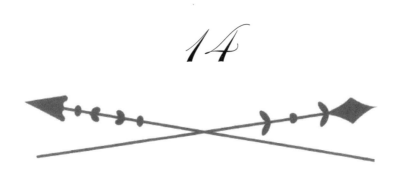

The meal at the restaurant was as filling as the sermon had been. It had turned out to be a most memorable service in many ways, not the least of which was their membership into the church. Lydia walked through the front door of The Rhododendron in a tizzy of countless thoughts, with Glenn's words about losing those dear to you at the forefront of them.

"Ward, I know you're not the kind of person who needs to hear these words often, if at all, but I must tell you how much I have loved being married to you."

"You *have* loved?" he winked with a grin. "As opposed to what? Are you planning on checking out on me sometime in the near future?" With that he pulled his tie from around his neck and laid it over the back of the sofa as he reached for the remote and the television guide from the paper.

"No, I simply felt the need to tell you how much I love you. That's all." Lydia knew full well why her need to share those words, but she had no inclination to share her reasoning with her husband.

Ward placed the paper and remote on a small table beside his recliner that faced the den's television and walked to where he stood face to face with his wife. "Don't you ever think for one moment that it isn't important to me to hear those words. I know I'm not a wordy person at home, but you mean the world to me. Being married to you is the best thing that ever happened to me." He then took Lydia in his arms and kissed her in a gentle and caring manner that she had forgotten over the years.

That simple act of love was all she needed to know that she truly was the love of his life. She tried with all her might to remember whether there was a time when the two of them had ever experienced a burning desire to be with each other. They had been high school sweethearts whom everyone knew would marry once Ward graduated from college. Lydia was sure she would be the "ideal stay-at-home Mom" but when, after several years, it became apparent that she was not to bear children, she gave into the lifelong goal of teaching children. That was when she finally went to apply at the local county education office as a teacher's aid.

"Had I known that I'd never have children of my own, I'd have gone off to college when you did," she'd shared with Ward the night that she filled out the application.

That was the last time she could remember when he'd taken her in his arms and let her know how perfectly satisfied he was with her just the way things were between them. *That is, until we came here and finally owned a home of our own.*

Lydia watched Ward's steps as he moved back to the chair

and settled in a reclined position to watch television. She knew that within minutes, he'd be asleep and that the screen was merely an excuse to fall into a Sunday afternoon nap. There had been many Sundays when she'd joined him, but today, there were other letters in the bundle to be read.

Philip and Francie were due for another visit soon and she wanted to have read as many of the letters as possible before their arrival. She wanted to know the innermost thoughts of the two individuals who had lately become her own family, or so it seemed.

Feeling the beating of the African drums within her own soul as she walked past Glenn's writing desk, she felt it was going to be a wonderfully relaxing afternoon of reading and anticipating the couple's fascination with each other with the opening of each envelope. Lydia poured herself a tall glass of lemonade, took the pile of letters bound by the pink ribbon from the desk drawer and sat down in Eugenia May's comfortable chair for an uninterrupted afternoon.

Somehow, the fact that her own Ward was in the next room, also having a relaxing and uninterrupted afternoon, filled Lydia with a wondrous sense of peace and comfort that she'd not encountered in a long time - *if ever*, she mused - as she read of a developing and beautiful courtship between a man and a woman.

Wembo Nyama, C.B.
October 2, 1927

My dear 'Gene,

I was hoping to get the opportunity to make some greetings for Thanksgiving but that plan has had to take a second place in the multiplicity of things commanding my time and energy. For this reason this letter is going to have to bear my greeting to you although I fear that it will be late in reaching you. "God makes us thankful for friends who pave the way for a closer walk with thee" is my prayer at this Thanksgiving time.

Don't think I am willfully neglecting to write to you because I am not. I have been so rushed for the past few weeks that at times I have allowed myself to become irritated. I was very much ashamed afterwards and shall try to keep a better hold on my temper in the future. Yesterday morning was just a sample of how my time is filled. I arose at the usual hour and went to early prayer service just a little before six. It being Saturday was my time to have charge. Immediately afterwards I had to write some letters to send to Tunda by a man who had brought some boxes of the Lewises. I finished one letter and then had to stop and assign some special work which I was to have done. By that time the bell was ringing for breakfast. After breakfast I had to write more letters to go with orders for medical supplies, which I had just received from Tunda by a special man and which had to go back to Tunda before mailing. You see that is just one of the duties of the business manager. When I finished the last one I had to weigh out loads for men who had come to take things for the Lewises to Tunda. Transport man (agent) for this station is another one of my duties which has consumed considerable time lately. I then took about a minute to get a good breath before paying my teachers who were waiting on the porch. It being the end of the month they were very much in evidence. Next I had to count out some money for one of the departments as I am Mission Treasurer and "hold the bag." My bicycle tire was flat and had to be patched. The Boys Club had to receive money for rations. My personal boys were clamoring for their month's wages. There were several Mission Boys wanting numerous and sundry things. At last I closed up the office and went to dinner. Outside that I had little else to do yesterday morning. I had wanted to get some new materials ready for the school for the new week but as usual that had to be put off until a more convenient day. The truck has to have some work done on it also before I can start out on it for a trip which I have to make to Minga next weekend. That, too, is having to wait until the new week.

Everyday, of course, is not like this but I just wrote about it to let you see that practically every minute is commanded by something. I would also like to have something interesting for you to read but I have very little energy these days for the creative things.

Do you think I need a companion to help me? Some of the missionaries tell me that I do, but I don't know. It all depends on who that one would be.

But to become rational again, I want to tell you that I am deeply appreciative in a very personal way for all the contributions which are being made that I may remain in this field and carry on the work of the Lord, our God. I cannot reach out and touch each hand and tell that person in a physical way, but I do reach out my spiritual hand and place it upon each head and ask that God's blessing may rest thereon. I pray not only for those who give but for all those who want to give, and that God may see the heart of each one of the members of St. Paul Church and give it a spiritual blessing as well as a physical one. I am doing the best that I can to live up to what is expected of me, but I know that many times I fall far short of reaching it.

To know that you have been re-elected as Pastor's Assistant again for the coming year is very pleasant. I don't know of any young woman whom they could get that would fill the place in as creditable a way as you do. Accept my congratulations and best wishes for the coming year. I am glad to know that you are going to be in Goldsboro for more time to come.

I know something of just what you have been facing in trying to decide just what to do in regard to your music. I faced something of the same question when I was in New York City. I wanted to study voice there. There were so many good teachers there and I had the opportunity of studying with an especially fine one. However, I had to let them all pass by because the work that I had to do consumed all of my time. It is a question that you will have to decide for yourself. To study in that great field of music would be most pleasant indeed. The most important consideration which I believe that you have to face frankly is "Will further study of piano and pipe organ greatly increase your efficiency in your life's work?" If you can decide this in the affirmative then you should return to the conservatory and finish your music.

We do not have pipe organs on the mission fields out here, and I do not know of a single piano in this part of Africa. If there be one in Congo I do not know of it. I am going to do my very best to secure a piano of the smaller type such as is used in primary departments of schools and Sunday schools. Provided the freight will not be too exorbitant I am going to bring it back with me to Africa when I return from my first furlough. All I have at present is a small folding organ but at times I imagine it is a great pipe organ.

The dry season is about at an end and we are now beginning to have fierce storms which are heralds of the rains. Last night a marvelous one, and I mean that in its real sense, came up just after supper. The lightning flashed in a most awe-inspiring way, the thunders crashed and rolled, and the wind blew. It was a wonderful sight to see the heavens, all dark and murky, suddenly pierced by a blinding flash followed by a deafening crash, and the low murmur of the distant rain.

The natives have strange stories about the storms. They were telling me this morning that the lightning is an animal something like a sheep and that it picks out some people that it wants to kill and it never fails to find its mark. They think that someone is killed by each flash of the lightning. The lightning always picks out someone wearing white clothing if such a one can be found, and those who are not in their houses. Whenever a storm comes up and they are away from a village they will try to get to one. No matter how hard the rain may come down they will not stop until they reach their destination. I told them this morning, a group of boys here at the house, that the lightning is no animal. They replied that it is because I do not know, but that some day I shall see.

I must stop now. However, I must now get to work. I am enclosing a sketch which I wrote a few days ago which tells something of the customs of the people when death comes. It is not complete but just contains a few observations which I have made.

May God bless all of you in the work which you are doing in the home land, and may He at all times be near to counsel and guide you.

Very sincerely,
Glenn

Sunday afternoon? Again? It seems that Glenn, too, enjoyed his restful Sabbaths in the Congo with these same letters — except by way of writing them. Sundays must have been his only day that allowed moments of free time for writing.

And it appears that our Glenn and 'Gene were both musicians. No wonder the beat of the drum was so strongly calling to me each time I passed the writing desk.

Lydia quickly moved to another letter, eager to see the outcome of 'Gene's decision about her study of pipe organ and piano at the conservatory. She checked the date of the letter, noting that the past three had been written practically a month apart.

Let's see, if it took three months to get there and three months to get a reply, that would be only one correspondence every six months. It appears our couple has resorted to hearing from each other once a month.

She looked at the other three piles of letters, also tied together, each with a different color of thin ribbon. *From the looks of those, I'd estimate that the correspondence grew as did the feelings between the couple.*

Lydia noted that the next letter she opened, like several of the last ones, did not have a salutation to anyone. She took a quick glance at the envelope to see that it was a report of the work being done at the mission. The impressive letterhead amazed her, for it was not at all what she would have expected from one who was working in the midst of such a primitive tribe. As she looked at the formality presented by the heading METHODIST EPISCOPAL CONGO MISSION with the words DEPARTMENT OF EDUCATION underneath in a smaller size, it soon became apparent to her that Glenn Edgerton had given his entire life to educating people, either in Africa or in America. The comprehension of that point made her think of Ward Mason, with the student to whom he'd had the greatest impact being Lydia Mason.

There is a calling to every occupation. Her awareness spawned several minutes of exploring truths and their philosophies, with the outcome being a deeper appreciation for not only the work of Glenn, but of her own husband. Lydia began to wonder how many students Ward had taught or mentored during his career. She was sure that it was nowhere near the number of the ones on the list of the writer of the four stacks of letters, but it had to be a great many.

And the ones that they've taught all had the opportunity to go out and teach others. "Education bearing fruit," she uttered as she began to read the report that told of taking a new missionary to Minga Station with the truck breaking down on the last half of the seventy-mile jaunt causing it to take them nearly thirteen hours to make the trip. After two days of trying to repair the truck, making no progress without the new parts that would have to be ordered, Glenn was able to take the "wheel" bicycle of one of the missionaries stationed at Minga.

"The return trip took nearly twelve hours, in nearly unbearable heat and then torrential rains, which actually packed the dirt and made the remainder of the trip easier. I have been on many trips but I have never had boys who were more faithful and loyal than the ones I had on this one. They were men from Minga and whom I did not remember that I had ever seen previously but they did just as much for me as any one in our village here would have done. One will have to go a long way before he will find a people with a deeper loyalty than the Otetela among whom to work."

His boys, Lydia had read, had to walk alongside the bicycle – "the wheel" – the entire time and carry the lunch and water and help get him through the streams and hard places. They stayed right by his side the entire time, on foot, as he made the trip that look a few minutes less than the trip in the truck."

It seemed ironic to Lydia that as she sat watching the Tour de France, she also sat reading about a missionary making a daylong seventy-mile journey bike trip. She recalled the words of the children's sermon that had been given the past Sunday at church. The associate pastor had brought in a bicycle tire that was flat to use as his example to the children. His point had been that the tire could not work without air, and that the bicycle could not work without the tire. "Like the bicycle," he had said, "the various parts are like the church as a body, and without one of the 'limbs' nothing would work."

Lydia envisioned the hot sun beating down on men who were walking for seventy miles for twelve long hours. There was no way she could recreate the toil of that scenario in her mind. But what she could see was the lone white man, in his riding clothes and a safari hat to protect him from the sun, with the natives accompanying him and carrying water and food and drink for them to make it through the day, just so that they could enable a man to work and also restock with food and drink for the next day's journey back to their home village. All this for a strange man because they were asked by another man whom they trusted.

All like the parts of a bicycle working together. "One will have to go a long way before he will find a people with a deeper loyalty than the Otetela among whom to work," she read again. It was difficult for her to imagine how well the people – the missionaries and the natives – were able to build such a trust with the obstruction of the communication barrier.

Love speaks volumes, she mused with the hint of a reflective smile on her face as she opened the next letter.

Wembo Nyama, C. Belge
November 1, 1927

My dear 'Gene,

Your dear card written from Lake Junaluska August 4, 1927 arrived bringing all the joy which you entrusted to it. It found me very happy indeed, and if you were so happy as I, you experienced real joy. There is much joy to be had in doing the will of Him that sent me.

Shortly after your card came I had a letter from Stella. I want to write to her soon. You know how little time I have for writing these days. She told me about your having gone to the conference at Lake Junaluska and how later Mrs. Beulah and Sonny went up and came back with you. It is beautiful up there and I am sure that all of you must have had a lovely time.

The atmosphere here tonight is very suggestive of the mountains. We had a storm this afternoon and it became very cool afterwards as night fell soon after the rain ceased. However, it is very delightful and makes one feel like doing lots of work.

I hardly can realize that before this letter reaches you Christmas will have passed, my second in Congo. The time has flown past and I have done so little to show for it. I hope with the New Year I shall be able to do more real work in bringing others to Jesus. Oh, they need to know Him so much and to take him into their lives. I pray daily that others may hear the call to come to serve this people.

Lydia's eyes skimmed over the rest of the letter that told of a young albino girl that had just entered the Girls' House at the mission. Glenn also rejoiced about a couple he knew, Dr. and Mrs. Moore from Raleigh, North Carolina, who were on their way to an assignment at Wembo Nyama. Simply from the tone of his words, it was clear that his love for the unknown albino girl in Africa was just as strong as what he held for the acquainted couple from Raleigh. She sat back for a moment and wondered how many other people, especially given that point in time, could have felt that same outpouring of love.

Suddenly the decision of joining a church where one felt that he or she belonged no longer seemed such a monumental commitment. *But,* as her eyes turned back to reading, *a decision that leads to that same outpouring of love,* Lydia heard from somewhere in the distance with the beat of the drums.

Well, dear, I wonder what you are doing tonight. It is hardly dark there yet, perhaps not even twilight. I remember how soon the sun used to go down in autumn and how long the twilights were. I used to love the sunsets in the autumn but I have seen some of the prettiest ever here. I wish that you could see them, too. Perhaps – but then I must not let myself think what lies in the future. It is enough to live in the present.

I wish that it did not take such a long time for letters to go and come even though I know it is useless to do so, I hope that there is a letter on its way to me from you now. With the best of wishes,

Your friend,
Glenn

Well, Glenn. I'll say one good thing for you. You've passed the tenacity test with flying colors. Sonny's still in the picture and you're still carrying a torch. But then, I guess the very idea of being a missionary in Congo takes more dedication and commitment than the average person has. If they give an award for the one who hangs in there the longest, you'll surely receive the prize. She paused. *And I hope the prize is 'Gene.*

Lydia found herself wishing she could call 'Gene and tell her to get on with the program. She also made a mental note to ask Ward if he would have hung around and waited for her if she had turned to one of his best buddies from high school while he was away at school.

But then, you must remember that she was already interested in this Sonny dude before Glenn walked into the picture. Or at least that Sonny had made himself a visible presence before Glenn became the "fellow of everyone's eye"— or at least in the eyes of all the available young ladies — through his departure for Africa, a true "worldly" adventure. Especially in the eyes of the young ladies of rural eastern North Carolina, she snickered, recalling how the girls of her school all turned their fancy to some guy whose family had just moved from New York. He immediately became everyone's heartthrob because he had been more places than the other boys from her small community.

Lydia took a sip of the lemonade and reached for the next installment of the courtship, which she immediately noticed was written on another Sabbath, exactly a week before Christmas.

Wembo Nyama, Congo Belge

Dec. 18, 1927

My dear 'Gene,

Again it is Sunday the last one before that which marks the anniversary of our Lord and Savior's birth nineteen hundred twenty-seven years ago when he was laid in Bethlehem's manger. Many have been those who have heard the glad story bearing the Good News but countless numbers still remain untold. Would that there were more to tell the Story!

Your two letters of October twelfth and twentieth have been received and I appreciated the both of them very much indeed. I appreciated them all the more because you wrote them as you did – in your own way.

The one contained a clipping from the "Christian Advocate". You said that you were sure that I was interested in the favorable publicity you have been giving me. Yes, I am but only to the extent that it bring the work of the Lord in this far-away land before the eyes of those at home. If you don't mind, I'd like to just interject a comment here on Miss Beauchamp's letter. To her the appointment as the new business manager of the mission might seem to be "a most flattering one" but we do not look on them as "honors" but opportunities for further service. Really, I should have far rather been allowed to carry on just the work of the educational department and it is a big work, too. But as I was called upon to accept the responsibility, and I don't deny for a minute that it is a great responsibility, I accepted it to do the best I could. The Lord has richly blessed me with added strength to fulfill this extra task. I could never have done what I have accomplished since May within my strength alone.

I was impressed to read in your letter which appeared as a preface to Miss Beauchamp's letter these words from your pen "we want every leaguer in the NC Conference to pray that he may be given strength, courage and wisdom in rendering loyal service as a Christian missionary in a non-Christian land." Oh! How the prayers of those back home do help us and how much we do need them! I am sure that a prayer must have gone out from your heart as the hand pictured these words. Please accept my deep thanks for all the ways in which you have helped in the work out here, by your talks, writing and other ways.

This morning Miss Armstrong and I took a group of boys . . .

"Ah, Miss Armstrong, good morning! What a lovely morning it is indeed." Glenn opened the truck's passenger door for his sister servant to Congo.

"It is a lovely morning, but I think that about every morning that I go to the Leper Colony. Those patients are a blessing to me. You'll see once we arrive there, and be surprised to see how happy they are – much more so than many who are more fortunate and richly blessed. It's impossible to describe the suffering that some of them must endure and the conditions of some of the bodies. Like I said, you'll see once we arrive.

"I can't thank you enough for going with me and taking our school boys to sing for them. The added gift of your lap organ will be a real treat for those in the Leper Colony."

"You are quite welcome, Miss Armstrong. I've selected a number of hymns and some carols so that I can play and give the boys a little breather between songs. I thought it would be a nice touch to have Christmas music for the patients along with our prayer service for them this morning."

"That should be lovely. Thank you, Mr. Edgerton."

"From what I've heard, you've spruced up the Leper Colony to make it look quite beautiful for the patients there."

"I've done what I can. I feel like they need a pretty place, a place that is conducive for making life happier since they have only a few more years to live on this earth."

"I think it's indeed wonderful that the mission is sending someone out each Sunday to talk to them, in addition to the daily visits. They need to continually hear of the love and grace of our Lord and Savior, just like the rest of the people around the world.

It thrills my heart to hear you speak of their happiness. I often times find that among the sufferers on the earth. They are true examples of happiness in Christ."

Glenn began to sing the words of the third stanza of *O Little Town of Bethlehem*, calling to Miss Armstrong to join in. "How silently, how silently the wondrous gift is giv'n . . ."

With her mind years away in a foreign land singing Christmas carols to lepers, Lydia placed the folded letter back into the envelope, her fingers feeling another piece of paper. She pulled on it to discover a Christmas greeting on typing paper that had been colored a pale blue. Glenn had used shades of pink and blue to outline the mountains of a sketch he had drawn, and to decorate fancy oversized capital letters that began each strain of the poem that had been typed on the paper.

How was he able to do this? Lydia questioned as she unfolded the rest of the sheet that had a beautiful radiating star at the top, also in color.

The star that shines at Christmas time Again with light proclaims
The message of the heav'nly clime. "Behold, the Saviour reigns."
Throughout the earth its rays will glow, To comfort, to reveal;
To shine and ev'ry joy bestow Where'er one doth appeal
For aid to tread the narrow way Like Him of Galilee.

*Receive the light and ever pray That some one else may see
A way to serve, and banish strife And know the crown when won.
The Father and Eternal life Through Jesus Christ, the Son.*

J.G.E. 1927

Lydia felt a ripple run through her. It wasn't that the poem took her breath away, but rather that one person should choose such a life of humility, as did Glenn Edgerton, to go and serve others. She thought about his words from the letters. What he did was not a matter of going to a foreign land and being the big brother who walked in with a better idea and tried to bushwhack his ways on others, feeling that he was superior to them. Glenn, Lydia had learned through the letters, tried to connect with the natives and serve them, truly serve them.

A servant to His Master, setting an example for others to also be servants of that same Master.

She retreated to the den and her recliner and took a rest on this blessed Sabbath. Lydia had decided that after dinner, she had two tasks. One was that she would look at the morning's church bulletin to see if she saw any opportunities for a women's mission group for which she could become involved. *What was it Glenn called it in his letters? The WSCS, that's it.* The other was that she would write a note to those who had encouraged and inspired her through life, the first one going to Ward. *I'll hide it inside his brief case so that when he gets to the university in the morning he'll find it.*

15

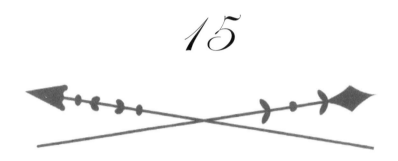

Ward kissed Lydia as he grabbed his briefcase and headed toward the door.

"I don't know that I've ever seen you look so happy," he commented, glancing back at her. "Or is it that you're already settled in and pleasantly content here?"

She smiled, not about to share her little secret of how the letters from Glenn were touching a flame inside her that she wasn't sure had ever been lit, and certainly had not been fanned. "I'm sure it has everything to do with the environment. There's something unique, special, about this house."

"If I'd have known you'd be this way in a house, I'd have bought one long ago. Whatever it is about this place, it looks good on you."

"Thank you." Lydia's eyes gave a long discerning look at the husband she was coming to know anew through the letters. "Just for that comment, I'll fix your favorite dinner of pork loin, baked with dried cranberries."

"I love you, Lydia," he spoke, taking the time to actually look *at* her as he headed out the door for his brisk walk to the Education Building from Howard Street.

"I love you, too, Ward," she replied, thinking of how long it had been since he'd left for work in that manner.

Is it that Glenn's influence in my life is making a change in Ward, too, or is it that he hears the beat of the African drums in his own way? For whatever reason, I'm glad I hid the note in his brief case.

She gave up on analyzing the situation and chose instead to grab her coffee, with lots of cream, and visit the writing desk. It dawned on Lydia as she untied the ribbon and reached for the top letter in a new stack that the beating of the drums that she'd first heard were now only audible as she read the letters. *Like the spirit of Africa and these letters are truly a part of this house.*

Her eyes drew her attention out the window and up the mountain. At the top of Howard's Knob sat the base of a giant windmill that had been in use for several years during the seventies. Although at one time it had been a gargantuan mechanism, with the NASA logo on the side of it, it now sat completely still and silent. *Because it receives no power, it therefore generates no power*, reflected Lydia. *Like people who walk in darkness. They don't allow Christ into their lives and they can't set the example of Christ.*

She picked up the next letter and opened the envelope. *These letters were certainly energized by a power – a far greater Power that will never allow them to become still and silent.*

Wembo Nyama, Congo Belge
Jan. 21, 1928

My dear 'Gene,

 This is the first letter I have written to anyone since Christmas, not even one to my homefolks, and I haven't yet become accustomed to writing an 8 instead of a 7 for the year.

 I must say your note was indeed a great surprise. It was of November 22nd and told of your resignation from St. Paul Church in Goldsboro. I could hardly believe it when I read it and I cannot help but wonder of the cause and be curious about it also, as you said "my heart is still there and probably always will be." I can imagine a few things, 'Gene, but imaginations are not worth anything at all in trying to solve a situation.

 I am very glad that you wrote me of the changes in your address as I probably should have gone on writing to you at Goldsboro, that is, the few times that I could find to write. I hope that they may be more frequent in the future. I shall be very anxious to know of your plans and shall look forward to your letter telling me of them.

 You may perhaps be wondering what I have done since Christmas that has kept me from doing any writing. It has happened in a very unusual manner . . .

"Mr. Edgerton, I've received word that Miss Armstrong and Miss Foreman want to visit a hospital at Bibanga. It is a Presbyterian mission station where they are doing a great work with sleeping sickness patients and with surgery. I'd like for you to accompany Miss Armstrong. Miss Foreman, the nurse at one of the other Methodist stations, will meet you halfway between here and Minga and take you the rest of the way. I'd like for you to go with them for safety reasons.

"You'll be leaving here the morning of December 23ʳᵈ and should be back within 4-5 days. I appreciate you giving of your time to advance our medical knowledge and facilities. Your work is greatly appreciated."

Oh, but that I could stay here and work on the development of the education program. God, I'm praying that you will soon send help with the business office so that I can dedicate myself more to the task for which I came here. Yet, I know that I'm your servant and you will place me where you need me. Let me find comfort in knowing that you need me in so many areas.

Glenn was so distraught over the news of 'Gene's resignation that he could hardly think of anything else. *What could have prompted her to leave? Was it Sonny Ledford? Did she become deeply enthralled by him?* He could not believe that was the case given her kind and encouraging letters to him. *Perhaps she doesn't care for him and she felt the need to have space between them.*

The young missionary turned to his Father. *Or, knowing what a fine and decent young woman she is who wants to serve you to the best of her ability, maybe she followed your direction for her life to another position.*

Oh, that I could talk to her. That I could look into her eyes and hold her hand.

His mind drifted back to the Sunday before he left for New York when they had gone riding for hours and she sang to him. *I must write to her right away and find out what prompted her decision.*

"I'll be loving you always . . . ," he hummed.

"Hello, Miss Foreman," greeted Miss Armstrong. "Thank you for agreeing to meet us here."

"I was delighted to be able to go with you to Bibanga. I, too, want to know more of the work they are doing there. It has become quite famous, especially among the mission stations."

"Please allow me to introduce you to Mr. Glenn Edgerton, a co-worker of mine at Wembo Nyama, where he is in charge of the business and the education."

After the three exchanged greetings and resituated the bags of Miss Armstrong and Mr. Edgerton into the Ford that Miss Foreman had brought, the group headed to Minga where they stopped to spend the evening.

The following day, December 24th, they reached Lusambo where they spent Christmas Eve and Christmas Day with Dr. and Mrs. Ham Moore.

"Mr. Edgerton, it's so good to see you again," was the greeting Glenn received when he reached the Moore's.

"Bettie?"

"That's right. I was Bettie Bass before my marriage to Dr. Moore. After our marriage, I came here to serve with him."

"I must say, the beauty of the trip on the way here from Wembo Nyama is beyond description."

"You're entirely right, Mr. Edgerton," acknowledged Dr. Moore. "We love it here and feel blessed to be located in this area. I don't know that I've ever seen a more beautiful place on the earth."

The Moore's were a most gracious host and hostess as they provided a wonderfully memorable Christmas gathering for their American friends.

"I don't believe this could have been any better had we been home," exclaimed Miss Armstrong, joined in agreement by Miss Foreman.

"Yes, it was quite lovely," said Glenn, thinking of the celebrations that were being held back in eastern North Carolina, and of one particular young lady and wondering how she was spending the holiday.

The next morning, Mrs. Moore, who also wanted to learn of the procedures used at Bibanga, joined the threesome. After a hard day's travel, they reached the hospital on that evening, a Tuesday, where they stayed until early the following Saturday morning.

"Thank you for agreeing to come with us, Mr. Edgerton. I'm afraid we'd not have been allowed to come had it not been for your presence with us."

"You're most welcome. Although surgery and the medical profession are both far out of my field of expertise, this was a most helpful and informative trip. It helps me to have a feel for the other areas of work at the mission."

Miss Foreman, who took turns maneuvering the Ford with Glenn, finally pulled into Lusambo around nine o'clock that evening.

When Glenn arose the next morning, anxious to be on his way to Wembo Nyama following the morning service, he learned that both Mrs. Moore and Miss Armstrong had been taken sick with dysentery.

"Not a *real* serious case," Dr. Moore informed him, but bad enough that I'm afraid they will both be bedridden for two weeks.

Glenn tried to pacify himself with the beauty of the area and do as much planning for the school as possible in his head. It was late one evening when Dr. Moore approached him to inform him that he felt Miss Armstrong would be well enough to travel by morning. He was up early the next day, helping Miss Foreman pack the Ford as they prepared to leave for Minga.

"I'm sorry, Mr. Edgerton," called Dr. Moore. "We've just gotten word that a big bridge is out on the way from here to Wembo Nyama. I'm afraid you'll have to stay here for a while longer until the repairs have been made."

The mounting pressures of being so very far behind were beginning to fray at Glenn. *If only I had a means to at least write my 'Gene.* Even the beauty of the area was not enough to keep his mind off his work and the speculation of whether there was any mail for him back at the mission.

It was another two weeks before the bridge was cleared for travel. Glenn finally made it back to Wembo Nyama on the Saturday evening before the school started back on Monday morning. In many ways, it had been a long and cumbersome trip for him, but in others, it kept his mind on things rather than work for the most part. And when he returned, he was most grateful to discover a note from Miss Bennett waiting for him on the writing desk. In it she informed him of her resignation from St. Paul.

The next morning, Glenn learned that his return to Wembo Nyama had brought some most positive changes.

"Mr. Edgerton," stated one of the other notes, "we have a new girl, Miss McNeil, who has just come to us. She has some experience in bookkeeping and we think she would be a great help to you in the office work."

It was only about the middle of that morning when Glenn ascertained that with the help of his new assistant, he would be able to get out his quarterly reports in spite of the delays with his recent trip to Bibanga.

Further elation came when he saw another note. "Mr. Edgerton, Dr. Moore will soon be able to take over the business department, so you shall have that weight off your shoulders."

"Glory, glory, hallelujah," Glenn burst into song when he read the note.

One of his personal boys came rushing into the office to make sure nothing was wrong. He even enjoyed the experience of trying to explain "how right" everything was. Glenn was unsure of how to communicate that he was so happy because he was so interested in his educational work and he would soon be able to devote his time wholly to its development.

I can't keep my mind from wandering back to the fact that you have left Goldsboro. I wonder what has become of Sonny Ledford. I suppose I have no right or should not with propriety mention to ask about him. You never mention him and occasionally I find myself wondering if he holds the same place in your life that he once did. It takes such a long time to find out what one wishes to know, but then I suppose I ought not to want to know in such a hurry about what is happening on the other side of the world.

My first term is half gone and it will be only eighteen more months before I shall be preparing to go home on my first furlough. I wonder what those eighteen months will hold for me and the few months of my furlough.

I don't know why I should look forward so much to your letters. They are never very long but somehow they always hold a little message or bear a little thought that seems to be just what I need.

I hope that you are going to be as happy in your new surroundings as you were in your past and as I am here. Best wishes.

Sincerely,
Glenn

I wonder what has become of Sonny Ledford, too.

Lydia reflected on Glenn's Christmas holiday and the fact that he had been away from all those he loved. Then, almost as if they could have been in Glenn's voice, she heard the words, "No dear Lydia, I loved all those who were around me. I was away from the loved ones of my past."

She began to wonder whether she could have as easily adapted to a not only different, but very strange, setting where she would have been surrounded by people with whom she had no means of communication. The impact of his situation was beginning to sink in as she envisioned the holiday dinner where several people, not really friends but merely acquaintances or people connected by the same homeland, sat together at a table and shared what they could find to eat in a foreign country. *And not only a foreign country but a primitive culture.*

Lydia's heart filled with an emotion that she didn't even understand, one that she'd never experienced before. She could not tell if it was joy for Glenn's attitude and his heart of servitude, sorrow for the fact he was away from his home and loved ones on a holiday – one that was clearly significant to him through the words of his letter, pain for the fact that he longed to know the love of a woman he barely knew except through her letters, security that at least he had some "home" folk around him, peace with the example he was able to show through his way of dealing with the situation. Her mind, her heart and her soul seemed to be going in their own directions, none of them having an idea which way to actually go. She suspected that had more to do with what was actually going on inside of her at The Rhododendron in Boone, North Carolina, rather than solely what was going on with Glenn in the Wembo Nyama mission station of the Belgian Congo of Africa.

Feeling the need for a break, she wandered outside to take a walk hoping the exerted energy of climbing hills would clear her mind of all the thoughts rushing through it. However, it mattered not where she ventured, the vision of the huge powerless windmill stood tall before her – literally – atop Howard's Knob.

16

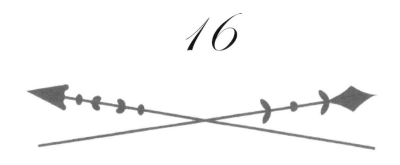

Wembo Nyama, C. Belge
March 4, 1928

My dear 'Gene,

Your letter written the day following that which com-
memorates the birth of our Lord has just reached me. I was
very happy to hear from you again and to know what you
have been doing since you left Goldsboro. It was very good
indeed that all of you could be together on Christmas Day
and in the place which seems so much like home to you. We
were all together the last Christmas before I sailed but only
God knows when we shall be together again. I have written
some few weeks since how I passed this great season of the
year and for some reason it seems that it is still December. I
suppose that it must be because with each letter I have said
something about what happened at Christmas time.

One night this week we had one of the worst electrical storms I have ever experienced. Two clouds coming from different directions met just above our mission here and I have never seen such terrific lightning. A blinding flash struck my house and I suppose that the house would have burned had it not been for the lightning rods and the wet roof. I was standing almost directly under the spot where it struck and the crash was so tremendous that I hardly knew what had happened. When I came to my senses I was facing in the opposite direction. I was completely unnerved and for the first time since I have been in Congo I was frightened. Another flash struck a small tree about thirty yards from my house and near the kitchen of the house next to mine. Another one struck almost as near, and also a fourth.

I had undressed and was ready for bed but had not laid down. I kept running from one door to the other to see if any of the other houses were on fire. I did not really know until the next morning how narrowly I had escaped. I know that I should not have been afraid and that God was in it all. In my mind I wasn't afraid but my physical structure was completely unnerved. The flashes were so near that I could hear the crackling of the current in my room before it exploded. I am so thankful that I was spared with only the shock that I may continue to work for Jesus among these people.

For the past few days I have been taking stock of myself and what I have tried to do. I seriously began this night previous to the one of the visitation of the storm. I have done so little and I have failed so miserably in bringing these boys and girls closer to Jesus. My life has not been what it should have been and what it should be. If God will only spare me, I am going to live more fully for him and be more consecrated to His work. When you speak of the "wonderful work" that I am doing it is encouraging and gives me a greater determination to try not to be such a complete disappointment to my Savior and to those who have trusted me to do their work out here. Oh! Pray that I may be given the Grace and Power which I need.

Don't wait so long the next time to write. It is such a long way out here and sometimes it seems it takes letters a very long time to come.

With every good wish and a prayer for the great success and happiness in your new work in His service.

Your sincere friend,
Glenn

Lydia didn't realize until she stopped reading that she had tears streaming down her face. She had been deeply touched by Glenn's plea to do better with the African boys and girls. *Doesn't he realize that he's been so busy with all the office work as the business manager and with trips like the one to Bibanga that he's not had the*

time to dedicate himself to the teaching part of his work?

Her heart called out to her to read a Bible story that she had not thought of in years. She knew so little about the Bible that she had no clue as to where to look for the story, but it was the one about letting the little children come to Jesus. *What was that word the scriptures used?* She tried hard to recollect.

Lydia looked through all her belongings to find another Bible – knowing that Ward's had gone to work with him in the briefcase, for she had placed it there with her letter. She was frustrated and embarrassed in front of God that she cared so little for it that she didn't even know where it was in amidst all of the boxes that had been placed downstairs in a corner. Then it struck her that she shouldn't choose now to be embarrassed. *God already knew of the Bible's insignificance in my life.*

She realized that she fully understood Glenn's plea to God from the letter. It was the same plea that was going on inside her now. It was the same plea that had gone on inside Ward on that day in Charlotte when he took the turn that bore the stained glass window.

Where is that Bible? The tears began to pour down her face as she felt such hurt and pain for the poor young man who was stranded in a foreign land and who felt such a hunger inside to do such a good work on Christ's behalf.

Lydia recalled a hymn that Glenn had mentioned in the first letter. She quickly ransacked through the pile of letters to find it and began to search for the title. "'Tis So Sweet to Trust in Jesus," she read. The title rang a bell and she vaguely recalled its tune, but she knew none of the following words of the hymn.

She read the title again and stopped. *What more words do you need?* Lydia reasoned. *Those were the only words that Glenn had to hold near to his heart to feel God's control in his life and work.*

The woman once again felt the moisture on her cheeks. Try as she might, she could not list one time in her life when she had trusted Jesus to take care of her. Sure, she'd heard people at the church make comments about that, but she'd never seen the need. Her life seemed just fine as it was. She and Ward had never been able to have children, but otherwise, they had an okay life.

An okay life! The words screamed at her as her subconscious caught what her mind had thought. *Why do you want to be content with an okay life? There's a lot more to life than "okay!"*

The doorbell rang.

"Not now," she wanted to yell.

Lydia dabbed at her eyes with the hem of her shirt and went to open the door. Phillip, along with Francie and David stood there, each of them with their arms full of memorabilia to share with the new owner of The Rhododendron.

"I'm sorry," she apologized. "I must look a mess." She'd been so deeply engrossed in the letters and Glenn's emotions and struggles that she'd completely forgotten the promised visit from her new friends.

Francie immediately noticed the tear-streaked face, as did Phillip, but neither of them said a word about it.

"We brought you something," David spoke excitedly as he moved between his parents and held out his hands.

"Well if you aren't a sight for sore eyes," Lydia managed as she reached out to take the old and cracked leather bound book from him. *Hopefully they can't tell how sore my eyes really are!*

Phillip and Francie looked at each other, both of them noting that her statement was more than proverbial words.

"It's the Bible that my great-grandfather used in Africa," David went on to explain. It's one of Dad's most prized possessions, but we talked about it and all agreed that it belonged with the writing desk and the letters."

"Suffer," mumbled Lydia.

Phillip and Francie looked at each other again, each of them with concern in their eyes for the woman in front of them.

"Excuse me?" David asked, a puzzled look on his face. The word was not exactly the thanks that he'd been expecting.

"Suffer the little children to come unto me," Lydia said with great pride and confidence. "That's the verse that your gift made me think of." *And it's also the word that I had been searching for prior to your arrival.*

Suddenly Lydia realized that the appointed time of her guests' arrival was the answer to her plea to God from a few minutes before. They had come bearing a Bible, which in turn miraculously reminded her of the word for which she had been trying to remember. "I can't tell you how perfect your timing is," she smiled, a look of genuine relief replacing the panic-stricken face that had greeted them at the door.

Again Phillip and Francie glanced at each other, this time both of them with a smile on their faces as their fears about Lydia were removed.

"Please sit down," she invited. "There's something I'd like to share with you." Lydia recapped the past few minutes for them, giving them an insight into her disheveled appearance from when she opened the door. "You were the answer to my plea to God, my prayer," she sighed.

Phillip reached out and took Lydia's hand. "Lydia, you're an answer to a prayer for us, too. We had so hoped that this house would fall into the hands of someone who would love and care for it with the same admonition as my grandparents. It's apparent that is the case with you. We're so relieved to know how much you treasure the letters."

"And we hope, especially after the story you just relayed to us, that the Bible will mean just as much to you."

"Oh, yes," Lydia assured them. "And rest assured that if anything . . . anything at all happens to me, I'll make sure that Ward gets it back to you."

"Let's not worry about that now," Phillip replied.

"I guess you're right," nodded Lydia. "As your grandfather said in one of the letters to 'Gene, it is of no use to worry about the future." She smiled. "How rude I am. I didn't even bother to tell you how much I appreciate this - shall we say - loan."

Before anyone had a chance to respond, she asked, "Phillip, do you know a hymn called *'Tis So Sweet to Trust in Jesus?*"

"Yes, that was one of my grandfather's favorite hymns. Why do you ask?"

"He mentioned it in the very first letter that I read, and then just before you came today, I was reading another letter and I remembered him having mentioned a hymn. I went back to find the title in the letter, but I'm ashamed to admit that I don't know any more of the words than what's in the title."

"'Tis so sweet to trust in Jesus," sang Francie, "and to take him at his word; Just to rest upon his promise, and to know, 'Thus saith the Lord.' Jesus, Jesus, how I trust him! How I've proved him o'er and o'er! Jesus, Jesus, precious Jesus! O for grace to trust him more!"

"That was lovely, simply lovely!" exclaimed Lydia. "It's so helpful to know of the words to which Glenn was referring in his letter."

"There are actually more words, but I don't know the rest."

"David," Phillip called, "run out to the car and see if the hymnal I used yesterday still isn't in the back seat."

It wasn't but a minute before the child returned with the book in his hand, already turned to the right page number.

Phillip read the rest of the words to Lydia.

"Oh, how beautiful those words are. I especially like the ones that said, 'Just from Jesus simply taking Life and rest, and joy and peace,' and 'And I know that He is with me, will be with me to the end.' There truly is a peace in them. And just from the letters, I can get a visual image of Glenn, knelt after the storm which he mentioned in the letter, praying, 'Jesus, Jesus, precious Jesus! O for grace to trust him more!'"

Her eyes were again beginning to tear up. "Now you see why I appeared so distraught when you arrived. It's the strangest thing. As I read the letters, it's almost like I'm right there with your grandfather, and in my own set of circumstances, feeling what he felt to some extent in Africa."

"That's what faith is all about," explained Francie. "We all have trials and struggles in life, no matter what our career and no matter whether we attend church or not. No matter how much we try to follow God's word and apply it to our lives, there are going to be storms in everyone's lives. It's those words of that hymn that allow people to keep going, though. To keep their chins up and be able to face each tomorrow."

"You know," began Lydia, "I never realized until I moved into this house the truth of your statement. The odd thing is that I'd never had a bad life. I don't recall any real struggles or incidences in my life. Ward and I have loved each other from the beginning. As I thought the very minute before you came, we've had okay lives. That's when I came to the rationalization that okay wasn't good enough."

"Sadly," continued Francie, "too many people go through life just like you mentioned. They never know what they're missing until it's too late."

There was a period of silence as Lydia visibly took in Francie's words, Glenn's words and the words of the hymn's author. No one interrupted her deepness of thought until she finally spoke again. "There's a reason we bought this very house, isn't there?"

"I highly suspect there is," smiled Phillip with a reassuring expression on his face.

The afternoon was filled with pleasant conversation and relived memories of Glenn and 'Gene until at last Phillip again sent David to the car. "We didn't bring a lot of the things we had planned to bring," Phillip apologized, "but that's because we wanted you to first get to know Glenn and 'Gene through their letters. We thought that would give you a much better picture of them than anything we could bring. However, there is one thing we wanted to show you."

"We'll bring the other items we mentioned at another time," promised Francie. "After you've had a chance to get through all the letters."

David came bouncing through the door with a huge wooden object of dark brown wood, beating on it with each step.

"Oh my!" exclaimed Lydia. "That's it! That's the sound that I'd hear every time I walked by that desk before I sawed into the lock. Now I only hear it when I read the letters." She stared at David and the object in disbelief.

"This is the African drum the natives carved out and gave to my grandfather," Phillip explained. "It's made from African mahogany. Look inside it."

Lydia stared at him and at the drum for a moment, not sure she was ready to see what she'd been hearing.

"I don't understand," she said. "How could I have possibly heard that drum when it was at your house in Charlotte?"

"I don't think it's the drum you actually heard," suggested Phillip. "Possibly it was the strength of those letters wanting to be read, to be heard, and the spirit of the drum that was behind them."

Francie moved to Lydia and put an arm around her. "Sometimes there are things we simply can't explain. We have to accept them as God gives them to us. I think this is one of those things." She smiled an understanding smile that spoke of a real friendship and bond. "I believe that you have a lot more in common with Glenn and 'Gene than you know, and I believe these letters are going to prove to be a source for that. That's why I think this was the house with your name on it, and that's why I think you heard the sound of the drum. It was a beckoning . . . a calling."

Lydia returned the smile. "I understand precisely what you're saying. I'm not sure I could have said that six months ago, but now I do."

"We'd better be going," Phillip said as he rose from his grandfather's old armchair. "We need to get David back. He'll have school tomorrow."

"Thank goodness for these long weekend vacations," added Francie. "We'd never get any time together."

Lydia hugged David. "Thank you for sharing your time of vacation with me."

"This was fun. It was the only time that I got to play the drum without getting yelled at," the boy admitted, causing the three adults to burst into laughter.

"Come back anytime," invited Lydia.

"We will," accepted Phillip. "And thanks for your open invitation. You can be sure that we'll take you up on it."

Francie turned back when she got to the car. "If you ever need to talk about any of this, please feel free to call me." She went back to the front door and handed Lydia a business card. "Here are the numbers where both Phillip and I can be reached at anytime. Don't ever hesitate to call."

"Thank you," nodded Lydia, knowing there would be no need for the numbers. "That's a most gracious offer."

"We mean it," emphasized Phillip.

"I'm sure you do," Lydia smiled appreciatively.

She closed the door with a feeling that she'd been accepted into a wonderful loving and caring family. Sure she would never have need of the card, she didn't want to dispose of it since it had been such a nice gesture. Lydia opened the drawer where the letters had been hidden and placed it in a back corner of the desk.

A quick glance at the clock on the stove told her that she had exactly enough time to read another letter before getting dinner ready. The droll of the distant drum as she sat in 'Gene's old armchair set the tempo for her eyes to take her on a journey through the letter.

Wembo Nyama, Congo Belge
August 25, 1928

My dear 'Gene,

For months and months I have waited expectantly for a letter from you but none has arrived to let me know where you are nor what you are doing. Perhaps I should continue to wait for your letter before I write again, but somehow I feel that I just must write to you and that I must tonight.

'Gene, dear, why did you stop writing? Don't you know that I just loved to receive your letters and that I looked forward to their coming so much? The last one that came

from you was written shortly after you left Goldsboro. 'Gene, where are you and what are you doing that has caused this prolonged silence? Have you ceased to care for me at all or did you decide that it would be impossible to ever care for such a person as I am and that you'd best not let there be a beginning? Won't you write me right away and tell me all about it? Is there someone else who has come into your life, or was there before, to whom you have given your whole self?

There are so many, many things that I want to talk to you about. I wish so much that I could see you for even a short while. There have been many things I've wanted to say but which I have kept back and even now needs must refrain from giving utterance to.

I had hoped that the time would soon draw near when I would be going to America and that I should soon be able to see you again. But I fear now that the time is longer than I first thought. Can you keep a secret for me? I call it a secret because I have not yet told the home folks. The reasons that I feel the time is longer than I once did is that I am expecting to stay four years instead of three. The bishop said that he would like for me to if my health continues good.

My health has been splendid all the time I have been out here. In fact, I've gained so much weight that I hardly know myself. I am now in the first month of my third year and I just can't realize that it is true. The home call is strong but I hate to think of the day that will come to take me away from the natives here.

'Gene, dear, must I wait these two more years before I shall reveal to you the longings of my heart? It is full now to overflowing with that which it wants and craves to express. Dare I tell you now? It is almost beyond my control but I must refrain this once again. Perhaps there'll be a letter from you soon.

Good night, 'Gene. May God keep and bless thee.

Your sincere friend,
Glenn E.

Can she not feel his love for her? Can she not know that this dear of a Southern gentleman is fighting every emotion inside him with all his strength to keep from telling her how he longs for her love in return, just so that he can wait until he returns to the States to tell her in person and to see the look on her face?

The turning of the doorknob interrupted Lydia's thoughts when she turned and saw Ward. She jumped from the chair and threw the letter on the floor behind her.

Before she had time to apologize for not having dinner on the table, he grabbed her, spun her around in the air and said, "You're beautiful. Not just on the outside, but you're a beautiful person. If I weren't already married to you, I'd ask you to marry me all over again."

The letter she had written to Ward had completely slipped her mind until she began mentally scrambling to figure out what had caused such a burst of excitement from her normally sub-dued husband.

"I never knew what an impact a simple letter could have on someone," he admitted. "I was so overwhelmed and overjoyed at seeing your words this morning that I've looked forward to coming home to see you all day. I even assigned my classes to write a letter to the person who had impacted their desire to teach the most."

Ward spun Lydia around again. "And I'm glad I caught you before you got in the kitchen. We're going out to dinner this evening at the Makoto Japanese Restaurant."

Lydia stared at the piece of paper that lay on the floor beside the chair. *Glenn wasn't the only one who was touched by the letters of his lady,* she smiled.

Maybe our life isn't just "okay" after all!

For the first time in Lydia's life, she felt that she had trusted a greater Power and that greater Power was proving her trust. *Just like in the words of the hymn.*

"Give me one second to freshen up."

"You're beautiful just the way you are," he replied, pulling her hand as he rushed out the door of The Rhododendron.

17

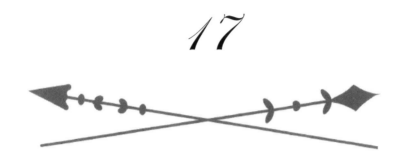

My dear 'Gene,

The moon makes this one of the most beautiful nights I have ever seen. Just at sunset a storm came up and a heavy rain fell. Then practically all of the clouds cleared away leaving everything clear and cool. I have just returned from a most enjoyable ride on my bicycle.

Due to the coolness I wore a coat. This was also a protection against the dampness. I wish that you could have been along to help me enjoy the ride.

Every blade of grass wore its necklace of diamonds made exquisitely beautiful by the moonbeams. On the tip of each leaf of every tree a fairy had hung a most gorgeous pearl. Darkness in its swift flight before the moon had dropped a blanket of stillness over everything. The moon, a glorious liner, was sailing merrily onward, bounding now and then over the wave of clouds which danced in its wake.

I wanted to ride on and on and enjoy to the fullness the beauty of it all. It is great to be able to enjoy such experiences alone but sometimes one wishes for a companion to enjoy it with.

A few days ago I received a letter from Stella. Among the things which she was telling me about our friends was the interesting news that this winter you will be teaching at Snow Hill. I can't realize that you are going to be so near Goldsboro.

For sometime I have been expecting a letter from you telling me something about yourself, but it is very slow in coming. In fact, I have heard from you but a very few times since you went to Durham.

Several times I have written letters to you and later torn them up as I thought perhaps you did not care to hear from me or did not care to have our friendship develop any further. At least, I judged this to be the case since you did not write to me any more.

Perhaps I should let this letter take the course which the others have taken and consign it to the flames. But I cannot. I must send it on its way and perhaps discover for me your desires for the future.

'Gene, please tell me and tell me frankly. Do you care for my friendship, or is it a case like many young men you have known in the past, just a passing acquaintanceship? Is your heart so devoted to some one man that it has not room for another? If so, please tell so, and I shall not attempt to intrude on those sacred grounds, for they are sacred in my code.

I have wanted to ask you this before but I have continued to hope that each mail would bring me some message from you. Perhaps I should be able to take the silence of the past for an answer, but somehow I must have the answer from you yourself. Perhaps I have no right to ask for an answer but you will not deny me this will you, 'Gene?

I shall be anxiously awaiting your reply.

Most sincerely,
Glenn

My, how the words have changed, Lydia noted. *Much like the phrases of Ward with me ever since that letter I sent him.*

With that thought, she wondered if this being the first letter in the third bundle had anything to do with the fact that its group was bound by a baby blue ribbon. *Or is this to signify his Alma Mater of Carolina?* she wondered. *A real possibility since Ward's favorite color is also Carolina blue.*

She was "tickled pink," as one of her favorite childhood phrases stated, that their mediocre existence had soared into a life of pure delight. *In many ways,* Lydia smiled, thinking how odd it was that they had reached near-retirement age before they ever conceived what a marvelous life they shared.

Ward had even begun to read the letters in the evenings and carry on discussions with her about how their lives paralleled with that of some missionary – who had become a part of their daily existence – in a foreign land decades ago. That time together had come to serve as a prelude to the Bible reading they had made a priority each evening before retiring for bed.

18

Wembo Nyama, C. Belge
February 3, 1929

My dear 'Gene,

Your letter of December 8th arrived yesterday and although it was very short I appreciated it <u>very</u> <u>much</u> indeed. It had been ages - - ages since I had heard from you and I was beginning to think that it would be ages more ere I should hear from you.

Even now I can't exactly decide whether I should be writing to you again so soon after the arrival of yours and whether it should be a long or short note. I would that my ability also lay in the realm of being able to express much in few words.

Suffice it to say, I am going to look anxiously forward to the arrival of your letters. You assured me that you will write more often hereafter.

The new year is already slipping speedily and silently away. In fact, one of the twelve months has already flown past and where has it gone? "Who knows, who knows?"

In another year I shall be preparing to go home as I am intending to leave for America somewhere about the latter part of February one year hence. I am due to go in July of this year but am going to stay eight months overtime, if God be willing.

Not very much news comes to me from St. Paul since you went away. Not very many even remembered me with a greeting this Christmas season. Never has the church officially remembered me with a greeting on any occasion. But out here on the rough out-posts perhaps we should be too busy spreading the Gospel to notice an oversight of this kind. What if God should forget us out here, even for a moment!

I am looking forward to seeing you when I get home. Write to me when you can.

Your sincere friend,
Glenn

What was that I heard last night on the television about people sending messages to our troops? I'm sure Ward will remember. I've never thought too much about it because I assumed that friends and families of the military persons would take care of writing to their loved ones.

As Lydia thumbed through the stack to find the next letter, she had a quick chance of heart. Rather than opening the letter, she reached for the local telephone directory and opened it instead.

When she received an answer at Boone United Methodist Church, Lydia asked for the number of the chairperson of the Women's Society of Christian Service.

"Women's Society of Christian Service?" asked the secretary. "I've never heard of that before. I'm sorry, I don't believe we have one of those here." Then she was quick to add, "But all of our women do Christian service, I'm sure."

Alice Balmer, a church member doing some volunteer work in the office, happened to overhear the conversation. "The Women's Society of Christian Service? I haven't heard that term mentioned in years."

"You know what that is?" questioned the secretary.

"I do. My grandmother was the head of it for years at the old sanctuary."

The secretary turned back to the phone. "Hold on, I have a woman here who may be able to help you."

"Thank you," replied Lydia.

"Hello," said Alice. "You're inquiring about the Women's Society of Christian Service?"

"I am."

"That organization is no longer in existence."

"Oh no!" Lydia exclaimed, her voice dropping.

"Are you familiar with our UMW?" Alice asked.

"No," she responded, her voice still saddened, "no, I'm not. You see, I only joined the church this past Sunday. I don't really know anything about the various organizations, and I only happen to know of the Women's Society of Christian Service through some letters I was reading of John Glenn Edgerton's, who was a member of Boone United Methodist Church."

"You knew Dr. and Mrs. Edgerton?" came the woman's enthusiastic response.

"No, I'm afraid I didn't actually know them, either, but my husband and I purchased their old house and found some of his old letters that mentioned the Epworth League and the Women's Society of Christian Service and how supportive those organizations were of him in his years on the mission field."

The woman's voice showed that she was now greatly impressed. "How exciting! Mrs. Edgerton was actively involved for years with my grandmother in the missions' programs. They were close friends. In fact, Mrs. Edgerton was a president for years and also a board member of our organization.

"I understand your confusion now. The Women's Society of Christian Service changed its name back in the sixties when the Methodist Church merged with the Evangelical United Brethren Church. After that, our women's missionary organization became known as the United Methodist Women, or the UMW for short. I happen to be the program chair for my circle. We'd love to have you come and join us and I'm sure that the entire group of circles in our church would love for you to come and do a program and tell them all about those letters."

"I'd love to come and visit with the 'circle,' as you called it. But I'm not too sure about the program," Lydia hesitated. "The letters are very personal and I'd have to ask Glenn's family about that first."

"You do know that Dr. Edgerton's grandson is our resource person for the UMW for all of our Conference, don't you?"

"Phillip?"

"You know Phillip?"

"I met him quite by accident . . . no, it was no accident at all, but yes, I met he and his wife and son. They've been here to visit a couple of times."

"That's unbelievable! Phillip is extremely involved with us through his capacity at the conference office and even more so through his love and support of missions because of his grandparents. You absolutely *must* come and be a part of our group. I can't wait to tell the other women all about you."

Lydia sat speechless. She had searched for an announcement about such a women's group in the past Sunday's bulletin, but because there was nothing about the Women's Society of Christian Service, she had no idea of where to turn. After this morning's letter, her conscience would not let her drop it. Phillip had told her about his work with Mission and Outreach, but he never mentioned its connection with the UMW.

"We'll meet on Thursday evening," continued Alice. "Why don't I come and pick you up and take you to the home of the hostess for the evening? I know exactly which house belonged to the Edgerton's."

"You don't meet at the church?"

"No, it makes us much more closely knit to visit in a home. We have refreshments and bond in a small group situation in a comfortable setting. It allows us to work better together and build stronger relationships. We get together with our entire unit once a quarter, and then have a couple of annual meetings. There are two wonderful opportunities for you to join us at Lake Junaluska for meetings of the UMW groups from all over our conference. They are tremendous events. I never miss one of those. And then there are also jurisdictional events, which include the different regions of the country, and national events."

"I can't believe I didn't know anything about this," Lydia said, feeling a bit embarrassed.

"Why should you have known if you weren't involved? You've still plenty of time to be an active participant. I'll pick you up at 6:30 on Thursday evening."

"Fine. Thanks. I'll be looking for you." She started to say good-bye when she remembered the original reason for the call. "Oh, excuse me, I nearly forgot why I called. I've gathered from these letters of Dr. Edgerton's that the women of the WSCS, as you called it, could send him cards and letters of encouragement. Does your UMW have the names of any current missionaries to whom I might send messages?"

"As a matter of fact, we do. The UMW has an annual prayer calendar that lists the names of missionaries we have throughout the world and their birthdays. Some of them even have e-mail addresses, depending on their assignments."

"Oh no," replied Lydia. "I want to send a real piece of mail that they can open and hold in their hands. After reading these letters from Glenn, it has reminded me how much I used to look forward to letters in the mailbox. That electronic stuff is fine for some things, but not this."

"What a noble way to express that," remarked Alice. "We actually have an extra copy of the prayer calendar here in our UMW box at the church if you'd like to borrow it."

"That would be great," accepted Lydia. "I'll be there to pick it up in a few minutes."

"Oh, and I almost forgot," rushed Alice, "my name is Alice Balmer. When you told me you joined the church on Sunday, I figured out who you were. I was here for the service when you made that commitment and the congregation took you in. Congratulations! Boone Methodist is a wonderful place to be."

"So I'm hearing from lots of sources," chuckled Lydia.

She quickly dashed out the door and drove the few miles to the church to get the prayer calendar. Alice had hung around to explain how to use the small booklet and to extend Lydia a personal welcome.

Lydia leafed through the pages passionately and made a pledge to earnestly pray for each of the missionaries on their birthdays and see how she could best get involved in sending them greetings on the holidays. *And during the year, too*, she reminded herself. *Don't forget them the rest of the year, either.*

It wasn't long before she was back in the living room of The Rhododendron, every part of her being exuding joy with her current project. She had simply wanted to find out how she could write a note of encouragement to missionaries in foreign lands. What she received was an offer of invitation, acceptance and spiritual renewal all at the same time.

I can't wait to tell Ward, she gloated, in amazement at how they had managed to get through their lives without the letters and the influence of John Glenn Edgerton.

She'd heard of ghosts who haunted houses before. *But this is a Ghost who saves houses*, she laughed aloud, thinking of how the "Power" of the "Ghost" had scared the snake right out of its skin!

When Ward came home that afternoon, Lydia was sitting in the floor with a circle of cards spread out around her.

"What on earth?"

"I'm so glad you're home. Do you remember what the TV reporter said last night about sending messages to our troops overseas?"

"Yes, I do. But what are you doing?"

"It struck me today as I was reading Glenn's letter that we get so bogged down in our everyday lives that we tend to forget about the people that are overseas, such as our missionaries or our troops who need our prayers and encouragement. We take it for granted that someone else will write to them or send them cards on their birthdays and on holidays, therefore, we don't do our part."

"From the looks of things, you must be planning to send a

card to every single person over there."

"Come and help me. I'm sorting through all these cards that I picked up last year on the dollar table. It doesn't matter how much they cost; it matters that we let them know we care."

"You're really taking this seriously, aren't you?"

"I really am," she stopped and smiled for the first time. "We never had children to pour our love on. This seems like a way we can share ourselves with others."

For the first time since Ward had walked through the door, he realized what an important task this was to his wife. "May I bring you a glass of lemonade and a plate of cookies? We can make this an indoor picnic!"

"Thanks!" Lydia's smile grew even larger. "I knew I could count on you."

19

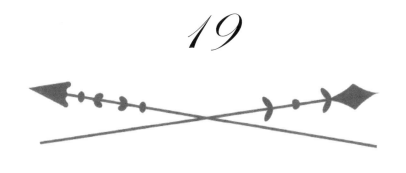

Snow Hill, North Carolina
April 15, 1929

My dear Glenn,

Your letter written February 3rd reached me today and my promptness in writing you will prove how power- fully appealing it is. Glenn, you just mustn't be lonely and discouraged and feel that you have been forgotten for such is certainly not true. I am glad however, that you feel that you can write me and explain it when you have lonely hours.

Somehow I can't believe you meant to send those let- ters, but am certainly glad that you no longer burn them. Please send on each one that you write. It simply thrills my soul to hear from you – but your letters are always too short! The personal element and extreme confidence in which your letters are written <u>and</u> <u>kept</u> is an experience that is most thrilling, and I only wish I might let some one person know my reaction when your letters come to me from so far away. It is great to know you as I do, and your <u>sincerity</u> is a perfect <u>virtue</u>. I'm sure I can never regret anything I may have written you. I hope I haven't encouraged you in any way – I haven't meant to because I don't think it would be quite fair to you, but I want to assure you that I consider our friendship more than merely a "passing acquaintanceship."

Assuring you of my constant thoughts and daily prayers that you may be strengthened and comforted in His service, I am

Most sincerely,
'Gene

Lydia wondered from the words of the letter if anyone knew of the relationship that was building between this couple with each passing letter. *'Gene is no longer at Goldsboro. Perhaps it became too difficult to hide her feelings from Sonny and Mrs. Beulah.* If Lydia was right in her assumptions, Rev. Daniel already knew of the potential for a budding love affair. *And was in agreement with it!*

She quickly opened the next "volume" of her "detective novel" to discover another note that had been written from 'Gene on the same day.

Snow Hill, North Carolina
April 15, 1929

My dear Glenn,

Please don't be disappointed and think you're getting a real letter for this is only a note to say I hope you are well and happy and are accomplishing great things in carrying on your plans. I have begun to write more often; I know you are surprised to hear from me twice in so short a time, but I believe if I were out there I would be mighty glad to get a letter from America regardless of whether it contained any startling news or not.

Now you've got the big fat picture. All these months he's been there begging you to write and you finally take him serious. What did he do to prompt this change of heart, threaten not to come home? Or to come and bring Miss Armstrong with him?

We have been mighty busy at school getting ready for the County Commencement and the Finals. You know what that means. School will "close" about May 21st. I am helping with the Senior Play. Then, I am the High School Librarian and I have lots of work to do there; statistics, etc. to work out. This has been a most pleasant year in many ways and I have thoroughly enjoyed Snow Hill. It is so different from what I ever thought it to be. We have already been re-elected but all the school folk in the state are mighty upset over the bill that has been passed by the recent state legislature. We don't know how many teachers we will be allowed to keep another year or just who. I can't explain the bill, but I'm sure you will know about it soon - if not already. I hope such an action will mean more to our N. C. schools.

I haven't been to Goldsboro since Christmas and I never see or hear from "Sonny" . . .

Lydia's eyes stopped and flashed back over that sentence. "I never see or hear from "Sonny.""

Woman, don't tell me that you don't want to unfairly encourage this poor man sitting all alone with his students in a foreign country all the way on the other side of the world. You've just given him the green light to proceed!

Lydia tried to envision a single woman at home in the small community of Snow Hill, North Carolina, back in April of 1929, a time that was swinging high in lots of ways, both socially and economically.

Not hearing from Sonny, huh? Maybe he gave up on her.

She looked down at the letter and recalled her own years of being in her early twenties. Boys who would come by the corner drug store where she worked could tell merely by the look in her eyes that all of her interests were vested in one young man. As she allowed her imagination to see a woman in Snow Hill and a man in Africa, it was easy to create a scenario of what probably happened.

Besides, it was already decided from a higher Power, Lydia acknowledged as she glanced up at the forsaken windmill, *'Gene was Glenn's mate for life, anyway.*

She sat back, contented and ready for a smooth ride now all the way to the finish. It would not be long before she could call Phillip and Francie and inform them that she'd read her way through the letters and was ready to hear all the details of three generations of Edgerton's.

20

My dear 'Gene,

Few letters have I received in Congo which brought me more happiness than the one which came to me from you in the mail last Saturday at noon. I have read and re-read it many times. Each time I enjoyed it more. 'Gene, it was just so full of yourself. I could see you peeping out from behind the words, smiling through the spaces between the lines, while pausing to put a dot over an "i" here and there. I felt as though you might have been a "Roxanne" leaving from her balcony dropping your words like jewels of dew which glimmered in the moonlight to me below in the shadows, receiving and feeding on each one.

Oh, 'Gene, you did not need to put it in words, it was

all there. It was there because it was you. How I have looked forward to and longed for the day to come which would bring this letter from you. And yet, it is true even though I first felt as though I were awakening from a beautiful dream. How I wish tonight that I might leap upon one of the shimmering moonbeams and nullify all time and space just to have a few minutes with you!

If I have been an inspiration to you, how many more times have you been an inspiration to me? All the noble words you have spoken to me have spurred me onward to become worthy even in a small sense of the tribute you have given to me. What would man be were there no angel in his life to urge him at all times to live up to the best within him! What would life be!

I am so glad that you told me more about yourself and what you have been doing since the last time you wrote. I wondered how it was that you came to be in Snow Hill. And to think what an honor to be the only Latin teacher in the whole of Greene County. Which do you like to teach the better, Latin or English? Of course you enjoy them both.

A letter came this week from Winnie Duke. Poor girl. She has been sick more than sixteen days since Christmas. The flu surely did deal her a hard blow. She is such a brave little soul and possesses one of the pluckiest spirits I have ever known. I am sure she is now up and at it again because nothing could keep her down.

Honest, 'Gene, I am ashamed to admit it, but it has been months since I have written to my boys at St. Paul. I believe they are the debtors as far as letters are concerned. I have written a few times and should have written more often if I did not have so much work to do. I wonder if everyone feels as though he has more to do than the other fellow. I shall not attempt to enumerate the many duties I have but sufficeth it to say I am busy every day from early morning until late at night.

You spoke of studying and enjoying so very much "The Methodist Evangel" by Dr. Goddard. I wish you could know him. He was with us here at our Mission Meeting in November and I had the opportunity of knowing him. After Mission Meeting was over I traveled with him for several days and honestly he seemed almost like a father to me. He is a great spirit and a most consecrated servant of God. Some day perhaps you, too, may have the privilege of knowing him.

I was so glad to have news of "Bobbie" Brown. It was the first I had had since conference and I hadn't the slightest idea where he had been sent. He is a great soul and I feel it was a great privilege to have had the opportunity of working with him that summer. He meant a lot to me and I'm hoping to have a letter from him soon.

Yes, I know Elmo and Mary Tabb. They arrived here in time for Mission Meeting last November. I had the opportunity of knowing them then and have seen them several times since then. They are not on the same station with me, but at Minga, about sixty miles form here. I believe that they will make good missionaries.

'Gene, how can I bring this little hour with you to a close! It has just slipped away and is laughing at me in all its glee as if to say, "You thought I'd tarry awhile but I have eluded you." The months are speeding by and just about a year from now I should be nearing America. Can it be true that it has been almost three years, just lacking one month, since the night I told you good-bye and rolled away on the rails!

But, 'Gene, I'm coming back some day, God willing it, and what a joyous day it will be. The months will pass more rapidly now than ever, knowing - - May God keep you and bless you each and every day.

Your sincere friend,
Glenn

At last! How I wish I knew what she'd said in the letter. Whatever it was, it surely was a boost to his morale. Has Sonny seen the door? I surely hope so!

Lydia heard the postman at the door. She jumped up in time to speak to him as he made his way down the steps to the street.

"Good morning!" she called.

The postman waved back, grateful for a kind word and a

huge beaming smile. *Makes the day go faster to know that someone actually cares.*

Lydia leafed through the envelopes and found a small post-card hidden between two of them. She flipped it over to see that it had been sent from Cambodia.

"My dear Lydia," she read aloud, "what a pleasant sur-prise to receive the card from you on my birthday. It is also such an encouragement to know that people in America are praying for us. Your kind note was a great inspiration to me. I hope that you will write to me again when you have the time. Sincerely, Claudia."

Lydia was so thrilled that she phoned Ward in his office, an act she rarely did.

"What's wrong, dear?"

"Nothing!" she excitedly screamed into the phone. "Nothing's wrong. Do you recall all those cards we went through and mailed to the missionaries? Well, of course you do," she an-swered for him. "I just received a reply from one of the women in Cambodia."

Ward had sensed the enthusiasm in his wife's voice even before her words. "That's terrific, Lydia. Why don't you read it to me?"

She was delighted that he'd ask to hear the message.

"And how long until you write her again?"

"As soon as I can turn on the computer. She has her e-mail address underneath her signature."

"I thought you were all against all this technological stuff. From the sound of it on the evening we worked on those cards, if

I remember accurately, you were a diehard advocate of the old stamp and envelope technique."

"That was before I got a response. This is just like having a pen pal in grade school." Lydia's voice, as well as her words, possessed the thrill of a young schoolgirl.

Ward laughed. "Ah, what would Glenn have done had he had that modern convenience?"

"Thank God he didn't! I'd never have gotten to know him or 'Gene." She paused as she reflected on her own words. "Isn't technology a shame, Ward? Think of the future generations. There will be no letters for young people to look at and paint visual images of their ancestors and all the beautiful things of the past. How horrible that we are totally obliterating the past of today for the future thanks to everyone's rush to "do it" or "have it" right this minute."

The joy that had been so evident in her voice moments earlier had subsided into sorrow.

"But dear, think of the joy that you've brought into Claudia's life. You, with your letters, are still making a difference in the lives of others. You are showing them that you care."

"You're right!" came the energetic reply. "Forget the idea of the e-mail. I'm going to send her another letter tomorrow. If Glenn had to wait three months for a letter to get across and another three for a reply, surely Claudia can wait for another few days."

"That's the spirit. You hang in there, love."

"I love you, Ward."

"I love you, too, Lydia. See you in a couple of hours.

What's for dinner?"

"Another one of your favorites. Swedish crepes filled with fresh strawberries and cream with ham on the side."

"Yum! What's the occasion?"

"You helping me so graciously the other evening with all the cards. I've not had a chance to formally say thank you yet."

"I believe you just did with the letter from Claudia."

A muffled laugh was all he heard from the other end.

Lydia sat in silence for a few minutes as she read back over Claudia's card and replayed the words of her conversation with Glenn. She thought how richly the courtship of Glenn and 'Gene had been blessed through the situation of the letters and having to wait so long between each one. *What a lesson of patience, and learning that the rewards of a chore are not always reaped "right now", that they had discovered through such a seemingly simple task as putting pen to paper.*

21

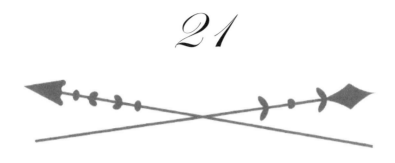

My dear 'Gene,

This is the Lord's Day and a blessed day of rest it is for me. It has been a most busy week that has passed; the opening week of school always is. Reorganization of classes, grading new pupils who have come in, caring for the details of the boarding department and many incidentals make an already crowded program more crowded. I sometimes wonder, however, if all of us do not work better under pressure.

But my work is destined now to be harder than before. Last week, I wrote you about one of our families having to go home on account of health. This week I must tell you about another. Miss McNeil, my co-worker in the educational work, is having to go home. Her health has been failing for some time and the doctors advised her to go home back in February. However, she has been making a desperate effort to regain what she has lost and to stay. The fight has been too great and the only thing left is to go to America if she ever hopes to regain her health. It is tragic and I feel deeply for her, but for months I have seen that it would be thus. May God raise up another to take her place.

I had a letter from home today telling me about Dr. Goddard's visit in Goldsboro but I was so disappointed when I read that Papa did not meet him. I don't suppose that he knew Dr. Goddard would be there at that time. At any rate he was out of town at some kind of agricultural meeting.

It makes me very happy when I think about our school this term. For the first time since I have been here practically every boarding school pupil returned. In addition to these about twenty-five new ones came in. This makes more than two hundred boys in the boarding department. In the whole school the enrollment is between three hundred and three hundred fifty pupils. Oh, how I hope and pray all of them may be led to Jesus and many of them be called as evangelists to take the "Glad tiding of great joy" to their people.

'Gene, I have thought of you so many many times since last Sunday. You have been with me constantly and I find myself in the midst of what I am doing wondering where you are and what you are doing. How true it is that one's thoughts know no time and space. Would that my thoughts could transport me physically as well as mentally as it sails o'er land and sea.

Your letter is almost worn with the reading of it. Every day it is read and some days more than once. Each time I wonder if it can really be true and if it is your writing which so enthralls me. But I know that it is because I see and I feel it. Oh, the joy supreme which it has brought to me. Heavy tasks seem lighter and multitudinous duties seem few, thanks to your words.

Just as I finished the above paragraph the bell rang for Sunday School. Of course I had to stop and go. To my surprise and joy I found every seat in my classroom taken and when I counted them there were one hundred six boys. It is a very large group to teach and I have to use the lecture method, in spite of how much I dislike it for growing boys.

Tonight I have been playing a few hymns since coming back from supper. I love my little three-reed organ even though I play it so seldom. Tonight as I played, my thoughts went wandering back to the night that a group of us went up to Beulah's after church and played and sang awhile. Do you remember it? Perhaps you don't as there were many nights when you went out there. I wonder just when I shall hear you again make the keys talk and sing, rhapsodize and then fade away into soft melodies.

Oh, 'Gene, if you only knew how much I want to hear from you, but more than that and most of all, how much I want to see you, to be with you and to have a long, long talk with you! Looking forward to this will make the months melt away as the snowdrift before a warm sun and a southern zephyr.

May God bless and keep you each day,

Most sincerely,
Glenn

Lydia wasn't sure whether she felt more horrible about Miss McNeil or excited about the number of boys in the school. *I'm sure that Glenn has much to do with the success and the growth of the school. Kids can tell when you really care about them. That's one thing that I'm sure is the same in any language. They know the difference between obligation of duty and sincerity of feeling.*

She was sure that if Glenn was able to write such beautiful words to a woman by whom he was so enraptured by, he could also express his concern and care for students in another land. It was his mission, his goal, and most of all, his passion.

Passion! That's it. That's what it is that allows him to love his surroundings so much. That's what allows him to communicate with the students when there are no words. They can sense his love.

She began to dwell on how enriching and rewarding it must have felt for him to realize the fruits of his labors in the number of students that had returned. Then, thinking of his humility in the letters, she wondered whether he even considered that he had anything to do with it.

He probably suspected that it was all of God and that he was merely the facilitator. Lydia caught what had just run through her mind. *And he was right*, she'd come to learn.

One hundred six boys? Her experience as a teacher made her aware of how demanding that had to be. *I can't imagine one hundred six boys who can understand me, much less who can't.* She was continually amazed at the magnitude of the communication barrier.

What's this? Lydia wondered as she opened the note that didn't have an envelope. She saw from its opening words that it was a letter, more like a journal entry, which Glenn had sent out as a report. *I wonder if they received one at St. Paul. I wonder if he sent one to 'Gene, too.*

It was then that she noticed the date. *March 1928.* That seemed rather odd for all of the letters were neatly in order, each period of letters tied into a specific bundle with a different color ribbon. Perhaps these got lost from the others. *Or maybe it took that long for these to get back to America.* That's when it struck her that the one she was reading was probably the one that had been sent to 'Gene.

Seeing how long the note was, she fixed herself an extra large glass of lemonade and grabbed a handful of freshly baked Moravian cookies, settled in the chair that officially belonged to the lady of the house and began to read.

METHODIST EPISCOPAL CONGO MISSION
DEPARTMENT OF EDUCATION

Wembo Nyama, Congo Belge
Near the end of March 1928

To get off on an itinerating trip is quite a task at any time but especially so when one has not been on the path for an entire year. The first term of school closed on Friday afternoon and that consumed the entire weekend with its many phases. This meant that there only remained Tuesday and Wednesday along with Monday in which to get ready to depart on Thursday morning for a two week's trip.

On Tuesday afternoon I went to a nearby village to see the work there so that it would make it possible for me to go further the day on which I started. Arranging everything so that it can be left for two weeks is quite difficult in itself to say nothing of the time that is consumed in packing boxes of provisions, wearing apparel, cot, canteens, and other numerous things which one must needs have on the path.

But at last I had the small trunks, etc. prepared to give to the men, and they had gone. About nine o'clock, after telling everyone goodbye, I mounted my wheel and turned it toward the north to go on my first itinerating trip alone. I left with the expectation of seeing no white person until I again returned to the mission, and perhaps my expectation will be fulfilled as I am now in the midst of the route and have seen not one thus far. Some times it is not a rare thing to meet company men on the path, or others.

By steady going I reached my first stopping place shortly after noon. This was the village of chief Shungu a Kei. He has a large village of perhaps four or five thousand souls, counting women, men and children. It is the usual thing for a native to think of only the men when he tells you how many people there are in a village. This village is one of the most heathen that I have been in yet. The chief has perhaps more than fifty wives which is the usual thing for powerful chiefs. But the village is filled with children and in the children lie the hope and the future of this people.

Because of the size of the village the evangelist has two places of assembly there. There is but one church which is too small but the chief promises to build another church near the second place of assembly. As I entered the village someone sent up a cry that a new white person had come and soon the huge street was filled with children who ran along on each side of my bicycle, some of them begging to push it and others telling them to keep away. All along the way to the rest house if a child should trip and fall a loud yell of derision would go up. They seemed to enjoy this and those who fall along the way did not seem to resent. When I came to the chief's house he came out to welcome me and to show the way to the rest house.

Our work in this village is very young but the evangelist there is a very courageous and enthusiastic worker for the Master, and he has made a good beginning to break through the heavy wall of heathenism there. He works hard and commands the respect of all the people. They know that he is a good man and that he is sincere in the work that he is trying to do for the people. We need more men like him and we are trying to equip them for the hard task ahead of them by the training in the Bible School at Wembo Nyama.

From Shungu a Kei to Umimnga, the next village which I stopped at, one encounters a most beautiful journey. A part of the time he is passing through small villages and between them spaces of grass-covered plains broken here and there by small clumps of trees, and now and then a lone palm tree standing sentry over the wide expanse about it and watching the decades slip by. When the journey is about half finished, still going toward the north, there is seen a most beautiful tropical forest.

This forest lies along the banks of the Lunya, a small, swift river of black water. As one enters it he follows the native path which has been built up by driving small sticks into the ground, digging the earth from the outside and putting it on the interior. This is held in place by the numerous roots of grasses which grow along the way. Of course the sticks have to be renewed periodically because they rot quickly in the water and shadows.

As one passes along through this dense growth he cannot but be impressed by the mass of tangled beauty. Huge trees which have made stilts of their roots raise their immense trunks and thrust them upward to the sky. Dangling from their limbs are myriads of serpentine vines which seem to be trying to pull them back to give their own a glimpse of the sunlight. Now and then appears a tree which was once a vine but due to its parasitic persistence it has long since claimed for its own the strength of the body which succored it and assumed its place in this dense jungle. Underneath, near the edges of the path where now and then a few rays of the sun have crept in at mid-day are clusters of coarse tropical lilies whose blossoms have neither beauty of color nor pleasing aroma. Bordering the path, and now and then thrusting themselves into the very path itself are many varieties of graceful and beautiful ferns such as only the tropics can give. As one passes they thrust out their fronds and caressingly beseech him to tarry a moment and contemplate of their rare beauty.

I had the opportunity to see this place of beauty under different circumstances. The onward journey was before noon when the sun was at its brightest. The return trip was after a rainy morning when the forest was still clothed in the thick shadows cast by the clouds. The onward trip was through a path dappled with gray light, the latter was only a mass of grey and green. Each held its own peculiar beauty and each was filled with enchantment.

All along the way as I passed through small villages I found boys from the school at Wembo Nyama who were home on vacation. In every instance they were soon near to give me a greeting and would run along by my bicycle singing their path songs until I was well out of their village and at times even until I arrived at the next village. It always did me good to see them and to know that they are well and happy and looking forward to the time when vacation will be over and they can return to the mission. In one instance they told me that they were tired of sitting all day and doing nothing and that they would be glad when vacation time would be over.

When I arrived at the village of Chief Umiunga it seemed as though all the children in the village turned out to meet me. A drummer from a village which I had passed through had relayed the message that I was coming and they were ready to greet me. Before I went to the rest house I stopped by the chief's house and gave him my greeting. Afterwards he came down to see me and we talked for a very long time.

It was Friday afternoon and I met with the evangelist in the school. We talked about his problems and tried to devise some way of remedying them. For instance the chief had sent off all the larger boys in the school and village to do some work for the statesman, and of course this had disarranged his classes. I gave him new material for the school, some to replace the old ones which were exhausted and additional new ones. The next morning was Saturday and although they do not assemble as a usual thing for school on that morning, they consented to do so as I would have to leave some time during the morning.

Saturday morning dawned cool and grey. By the time that I reached the church for early morning service it was raining. I stayed for school and by the time that it was over the rain was steadily coming down. Shortly after I returned to the house it began to descend in torrents and continued to do so all the morning. We had planned to get away about nine or ten o'clock and hoped that every minute the rain would hold up so that we could go, but it did not. It continued until shortly past noon, but when it did hold up we made our start.

When I reached the next village one of the first things which the chief had to tell me was about the death of his son which had occurred forty-three days before. The funeral rites were still going on and were to continue for three weeks longer. It was the first big funeral I have seen. All the people in the village took a part some time during the day whether there was rain or sunshine. The place where mourners assembled was directly opposite the house of the chief. It was surrounded by dead palm branches and on a stick in the front hung the hat of the dead man. All the women in the village and a part of the men wore grass wreaths on their head and skirts of closely woven loosely hanging grasses, symbols of mourning. In the afternoon and morning they assembled in front of the chief's house and engaged in all kinds of ritualistic and heathen dances accompanied by drums perhaps better termed tom-toms. Many of them carried symbolic sticks and in the center was one designating the rank of the dead man. Many of them had painted their bodies with mud in a most hideous fashion. The rites continued well into the night, and next morning they continued them in the downpour of rain.

It is hard for the message of Jesus to penetrate the

ears of such people whose ears and hearts are so tightly sealed by heathenism and superstition. But an opening has been made with the younger generation and the word of Jesus is making glad those hearts who accept Him as their Saviour. It takes courage for a man of God to stand up before a crowd of such people and proclaim His message when he knows only too well what is in their hearts. But, God be praised, there are such men among the land of faithful evangelists who labor for the Master day by day.

Returning to Shunga a Kei late Saturday afternoon I passed the night there. On Sunday I attended service both morning and afternoon in the two places of meeting and preached at one of them. In the afternoon service the church was packed. Every seat taken, children seated on the ground all about the front of the church, the aisle filled, and many standing on the outside. The evangelist delivered a very good sermon and I am sure many went away thinking about some things they had never bothered to think about before.

On Monday morning, after a session with the school, I left the village and went to the village of Chief Fundji, who is also called Lusamanya, which is about one hour and a quarter away by bicycle. I was greeted by the evangelist and the children of the village and escorted to the rest house. I made that my headquarters and in the afternoon went over to see the work of an evangelist in a nearby village. I took him new materials and helped him all that I could in the one afternoon. I returned to Fundji for the night, and the next day I spent in helping the evangelist there.

Wherever there were classes of those who were ready to be tested on the catechism, I heard them, and if they knew their answers well were put on probation. In some instances they were much better prepared than in others.

Late in the afternoon of Tuesday I departed from Fundji and started for Ngandemema which lay to the south and about an hour and a half or a little more away. When about half way there I met a messenger from the mission with letters for me. When he told me that everything was well at the mission I decided to wait until I reached the above-mentioned village to read the letters he had given me.

As I approached Ngandemema there were several Mission Boys out to meet and greet me. I appreciated their coming out to meet me and having them go on into the village with me. As I neared the center of the village where the home of the chief and the rest house were I met the evangelist. Nearby were his house and the uncompleted church. Although late afternoon was approaching and the sun was slowly sinking behind the trees, immediately upon arrival at the rest house I set about to see what the letters contained.

Sure enough they contained matters which it was necessary to answer immediately. My portable Corona came in very handy in this instance. I brought it forth and as I began to write upon it, it became a veritable sideshow curiosity to the natives. They marveled at the way I could use all my fingers in striking the different keys and at the way writing appeared on the paper. Another surprising and wonderful thing to them was the use of carbon paper. They thought that it was marvelous that I could make so many copies at one time. Finally the crowd became so large that I had to tell them to stand back and then as a resort to get them away without threats I brought out the soccer ball and sent them to play.

The evangelist in this village has a hard task just at present. He has been at this charge but three months and when he came he had few materials to work with. The church shed had never been completed - - only the frame work standing. He was holding services and school each morning and afternoon in the shadow made by his house, shifting the poles as the time of the day warranted, as these were their only seats. But I am sure that he will make a success of the work there because I knew his work at another place where he did a similar thing when the church blew down and he did not wish the work to lag until it could be rebuilt. However, I had a talk with the kapita, the chief being away, and the morning I left he had sent a goodly band of workmen to the forest to bring in materials for the completion of the church.

On Wednesday afternoon I went to visit the school at the village which was about an half hour or more away by bicycle. I would have gone there to spend the night but there are no accommodations for doing so and it was much better to return to Ngandemema for the night under the circumstances. I helped the evangelist all that I could. It was the poorest school that I had seen and had very little life. I returned to the other village in time for the late afternoon school there. When it was finished we had a great frolic with the *soccer ball.*

Each evening after supper all the boys in my caravan gathered about the house for the evening devotions. Sometimes the number was increased by the mission boys who happened to be in the village. At the service this past Wednesday night there were four or five, or perhaps six, I do not remember which as others came the next morning from nearby villages. It was very impressive to me as we gathered there in the soft light cast by the moon and lifted our hearts to God in song and prayer. Whenever I called on any of the boys to pray, they were glad to do so, and always before the prayer was over there was a petition that I might be given strength for the work before us and a ready tongue to speak the language of this people that I may more clearly teach them the Gospel of Jesus.

After breakfast on Thursday morning, and another session in the school, we "broke camp" and started for Lomembe which lay to the northeast. It was a very hot morning and the sun poured its burning rays mercilessly down upon us. We were all extremely sweltering when the village and rest house came into view just across a small stream on top of the hill. All the boys stopped to bathe as they always do when they are hot and come to a stream of clear water. It was very tempting, too, and looked so refreshing, but the lack of privacy thus by the side of the road made me postpone my bath until I had finally reached the house and some of the village boys had brought water.

The old chief, Lomembe, was very interesting in many

ways. He was very friendly and came to the house several times while I was there to talk. Once when he came I was eating, but I invited him in. Although no invitation was given to his numerous retinue they came into the house also. I gave him a sample of a few things I was eating and he pronounced them very good. He always gave some of each thing to his followers. I happened to be having tea to drink and not thinking he would like it I did not offer him any. He had perhaps been given some coffee at some time by some white person, and thinking this was coffee he asked for it. I gave him a little. He said that it was fine but I soon noticed that he gave the majority of it to someone else to drink.

From there I went north again for about an hour and a half on Friday afternoon, expecting to spend the weekend at Emungu. However, a few minutes after I arrived I had a talk with the evangelist and concluded that it would be possible for me to finish the work that I could do there in a much shorter time. After a few minute's rest I left the boys at Emungu and went to the next village, Okoka. It took about forty minutes on the wheel. Once there, I had the evangelist to assemble the school and spent the remainder of the afternoon with them.

The return trip in the twilight was very beautiful indeed. Before me was the sunset obscured behind a bank of clouds the rims of which were tinted with gold, silver and purple. On the one side were the wide stretching plains dotted here and there by an occasional palm tree and now and then by a clump of palms where there had been a village in *former days. On the other side the scene unrolled itself as a great brownish-grey carpet, sloping downward to the Lomani River several miles away, and finally losing itself in the majestic shadows of the trees whose tops seemed to unite sky and earth. Over all of this was thrown the changing shades of light as the day gradually gave place to night.*

Emungu was the first place on the itinerary where I had encountered mosquitoes. It had been such a pleasure to go to sleep at night and not hear the sound of their peculiar song when some unfortunate being was found upon which they could prey. But not so there. I was indeed thankful that I had a good protection in my netting, and also that I would be leaving the following morning.

As we were getting things in readiness to leave on Saturday morning, the thunder began to roll in the north and a heavy black cloud was gathering. We felt sure that we were in for a storm and we were going to do the best that we could to reach the next village before it broke. Part of the way we had to retrace our steps of the following day, and the boys did their best to try to get there ahead of the rain. The cloud was traveling in a diagonal to the path we were taking and we succeeded in keeping ahead of it, and soon saw that we would be able to reach our destination without delay from it. We were thankful, too, as we did not wish to be caught on the path by a heavy storm.

About ten-thirty o'clock we reached the village for which we were headed, Lusukula. Just before reaching the village we saw in the path the enormous tracks of a leopard, and fresh, too. At the village we learned that the nightly prowler had caught a dog early that morning and a goat in a nearby village. I don't think that I should have like to have encountered him along the way even though I had my trusty revolver with me.

I was very glad that we reached the village when we did and that the boys began to arrive soon afterwards. The nearer mid-day approached the hotter it seemed to get. About one o'clock it seemed to me to be about the hottest weather that I had seen in Congo. Everyone sought the shade, and a breezy spot if it could be found, and stretched for a long sleep.

Late in the afternoon I brought out the soccer ball and we had lots of fun. There was a nice open space in front of the chief's house to play. At either end the women soon gathered to watch and soon they were convulsed with merriment. Invariably when one of the young men or boys who had never seen a soccer ball before would attempt to kick it he would throw it into the air and kick into space. This always called forth a hilarious burst of laughter. Now and then when the ball would roll near the old men, one of them would grab it. They would pass it around, feel it and examine it until someone would pass it back into play. They thought it a marvelous invention.

On Sunday morning after breakfast we gathered in the church for the morning service. The little church was filled to capacity and a few were standing. The chief attended also. I was glad to see him there as not many of them go to the services. I tried to bring them a message centered about the transfiguration of Jesus. Although I realized that I was making mistakes in the language, I put my whole soul into what I was trying to say, and let the Lord speak through me. I feel that the service was not in vain.

After the service was over, I went back to the house and the chief came over and talked awhile. I then wrote a few letters. When I brought out my little Corona it was a big drawing card as it had been at other villages. They marveled at the way it could write but I think that the thing that interested them perhaps the most was the little bell. They soon discovered its location and then they would look and listen for it to ring. When I would stop before I reached the end of a line and return, they seemed to be just a little disappointed that they did not hear the bell ring.

Late in the afternoon we again gathered in the little church for the vesper service. One of the students in the Bible School who was on the trip with me gave the message. It was a quiet service and fitting at the close of the day.

In the evening we gathered about the sentry's fire and sang hymns. Several of the villagers joined us and sang with us. One of them was a young man who used to be an evangelist for our church but who is temporarily out of the work. He talked with me about the work and attended every service which was held while I was at the village. We are hoping that he will again find his way back into the work some time in the near future.

Monday morning I spent with the evangelist in the

school and found one of the best organized schools that I have seen in an out-station. That afternoon I left for Yeta, the last village I was to visit before returning to the mission.

The path trip to Yeta furnished a few interesting things. About half of the way there we came to a small forest which bordered each side of a small river. Just before we reached the forest we came across the remains of a python which the boys said a leopard had killed a few days before. Only a few pieces of the skin remained. We were then about to enter the forest when we noticed the trail which an elephant had broken through the tall grass and crossed our path. The nearer we came to the river the more signs we saw which indicated that a herd of elephants had been there, apparently that day or the day before. Many small trees were uprooted, and places trampled down. We crossed on over the river and before we reached the farther edge of the forest, one of the boys stopped and indicated that I should listen. In the distance I could just hear the elephants "talking," as the boys said.

When we reached the village we were talking about them and the people told us that it had been only the afternoon before that the elephants had been at the places we had seen and that they came there very often. They were not the last signs of them that I saw before I reached the mission but I was glad that I did not encounter them. I had no high-powered rifle, and that is the only weapon to cope with them.

The work of the church was nearly at a standstill in

the village, due, I think, partly to the lack of initiative on the part of the evangelist. He is a good man but did not seem to be able to instill in the people the desire to attend school, although they were a little more concerned about attending the church service.

As the sun went down on a typical African scene with all its beauty, the moon began to rise above the eastern horizon. It was not quite full but soon its soft rays were mystifying all beneath them and bringing rest to the tired world about us. When our evening songs were ended we soon noticed that a storm was approaching and that soon the moon would be blotted out and the earth left in inky blackness.

We did not have long to wait and by the time that everything had been put in readiness for the storm it broke. The first cloud did not last very long and soon passed away, but close upon it came two others which met and there was a great display of lightning. Flash followed flash rending the heavens asunder followed by deafening crashes of thunder. Soon the rain began to descend and the lightning to grow less fierce but now and then the prolonged rumbling of the thunder would make the very earth tremble.

The rain continued all night and the next morning dawned grey and dreary and appeared as though we were in for a rainy day. However soon after breakfast it held up, and although it was very cold we packed the things and turned our faces toward the mission. All the way along the streams were out of their banks having been swelled by the downpour of the night before. For the first few streams which

I had to wade my path boots kept out the water, but it soon began to seep through. In some of the places the poles had been washed away. In these cases, I would wait for the boy to take my wheel across, come back, arrange some other poles which happened to be there, and then holding to his shoulder or to some other small boy who happened to have followed I would cross, taking all precaution not to slip, for that meant getting into water above the top of my boots.

In one village a crowd of boys and young men ran along with me begging me to send them an evangelist. I could hardly bear to tell them that we had no one now whom we could send. The best that I could do was to tell them that perhaps one of the students who will graduate from the Bible School in June would go to them. God is working among these people and our greatest need is to train our Christian youth to go out and take the Gospel of Jesus Christ to their people. They are the ones who can best do it, and our greatest prayer is that we may have the strength and direction from on High to educate and prepare those who come to us for a greater service.

I reached the mission shortly after noon. I had been able to see it for some time from a nearby hill and it did my heart good to think that our station and village was a living emblem of the coming of the Kingdom of Jesus Christ upon earth. Those on the station were somewhat surprised to see me as I was not expected until late in the afternoon. I was glad to again be back and to see everyone again. It had been two weeks since I had left and my only companions were the

natives. They were faithful throughout the trip and not one
moment had been a lonely one.

    *May God bless this people, and may we, each and
everyone be a blessing unto them.*

    Lydia sat spellbound for a few minutes as she realized
that her entire being had been transformed from 'Gene's chair in
The Rhododendron of Boone to the distant villages of Congo,
Africa. The drums that had signaled from one village to another
that "the white man, the great evangelist" was coming were the
same drums that had signaled her that he was here - *in this place.*
Glenn Edgerton was alive and breathing within the confines of
The Rhododendron. His words, hidden inside that writing desk,
were still just as vibrant and powerful as the day they had escaped
from his pen "on the path" in Africa.

    *No wonder I heard the beating of the drums. They weren't a
real sound that I heard. They were instead a sprit, a Presence, that I
sensed through the work of Dr. John Glenn Edgerton.*

    It was with great elation that Lydia picked up the phone
and dialed the number for Alice Balmer.

    "Alice?" she asked when she got an answer. "This is Lydia
Mason. You will be thrilled to know that I have decided to accept
your offer and do a program on the mission work of Dr. Edgerton
for the circles."

"That's great news," came the energetic reply. "I took the liberty of calling our president at the church about this. She was so enthused that she's already gotten in touch with our district UMW president who I'm sure will be contacting you. They'd love for you to do something for the entire district at one of our upcoming meetings. This is wonderful. Thank you for the call."

"Thank Dr. John Glenn Edgerton," said Lydia. "It will all be in his words."

23

Lydia had been so deeply engrossed in the wilds of Africa the afternoon before that she leafed through the letters to see if she could find another report. It had taken her on a journey far away from home, all in the secluded comfort of 'Gene's chair. She was sure that was not the first time the occupant of that chair had been in a foreign land. *At least in her dreams.*

There was another report from only three months later than the time of the one she'd read the afternoon before. What really caught her attention was the line on which Glenn always gave his location. This one said, "On the Path." Lydia was already conditioning herself for the trip to another time, another place, as she grabbed a large mug of coffee for the ride.

METHODIST EPISCOPAL CONGO MISSION
DEPARTMENT OF EDUCATION

Wembo Nyama, Congo Belge

On the Path.

It was almost eleven-thirty o'clock on the morning of June 15, 1928 that I started out on my second itinerating trip of the year. It was Monday and like all Mondays was filled to the brim in getting the week started off on the correct track. The boys with the boxes, etc. quitted the station much earlier than I did and were well on their way when I departed.

This was the beginning of my first trip with a motorcycle. I had gone gone on the big motorcycle last year with Mr. Anker on a trip but I had done none of the driving. In fact I had never driven one until two days before I left when I took out the small motorcycle which we have on the station and after a little instruction in how to start the engine, shift the gears, etc., I rode off with it and drove it about the compound a bit until I became familiar with its workings.

To go on a good road the first time it well enough, but before I had gone very far I found the path getting rough as I had expected. I had anticipated a part of the path and sent some men ahead to help me in getting across the first stream. This done I came to a village where I picked up two other men to go to the next stream to help me there. That one ran through a swamp and the path had not been kept up and consequently in places was only muck. This made going bad but I finally got across and went along. When I came to the next stream, which was not a very large one, I overtook my box-men and they helped me across. The next stream I had to cross was the largest of all with about eight or nine bridges. Here again I had to have men to help me across and I was thankful that it was the last one.

It seems almost like a paradox to say that I was caught in a shower of rain and got some what wet when this is the middle of the dry season. But this is the case. We had had no rain for more than a month but that small cloud came up and had I not reached a small village when I did I should have been wet more enough. However, it did not rain long and I soon went on my way.

When I came to the village of Chief Djulu one of the first people I saw was the chief himself. It had been some time since I had seen him, in fact only once since my former visit to his village more than a year before. I was glad to see him and he was very kind to me while there and did all that he would to make me comfortable. He is a very intelligent native and his village is one of the best kept in the whole tribe. The rest house, too, is quite pretty for a native house and well kept also.

That night after supper while sitting by the fire of the sentry, talking to a group of natives, I heard some women singing in the chief's "fence" as the place where he lives with his wives is called. He had told me that afternoon that one of his wives had given birth to twin girls about three months before. These with me said that the song I heard was for the happiness of the mother and the children. It was their custom to sing every night. Their weird song was accompanied by the shaking of a gourd with small pebbles or seed in it. The mother was the only mother of twins in the village and she had but one other child. He was a boy of about seven years and was there in the group with me. He wore some strands of grass which was a sign to everybody that he

was the brother of the twin babies.

It was almost eleven-thirty o'clock on the morning of June 18, 1928 that I started out on my second itinerating trip of the year. It was Monday and like all Mondays was filled to the brim in getting the week started off on the correct track. The boys with the boxes, etc. quitted to the station much earlier than I did and were well on their way when I departed.

This was the beginning of my first trip with a motorcycle. I had gone on the big motorcycle last year with Mr. Anker on a trip but I had done none of the driving. In fact I had never driven one until two days before I left when I took out the small motorcycle which we have on the station and after a little instruction in how to start the engine, shift the gears, etc., I rode off with it and drove it about the compound a bit until I became familiar with its workings.

To go on a good road the first time is well enough, but before I had gone very far I found the path getting rough as I had expected. I had anticipated a part of the path and sent some men ahead to help me in getting across the first stream. This done I came to a village where I picked up two other men to go to the next stream to help me there. That one ran through a swamp and the path had not been kept up and consequently in places was only muck. This made going bad but I finally got across and went along. When I came to the next stream, which was not a very large one, I came upon my box-men and they helped me across. The next stream I had to cross was the largest of all with about eight or nine bridges. Here again I had to have men to help me across and I was thankful that it was the last one.

It seems almost like a paradox to say that I was caught in a shower of rain and got somewhat wet when this is the middle of the dry season. But this is the case. We had had no rain for more than a month but that small cloud came up and had I not reached a small village when I did I should have been wet sure enough. However, it did not rain long and I soon went on my way.

When I came to the village of Chief Djulu one of the first people I saw was the chief himself. It had been some time since I had seen him, in fact only once since my former visit to his village more than a year before. I was glad to see him and he was very kind to me while there and did all that he could to make me comfortable. He is a very intelligent native and his village is one of the best kept in the whole tribe. The rest house, too, is quite pretty for a native house and well kept also.

That night after supper while sitting by the fire of the sentry, talking to a group of natives, I heard some women singing in the chief's "fence" as the place where he lives with his wives is called. He had told me that afternoon that one of his wives had given birth to twin girls about three months before. Those with me said that the song I heard was for the happiness of the mother and the children. It was their custom to sing every night. Their weird song was accompanied by the shaking of a gourd with small pebbles or seed in it. The mother was the only mother of twins in the village and she had but one other child. He was a boy of about seven years and was there in the group with me. He wore some strands of beans which was a sign to everybody that he was the brother of the twin babies.

We used to have an evangelist at Djulu (we usually call the village by the name of the chief) but we have none there at present. However, I met with those who wanted to come this morning for a service before I left. Quite a number came and I thought that it was well that everyone had not forgotten the word of God although left without a pastor. We are hoping to be able to send one of the new graduates of the Bible school there.

After breakfast I chatted with the chief awhile and then left for my next stop, Ona Dikondo. (This name means, the son of a plaintain, a fruit similar to the banana). The road was very good practically all the way and I made the trip in good time. The only village I passed through before I reached my destination was Wembo Lua. It was just about fifteen minutes from Djulu and I had made a side trip over there yesterday afternoon in order not to have to make a stop this morning.

The work in the school here at Ona Dikondo is not progressing as it should, due I think entirely to the lack of initiative on the part of the evangelist. He has the materials with which to work, that is, as many as I am able to furnish for the other evangelists, and there are not so very many children in the village, the majority of whom seemed to be in school. He should have had a good school if he had put more into his work and made it interesting and an incentive for the children to learn.

Much like here, Lydia reasoned, thinking back to her own years of teaching. *It was easy to tell about the work of the teachers, simply through the eyes and the attitudes of the students as you would pass them in the hallways or in the cafeteria. I wonder how the other teachers and parents perceived my students.*

She had paused because of a break in the report. *Obviously a new entry for a new day*, she mused as she continued to read.

June 23.

Night is fast coming on but I shall try to get in a work or so before darkness makes it necessary to light a candle. Four days have passed since I have had the opportunity to bring the account of my trip up to date. I am at the village of Otepa quite a distance from the place at which I last wrote.

On Wednesday morning I arose and went to the early morning prayer service with the natives. As the trip for the day was to be a very long one for the men, the boys came quite early and fixed breakfast for me and I ate before going to the service. They finished getting things in readiness to leave while I was leading the service and soon all of us were on the path. The way the natives had to go was much shorter than the auto road by which I was to go, but as I was on the motorcycle I could make the whole trip much more quickly than they.

After I left Ona Dikondo the first village which I came to was Okita Ngandu. We used to have an evangelist there but when the village was moved a year or so ago there was so much work in building the new village that they did not build a church, and as yet the church is incomplete. They have been begging for an evangelist and we told them that when the church was completed they would be given an evangelist again. I stopped by and chatted with the people a short while and saw the frame of the church which has been finished, leaving only the roof to be grassed. The way the people gathered about me you would have thought that I was a circus or some other similar phenomenon. They asked me about practically everything I had on, what everything cost, and it made me think of myself asking so many questions. My boy says that I can ask more questions about more things in the same length of time than anybody he has ever seen.

After leaving Okita Ngandu I passed through country which I had been over before, but never had it seemed so beautiful to me. The hills and valleys for miles and miles were shrouded in a mystic mist which gave them an untold beauty. Now and then the sun would break through the clouds and with its glistening brush tint the mists and other clouds in varying hues of gold, pink, yellow and purple. Only the brush of the Master Painter could portray the canvasses which thus unrolled before me as I passed along.

In places the slopes of the hills were more rugged and steeper than in others showing where the fingerprints of Mother Nature are still fresh from the fashioning of them. The hills were in all their glory and seemed to be enjoying the prominence which the valleys were giving them. But down below the valleys were smiling with the knowledge that they too possessed a beauty which always caught the eye of those who passed along and that if it were not for them there would be no hills.

To ride along while the new morn is being born gives one a great inspiration, greater I sometimes feel than any other part of the day. God is in it all, and everything is so filled with His presence that it cannot but glorify His Name. "The Heavens declare the Glory of God; and the firmament showeth His handiwork" is the way the man of God a long time ago expressed it as he experienced such a morning as this one. It was filled with all the promise that God is able to give to man through the material creation; filled with opportunities to make good where yesterday he had failed; filled with a reassurance of God's love to all mankind.

Such an experience is not easily erased from one's

mind and many are the days in the future when I shall again and again experience this great morn "in the inward eye."

When I arrived at my destination, Okandja Luka, there were several Missions Boys, who were home on vacation, to greet me. I arrived a long while before the men with my boxes and when noon arrived I had lunch from a little "snack" which I had fixed and brought along in my pocket. I talked with the people for a long while and then had a rest in a chair which they brought me from the chief's house. The chief, like many others in the district, was not home but gone to Lubefu for a conference with the state official.

Lumbelilu, the evangelist there has a very good school. The pupils seemed very much interested in the work, and I think that they derive a part of it from the evangelist himself. He had his classes well organized and was doing the best that he could to carry out the suggestions which I had given the last time that the evangelists had assembled at the mission for quarterly conference. He is to be commended for the work that he is doing. He is a servant of the Lord well "worthy of his hire."

The following morning I went to Okit' Oleko, a village not so far distant. It is a new village and has no rest house, consequently I had to stay in a native hut of mud and sticks. It was not quite completed but was very much more comfortable than it sounds. I was glad that it was fresh and clean. There are no palm trees in the village to protect one from the burning rays of the sun, and we were very glad that the sky was overcast with clouds the entire afternoon. A storm had threatened but it passed into another section.

Here, too, I found the work of the evangelist good, and the amount which his pupils had learned in the time that he had been there speaks well for him and bears testimony that he has been "laboring in the vineyard" each day.

The following day I had planned to go to Otepa, the next village in which we have an evangelist. But the trip was such a long one that I changed my plans and went only as far as Otete. We have not had an evangelist there for the past six months but are planning to send one during the coming month. I felt that it would be well worth while to stop there as I have quite a number of Mission Boys from there and the people would keep in touch with us better by a visit to them. I was glad that I stopped there and I think the time well worthwhile.

On Saturday morning we again had another long journey ahead of us and as usual the path which I had to go was very much longer. Practically the entire way was new to me but was fairly good. When about half way I came to the Catholic Mission. I stopped and visited a few minutes with one of their missionaries. We renewed our acquaintance which we made on a former visit almost a year ago. I did not stay very long as I still had a very long way to go.

When I reached Otepa, "which was almost like going around one's elbow to get from the fingers to the thumb" I entered one of the prettiest villages I have seen. The main street is long and wide and on either side is a beautiful row of palm trees. I have never seen so many palm trees in one village. There are hundreds of them, not only lining the streets but in groves behind the houses. I say, behind, but in reality it is the front as none of the houses open onto the street. All of the trees are about the same height and size and form a most pleasing setting for a village. Their shimmering, glistening leaves make them veritable jewels in the sunshine.

Chief Otepa is away from home like all the chiefs to whose villages I have been except one but he is on a different mission from the others. It seems that I have selected a very unfortunate time to go on the path if my purpose had been to see just the chiefs themselves.

One of our very best evangelists is located here. He opened the work here about six months ago and has truly made a splendid beginning. In the first place the people have built the nicest church here that we have in the whole tribe. It is not only the largest in any out-village but the best equipped and very well kept. Large numbers of people are present at each service, not only in the mornings but afternoon also, children and grown-ups, too. They attend school well also. This is all due to the efficient way in which the evangelist has gone about the building of the work of the Master. He has a vision and those among whom he works cannot but catch his spirit.

Although yesterday was Saturday and as a rule school is not held on that day, the children assembled because it was the only opportunity I shall have while here to see their work. During one of the reading classes I was helping the teacher, and we were questioning all the pupils. Some of them who had not been attending regularly had come just because I was there. When one of these was called on he gave the right answer accidentally without knowing what he was doing. A snicker from him and from several others betrayed the situation. To avoid another similar situation, while the teacher had his back to him and was busy with another pupil, he silently but swiftly made for the door. The teacher did not see him until he was beyond recall. Several others later on, I mean two or three, to demonstrate their ability at self-expression followed in this little fellow's steps. The others were too glad to have the opportunity to learn to try to get out. I was particularly impressed by the interest the majority of them manifested.

"Let them flow in ceaseless praise," Lydia recited from the stanza of the hymn she remembered singing at church the past Sunday. She now felt that phrase vividly at work through the words of Glenn from his reports she had read over the past two days. "Take my life and let it be," she sang, picturing all the words of the text she could recall in her head and making numerous similarities to how they descriptively fit Glenn in his missionary journey.

And how they fit you, too, my dear Lydia, she sensed, as if the drums had beat out a special message to her.

How enlightening that the villages beg for an evangelist. And how rewarding that the evangelist teaches the children for future generations to look to God and trust Him for their needs and in their decisions. Teaching the love of God through example.

Lydia had specifically appreciated the comment about the pupils doing so well and that it came directly from their teacher. It was the same thought she'd had earlier. Now she wondered if she had set the example of Christ in her years of teaching, given that she was not the most committed of followers.

She pondered over what the report would have been like had she had to account in such a manner for her students and the school surroundings in which they learned. *Would I have gone to the trouble that Glenn did to make sure that pupils from the other villages were getting the same fair chance?*

Her fingers fumbled aimlessly for a few moments as the question ran through her head. She had loved the occupation of teaching; she had loved the students; she had loved the way to pass the time of day and earn and income. *Was it a job or was it a calling?* she pondered leisurely until she again heard the call of the drums.

There was one more note that had been folded with this report. The minute she saw the salutation, she sensed her eyes welling up from the tears that were forming behind them. It was to Glenn's "Papa," the first one that she'd seen addressed to him.

Of course I didn't see the others because these are all the ones that 'Gene kept and did not burn. I wonder how 'Gene managed to get this one and add it to the collection.

Lydia felt confident that she could do a program for the

circle and for the other women who might be interested. *All I have to do is to read the reports. Glenn laid out all the groundwork for me himself.* She turned her thoughts back to Papa and wondered how it must have felt to have a son or daughter who loved Jesus so much that they gave their life to go and serve unknown others. *True disciples,* she mused.

More than that, she wondered what it must have been like to have a son or daughter away in some strange foreign country where no one knew what was lurking, and to receive a letter letting you know that your child was all right and that things were going well and that he or she loved you.

Or a letter informing you that there would be no more letters from your beloved son or daughter, she thought, remembering the earlier letter from the young missionary in China about the ones who were persecuted and assassinated.

The tears that had started to form were now dripping down Lydia's face as she wiped them to keep them from falling onto the paper and blotching the ink that had dried so long ago. As she began to read, she wondered how many other tears had fallen on these same letters. *Especially this one . . .*

Wembo Nyama, Congo Belge
November 25, 1928

My dearest Papa,

 I have just been thinking that one month from today will be Christmas Day and I can hardly realize that the time has been flying past so rapidly. Most rapidly has this month passed, so fast in fact that next Thursday will be Thanksgiving Day although it seems to me that it should be about the Thursday of the first week in November instead of the last. I suppose that it must be because so many things have been happening.

 In the first place our Annual Meeting began on October 21st, and lasted for eight or ten days. It was the largest annual meeting that we have ever had and there were more missionaries present than ever before, there being forty-one in all including the children. We had a very intensive program to cover and it kept all of us very busy indeed.

 Dr. O. E. Goddard, Foreign Secretary of the Board of Missions, and Miss Esther Case, Secretary of the Women's Work, were with us during the conference. They came to us from the office in Nashville and were able to spend several days on each of the stations here before the meeting convened. We felt particularly fortunate to have them with us at this time and we feel that their visit is going to be of great and lasting benefit to our mission.

 After the annual meeting was over it was necessary for someone to take them to the train. As was the case last year it fell to my lot to take them. But I did not have to drive the truck as far this time as I did last year. I drove it only the first day, a trip of about eighty-six miles, to Minga. But I was delayed about two hours and a half by the rain and then in the mid-afternoon I discovered that the front spring was broken. There was nothing else left to do but to fix it.

It happened that I stopped on the side of a hill where there was a lone house. There were three women there and as I had two boys with me I knew that I should not be totally without help. I had never seen a spring put in before and had never helped to put in one but I tackled the job with the few wrenches, etc. which I had. I was fortunate to have had an extra spring with me. You would perhaps have smiled had you seen the front part of the truck and put in the new spring. I did the best that I could and about an hour and a half after I began the work, I cranked the engine and was off again.

But this delay meant that I would have to cross the river on the ferry after dark and this I had wanted to avoid. But the marvelous sunset which painted itself in changing colors over the hills which I had to cross in the late afternoon was a full compensation for all my trouble. My soul was filled with the greatness of the Holy Spirit and my lips sang with the psalmist of old, "The heavens declare the glory of God and the firmament showeth his handiwork" (Ps. XIX).

As I had expected, darkness fell before I reached the river, but still God had prepared everything for me. I met the state official at the state post, Lubefu, near the riverbank and he rode down to the river with me and saw that I got across safely. Once on the opposite side of the river the old truck seemed to take on new life and climbed the hills as it had never done before. It was not long before the remaining fourteen miles to Minga were covered. I reached there when they were preparing to return to look for me.

It seemed very good to reach there with no more trouble than I had had. Mrs. Reeve had a good supper waiting for me, although it was then getting near nine o'clock. Mr. Reeve was waiting to eat with me and we surely did enjoy everything. When we finished it did not take me very long to get to bed and to sleep.

The next morning we got up and dressed and after a very good breakfast loaded up the cars and started for Lusambo. From then on I drove the Dodge which Dr. Moore brought out and which the mission bought from him just before his death. Mr. Maw, one of our new missionaries drove the Ford car. Dr. Goddard rode with me and I feel very fortunate in having the privilege to have become better acquainted with him. With Mr. Maw were Miss Case, Miss Foreman, who is returning to America on furlough, and Mr. Eash, the Foreign Secretary of the Mennonite Church, who was visiting several missions in Africa in addition to their own. He was with Dr. Goddard throughout his visit to our mission.

We reached Lusambo late in the afternoon after a most pleasant trip. While there we stayed at the Wescott Mission which took over the work of the Presbyterians and

Methodists last January. We had intended to leave early the next morning for Mutoto on the Presbyterian Mission, but were unable to get away before about noon due to some work which had to be done on the Ford. However, we made good time and reached Mutoto that night.

We thought that our journey was near its end because the railroad station was only thirty-five miles more away, and the train, according to the information given to us by the postmaster in Lusambo, would not leave until Tuesday morning. You can imagine our chagrin when we learned, only too late, that the train which they wanted to get was to leave at midnight that night. It was then too late to reach the station.

The next day we drove over to the station to get all the information we could and we learned that there was a train leaving at the time they had told us in Lusambo but it was going in the opposite direction. Dr. Goddard then decided to go on to Luebo, another Presbyterian station, and take the aeroplane. So on Tuesday morning we started for that place.

I had never been to Luebo and had always wanted to go because I had heard so much about it. It is the Presbyterians' oldest station on their African mission and has a great work going on. To be privileged to visit it during this term was beyond my fondest dreams and you can imagine how happy I was to reach there.

The missionaries gave us a royal welcome and made us feel so happy to be there. We spent the next day in seeing a few of the many very fine pieces of missionary work they are doing, such as their Industrial School and Printing Department, Hospital, Church, etc. We wanted to stay several days in order to get a look at everything but due to the fact that it would take us several more days to get back home we had to prepare to leave the following morning, which we did.

We retraced our way to Mutoto and spent the next day there in order to take Miss Case and Miss Foreman to the train. They were going home by way of South Africa and Cape Town and as they were not pressed for time they were going by the slow train to Elisabethville where they could get a fast train for the Cape.

After several days Mr. Maw and I again reached Wembo Nyama. It seemed like getting home to me and I surely was happy to see the place and all the people again. It seemed to me as though it had been a month since I had seen my boys in the school. We had been gone fourteen days and had traveled more than a thousand miles. It seemed very good to be able to go to bed that night and not have to think what time I was going to have to leave the next morning and how many miles it was to the place that I was going to. But I was more than grateful that I had had the opportunity to see all the many things which I had seen. I should like to tell you about all of them but I know that you would weary of reading about them before you had nearly finished, so I shall close.

God has been very gracious to me here and I pray

that His presence may continually abide with each of you and bless you. Much love to you all,

Your devoted son,
Glenn.

P.S. We are all overjoyed that Hoover was elected. We got the news by radio. It is a great manifestation that the best element still predominates in America and that all her people are not ready to bring back the liquor traffic under any circumstances.

Lydia wondered whether Glenn's father had actually been the one to take the letter out of the mailbox or if he'd had to pick it up at a post office. She wondered if the postman hand delivered it to him. And she wondered what emotions went into gear when Papa saw who had sent the letter.

I do hope that Glenn's family was a supportive and understanding Christian family, who prayed for him and sent him messages of encouragement.

There was a great deal of contrast between the letter to Papa, the reports to the African Conference and the church back home, and the letters to 'Gene.

I guess guys don't get into the writing thing, she reasoned, *yet his words to 'Gene are so tender and loving.*

Lydia read back over the P.S. to Papa.

It was a different time in history. Things were not the same back then as they are today. Men were not raised to show emotion. They were to exemplify the stronger sex.

Now she was really in a quandary over the attitude of Glenn's family to his service as a missionary instead of a teacher at home. *Or even more so, like all the men who lived near Sunnybrook Farm in Goldsboro, a farmer to take care of the family's rural land.*

Lydia went to the desk and wrote herself a memo to be sure to ask Phillip about Glenn's home situation in regards to the support he received.

As she began to place the letter back in its envelope, she noticed that this letter was actually the last one that had been written for 1928. Lydia considered that fact a great tribute to Glenn's Papa. A tribute that said, in itself, what Glenn thought of both his father and his Father.

24

Wembo Nyama, Congo B.
Friday night, May 10th, 1929

My dearest 'Gene,

It is getting late, (the clock hands stand at about nine twenty but that is late out here) and everything is very quiet. It has seemed like a fall day and as tonight is quite cool, all the natives are in their houses sitting close to the fire to keep warm. I suspect that the majority have fallen asleep as they get drowsy sitting huddled over a fire.

Our "cool" weather or winter is just arriving. There is not so much difference in temperature during the day but the nights during the dry season are quite a bit cooler than they are during the rainy season. We feel as though the dry season has arrived sure enough as we have had no rain now for more than a month.

I enjoy the cool nights to the fullest extent. They are most conducive to good sleep and a peaceful rest of sleep is most essential in Congo.

Tonight I had planned to work on the translation of a book for one of my classes. It is called "First Lessons in Health" and I think is quite good. I hope I can get the pupils to put into practice even a few of the principles set forth therein. But I did not work on it. I worked on my little organ instead.

For sometime several of the reeds have needed cleaning and I have been putting it off for a long time until I should have more time. But that never comes and I thought "better now than never." So I opened it and set about my work. I really enjoyed doing it. When I finished I sat down to try it. As my fingers wandered idly over the keys my thoughts wandered across the seas.

I could see you seated at the console of some pipe organ. I could hear the beautiful strains of melody which the many tongues of the instrument produced as they responded to your touch. You were so plain to me but suddenly my thoughts came back to make me aware that you are thousands of miles away and that I was only a missionary seated at a little folding organ in the heart of Africa dreaming dreams. What would life be sometimes were it not for the dreams of happy hours!

'Gene, oh 'Gene, how long will it take the months between to slip away and resolve themselves into bringing me nearer to you! I suppose it is more than I should dare hope

for but I do want to see you again; to look into those deep brown eyes of yours sparkling as you looked at me teasingly. Perhaps, I am only holding to the ideas which I have of you and that you may not be like that at all. You I am sure that you must be. You could not help but be; you who are 'Gene.

I have had such a good time in my work at school this week. All the pupils have seemed to be working quite hard and to be interested in their work. I have been trying to work in some new material and although it has been difficult yet I do not feel that I have altogether failed.

On Monday morning three members of our station left for America. Miss McNeil was having to go on account of her health. She could not travel alone and one of the families, their furlough being due in July, went with her. All of us have been taking on extra work as their successors have not reached the field. We are doing the best we can to keep things going until reinforcements arrive. May God keep them on their homeward journey.

Now 'Gene dear, good-night. May guardian angels their vigil keep about thy couch as thou seekest thy repose night by night.

Sincerely,
Glenn

No wonder Glenn was so adamant about the church getting a pipe organ installed after the fire. I had no idea that he was such a fine and outstanding musician.

Lydia sat back in the chair and closed her eyes. She knew the tune of *'Tis So Sweet to Trust in Jesus*. She began to hum the melody as she imagined it being played on the pipe organ at Boone United Methodist Church. What she heard in her head was a magnificent symphony of sound with the driving beat of an African drum in the background – an aural cacophony that blended the mainstream of America with the heart of Africa.

She was so absorbed with the music, and at the same time trying to imagine a male voice – which she perceived as that of Glenn – singing the words that she missed Ward coming in the back door from the garage.

"Jesus, Jesus, how I trust him! How I've proved him o'er and o'er! Jesus, Jesus, precious Jesus! O for grace to trust him more!"

Lydia kept humming, with her eyes closed, as Ward leaned down and kissed her on the forehead.

"So this is what you do while I'm at work all day? And I thought you were spinning the hours away in those letters!" he jokingly teased.

"Ward! I didn't even hear you come in!"

"You didn't hear me singing?"

"That was you?"

"Who did you think it was?"

"I'm . . . I'm . . . ," She sat up in the chair and shook her head slightly to get her mind back into the present. "I'm sorry. I guess I was so immersed in the words of this letter that I was somewhere else altogether."

"Hmmm," he responded lightly, "obviously. Perhaps in Africa? That must have been some heavy-duty letter."

"Oh Ward, it is. You must read it. You must read it now. It can't wait until our devotional time together tonight."

He laid his brief case on the coffee table. "Okay, if it means that much to you." Ward sat in Glenn's old chair and began to skim over the words.

"Would you read it out loud, please?" Lydia requested.

Ward glared at her with an "I'm not too sure about that" look.

"Please," she pleaded. "It is *so* beautiful. I'd love to hear it read in a male's voice."

He gently shook his head. "The things I do for you," he smiled.

She sat back again, this time her eyes on Ward, as he read the letter.

"Isn't that the most idealistic expression of love you've ever seen or heard?" she asked, once he had finished.

With his eyes still fixed on the pages of the letter, Ward nodded.

Lydia wondered if he was too choked up to speak but was afraid to admit it.

"Lydia . . . ," His eyes slowly glided up to meet hers. "Dear, I didn't know about these letters to start with . . . I mean you opening them and reading someone else's private life. If they wanted these letters burned, they surely didn't intend for them to become public knowledge." He gave her a glimmer of a smile. "But they seemed to draw you into them in such a constructive way that I saw no harm in you reading them. Then when you met Phillip and his family, I began to understand how moving and inspiring all of this had become to you. If I didn't know better, I'd think you'd found a long lost family."

Ward gave her the same assuring grin that he had in biology class. "But instead, I think you've inherited a family. A grand family, at that. It's rather extraordinary, but I feel most confident with you having this kind of experience with both the letters and the Edgerton's. For some reason, there's a peace about it. I can't explain it, but it's like I can sense that they are supposed to be a part of our lives right now, and it's written all over you that you feel that same way."

Lydia nodded. "Yes, I do."

"You thought that it was Glenn singing in your imagination, didn't you?"

She smiled sheepishly. "Yes." Lydia nervously fidgeted with the letter in her hand. "Yes, I did," she admitted.

"I don't think that's anything to be ashamed of. Those letters and the love between Glenn and 'Gene are affecting you in a positive manner. They're making a believer out of me, too, and I don't mean necessarily in a spiritual way. Granted, our religious behaviors are taking on new meaning, but I am seeing the love that developed between this couple also having an impact on our relationship.

"It's difficult for me to accept what is happening between us as solely a chain reaction of owning our first home." His words stopped suddenly.

"So you do feel it, too?" Lydia smiled, moving from her chair to sit in his lap.

"Yes. I feel that, like that missionary who wrote to Glenn from China, I'm not a terribly demonstrative individual. But lately, whether it's the letters, or this house, or becoming *actively* involved in the church . . . I have no idea why, but for whatever reason, I feel the need to tell you, and others around me, how much I appreciate them.

"And Lydia, darling, I don't think that even I knew how much I loved you until recently." Ward laughed. "I had so much fun with you that evening in the floor when we addressed all those cards to the missionaries and troops that I felt like a newly-wed all over again. I can't remember the last time before that when we simply sat, and laughed and talked about the things that really mattered to us."

Lydia laid her head against Ward's chest. Neither of them said a word for a good while as they basked in the love that had gone from a dying ember to a radiant flame.

She could hear the beat of his heart, much like the beat of the African drum. As his chest moved up and down with each beat, Lydia felt a security that she was sure came when two individuals fully knew each other. She suddenly grasped the beauty of the love they shared, and how beautiful it had always been.

"Ward, I love you. No one could have given me a better life than you have."

He smiled warmly and held her head against his chest for a long time.

25

It had been a long day, far unlike the usual days of Lydia. She had met Ward at the Boone Drug Store for lunch, which had become like the letters - a daily habit. He had even started going there on the way to his classes for a dose of morning coffee and the old-timer's Coffee Club, another activity which Lydia had rejoiced over with him.

For some unknown reason, she felt the urge to stop at the library and sit in the corner and read. The read turned into a therapy session with Olivia, she later realized. She'd reached the point that she was spending so much time in Gene's chair or "the museum" that she was having no contact with the outside world.

It was time for Ward to be coming home when she glanced up at the wall clock in the library and saw what time it was. As she was rushing downstairs to exit the building, she ran into Ward.

"My goodness, young lady," he grinned when he caught her rushing to get home and start dinner. "You're so pretty that if

I didn't already have a dinner date, I'd ask you out tonight."

"You have a dinner date?" Lydia asked, playing along.

"Yes, with my wife. We're going to the Japanese restaurant and then enjoying a quiet evening of sitting alone on our love seat with no television."

"Oh, Ward!" she softly exclaimed. "I love you."

"Don't say that too loud! My wife might hear you. She comes in here from time to time when she's not traveling abroad."

Lydia burst into laughter as she grabbed Ward and hugged him.

"Careful now," he warned. "Some of my students might see you and wonder what's going on. You might start rumors around the campus."

"Good," she laughed, hugging harder.

What she had feared to be a wasted day turned into a perfectly peaceful day and evening. It wasn't until after she started upstairs for bed that she realized that she had not even opened the drawer of the desk during the past twenty-four hours.

"I'll be right there," she called behind Ward.

"I knew I couldn't keep you all to myself for long," he teased. "I'll be waiting for you."

Lydia sat just long enough to read one letter.

Wembo Nyama, Congo Belge
June 21, 1929

My dear 'Gene,

This has been a hard week but it has been less hard than it would have been because of the arrival of you letter of April 15ᵗʰ. The mail was late and did not arrive until late Sunday night and I did not get mine until early Monday morning.

We have no doctor stationed here now although the need is desperate. Dr. Lewis, our doctor from Tunda, is here having been called over on account of the illness of one of our workers. He had planned to return to Tunda last Monday A.M.

On Sunday A.M. a white man, a trader, came in with an acute attack of appendicitis. We were not prepared for operating for after much consultation the doctor and Miss Farrier, our nurse, who by the way had been in bed sick for more than a week, decided to get together as many things as possible, sterilize them and operate Monday A.M. All this was done immediately and everyone helped who could.

Late Sunday afternoon the patient was so much worse that Dr. Lewis decided to operate as soon as possible. It was then about suppertime and as soon as supper was over they began to get ready. As none of the boys were used to operating with Dr. Lewis and none had had recent experience in operating room work, it was necessary for Miss Farrier to get out of bed, go to the hospital and assist the doctor.

We have two Coleman gasoline lamps here, one being mine, and had it not been for them I hardly see how we could have furnished enough light with ordinary lanterns and lamps.

The patient was put on the table at 8:45 and began to take ether. (Can you imagine me in an operating room? I had a bad cold but I held lamps and did anything else I could). The man did not go to sleep quickly. After the incision was made it was found that he was in a serious condition. There was so much inflammation that the appendix could not be located and removed. Dr. Lewis did all that he could for him. By the time that the incision was closed (with the exception of a drain) it was after twelve o'clock. Can you realize the patient had been taking ether for more than three hours? We took him back to the room, put him to bed and then started for home.

It was almost one o'clock when I got in bed. I had been up since six o'clock Sunday A.M. and did not get my usual noonday rest and nap as I was helping with the sterilizer. Had it not been for my cold I should have been feeling O.K. But I was tired out. Even when morning came I felt like a "wash rag."

But when I awoke I found your letter and one from my sister to cheer me. I intended to write you as soon as I could but have not been able to get to it before now. I have tried to keep going somehow. But one day and one afternoon I just hung around the house as I felt too bad to do anything, even read.

I wonder what you are doing this beautiful moonlit night. It isn't night there quite yet but it will be as soon as the old globe whirls around a bit more, and I'm sure there'll be plenty of moonlight left for you to have a bit. I think we have the most wonderful moonlit nights out here I have ever experienced. Oh, how I wish you could be here to go walking with me tonight!

'Gene, why don't you write more when I am just hungry for whatever you have to say? Is it because you want to tell me something and at the same time do not want me to know it and that you must "ring off" for fear you will tell me? I always feel that way when I have finished your letters and even more so after reading this last one. Perhaps you are wise in so doing and only time can tell but there is much hidden there which I can read although it be not expressed in words. You do not mind if I see it and feel it, do you? Because after all you know you put it there, don't you? No, it isn't imagination and I don't let myself go off into reveries because life is too real to do that.

No, I don't think you'll regret anything which you may have written me or which you may write to me. I shall take it all at its face value and for what it is really worth. It would not be fair to either of us to do otherwise. One never regrets true and real friendship and sometimes I have known them to ripen into something deeper. We shall be only friends, but nevertheless true friends, and see what the future holds in store.

The months are growing fewer which intervene between the present and the time when I shall be leaving on furlough. There are only eight more now. "Throw in" two more for the voyage and then - - well, then you and I can take a stroll in the moonlight on just such a night as this.

Good-night and may God bless and keep you.

Most sincerely,
Glenn

Ward had already fallen asleep when Lydia reached the bedroom.

"Poor thing," she commiserated as she lay down beside him. "He's working so hard trying to make a good impression on his colleagues and be a good mentor to his students." Lydia smiled. *He looks so handsome.* She reached over and brushed a piece of hair away from his forehead. *Just like that day in biology class.* The adoring wife gave her husband a gentle kiss on the cheek and whispered, "Good-night and may God bless and keep you."

26

My dear 'Gene,

This week has been another nightmare for me but I am glad that it is about over. The man I told you about in my last letter, who was operated on, died on Monday morning of this week. It was a horrible death and a very sad one too. He died here at the hospital among strangers and the only white person who had known him had been away for the day Sunday, and reached him too late to be recognized. The saddest part was that he has led anything but a clean life and died not being a Christian. It must be terrible to have to go to meet one's Creator and Master as he went. May God have mercy on his soul.

Monday was the closing day of school and would have

been full enough had there been nothing else. The boys in the boarding department were very anxious to go home. By working until I could hardly stand on my feet I finished up everything about ten o'clock that night. It did not take me long to go to sleep after I got in bed and I rested well knowing that there would not be so much to do on Tuesday.

The remainder of the week I have decided between the evangelists, who are here for their quarterly conference, and the work on my books in the office. I would not have been fatigued at all by any of it had it not been for a cold which has been hanging on for two weeks now.

Next week I am hoping to almost finish my work on the books and get off my financial reports for the Second Quarter to Nashville. It surely will be a great relief and joy to me when this is done. It will mean that much finished.

One is grateful for Friday night once in a while when there aren't a million and one things to be done. There is always a plenty to be done all the time but I occasionally let a few things slide as I have tonight.

I have wanted to write to you all the week but I have been unable to do so. Your letter of April 25th was indeed a great surprise and a great joy. I had not expected another one quite so soon, judging from the past, but I was so happy to have it. I just hope you keep on writing like this.

Your words "I believe if I were out there I would be mighty glad to get a letter from America regardless of whether it contained any startling news or not" bear more truth than poetry. Oh! they are too true but so few people have stopped to even think of it. I sometimes wonder why the majority of people at home either don't write at all, or wait for an answer. We, out here want to write but so often have little time to do so. How just even a card bearing a greeting or a word of cheer helps to lighten the tasks of a day!

But 'Gene, I must tell you, your letters are beginning to mean more than that to me. I am beginning to look forward to them for the real worth they are to me. I am finding in them the unconscious revelation of a true and understanding friend. They are an inspiration to me because they are a bit of your own dear self.

I must say good-night but it is with a wish and prayer that God may keep and richly bless you.

Your sincere friend,
Glenn

I guess I know what this means, Lydia decided as she moved to the freezer. *Ward's favorite dinner of pork loin with cranberries. I'll throw together a sweet potato soufflé and green beans and then after dinner, we can spend the evening on the floor with cards again.*

She yearned for another evening of nothing except time with each other. It had seemed most bizarre that on the evening a few weeks before when they sat in the middle of the floor with a pile of cards and a list of names and addresses, it proved to be the most "quality time" they had shared in a long while.

And to think that happened as a result of us sharing a small bit of ourselves with those who are serving others in various ways around the world.

"I brought you a present," Ward called as he came through the front door.

Lydia wheeled out of the kitchen at the sound of his voice. She peeked inside the brown paper bag to see a container of fudge ripple ice cream, her longstanding favorite flavor.

"I thought we might like to have some dessert later while we were using these." He reached inside his shirt pocket and handed her a small envelope.

"Stamps?" Lydia cried in surprise after opening the envelope. "How did you know?"

"After your phone call today, there was no room for doubt. I immediately went to the post office and picked up some stamps for all the cards that we're going to address this evening. The ice cream was an afterthought. I knew you'd have something special for dinner, and from the aroma coming from the kitchen, I'd say I was right."

"So you think the food is simply a bribe to get you to help

me?" Lydia asked playfully.

"Not a bribe. Merely a show of appreciation." He placed his briefcase on the coffee table in the living room. "Look at the stamps. I even got the small sheets with a design that I knew you'd like rather than a roll."

"If I didn't know better, Ward Mason, I'd think you like this project as much as I do."

A boyish grin broke out on his face. "It wasn't the cards. It was the thought of being alone with you in our own house for a quiet and relaxing evening. There was a very therapeutic feel to selecting just the right card for each person on the list and writing those few words in each one. I never knew signing my name could be so much fun."

"Uh-huh, I knew it!" Lydia boasted.

"I guess my attitude doesn't leave much room for doubt either, does it?"

Lydia shook her head while putting the ice cream in the freezer.

"You know what I realized this afternoon after your call?" He continued when he saw the puzzled look on Lydia's face. "I think that I was secretly looking forward to another evening with those cards. That was the best evening we've spent alone in longer than I can remember. And the thing that's most ironic is that we weren't really alone. We were sharing all those notes with other people."

"Ward, you are that same dear sweet person that I fell in love with back in the tenth grade." Lydia offered her husband an appreciative smile. "Thank you for not changing with age."

He hugged her in a long embrace until the timer on the oven went announcing that the roast was ready.

"Here, let me get it for you," Ward said. "You go and get the cards so that we'll be ready to get to them as soon as we eat. I'll even take care of the dishes after dinner."

"What did I ever do to deserve you?" Lydia asked as she went down the hall.

"Love frogs?" was his joking response.

As he placed the baking dish on the trivet on the table, Ward made a confession. "Lydia, do you remember saying that moving here had proven to be a great education for you? It was one of those afternoons when you'd been at the library?"

"Yes, I certainly do remember. Those letters are always sending me to the reference department to hunt for something."

"I know how you feel," he added, placing the other dishes on the table. "All this education I have and the fact that I've been in the education field for years should account for something. But lately, I feel that I'm learning a lot of things that I never knew before."

"Such as?" she asked, placing the napkins and silverware on the table.

"The same things you've been learning through those letters, I highly suspect. But even more than that, what a gift I'm receiving doing for others. Small things like those letters. That was a terrific feeling when I dropped all those off at the post office the next morning. When you called today with the message about Claudia, I think I was as excited as you were.

"And the thing I find most phenomenal is the way all of

those feelings and those small things are pouring over into my work with my students. I've always had a good rapport with my colleagues and students, or so I thought, but that seems increasingly so here."

Lydia recognized every word with her own being. "I think you're exactly right," she admitted.

"What's your explanation?" Ward quizzed Lydia.

"You're the educator here. Why don't you tell me?"

He took a deep breath, trying to collect his thoughts and make an intelligent assessment. "I think you're right about the Spirit, the Presence in this house. But I don't think it's that we've let it into our house. I think we've let it into ourselves. Our physical houses."

"What a beautiful thought. I agree completely," Lydia stated as Ward pulled her chair out for her to sit down at the dining table.

The cards turned out to be the perfect compliment to the dinner and the ice cream. Claudia's was the first note that they wrote and they even included a picture of themselves that had been taken for the recent pictorial directory at the church.

"Here's a name for someone in Kentucky," noted Ward. "I thought missionaries went to foreign countries."

"We need missionaries all over the world, Ward. You

wouldn't recognize most of them to look at them. They don't come with a stereotype appearance and they don't walk around with some oversized cross hanging around their necks."

Ward looked up, taking in Lydia's words.

"In fact, they don't look any different from us. Let me tell you what I've found to be the most shocking realization through my UMW meetings. There are many missionaries from other countries here in the United States. We need a lot of work here, just like in other countries."

"Other countries send missionaries here?"

"That's right. I found that hard to believe, too. Even though I didn't know a lot about church, I did know, or so I thought, that missionaries were all people who had never done anything wrong and went to live in some foreign land."

"You mean that's not right?" Ward asked, letting her know that he'd been raised with that same ideal of a missionary.

"Where do we get those misconceptions?" Lydia wondered aloud. "No one lives a perfect life and we need help in many areas of this country, too."

"What do you suppose this missionary does in Kentucky?" Ward questioned.

Lydia shook her head while stuffing another card into an envelope. "I'm not sure."

"Why don't you ask Alice or check into that at your next circle meeting?"

"I will. Wouldn't it be great if we could actually go and do something to help at a mission somewhere? Kentucky is not so far away."

"Can people do things like that?"

"I'm sure they can. You wouldn't believe all the ways in which people can help with mission work from their own living rooms. Just like us and these cards. Ways that take little or no effort at all."

"If all of them make you feel as good as sending these cards, find out about some more of them." Ward looked again at the name and address in the prayer calendar. "It says here that she works at a place called Red Bird Mission. That's certainly an intriguing name for a place. I like it already."

When the last card had been addressed and stamped, Ward took Lydia's hand and led her upstairs. "I think I'll check out this Red Bird Mission on the internet tomorrow. Who knows? There might be something we could do for them."

"Oh, Ward. I'd forgotten how very much I loved you."

"Loved me?"

"You know what I meant."

"You're right. I do. But I like to hear you say it."

Lydia decided that it was also time to send another note in Ward's briefcase. *I'll take care of that tomorrow morning while he's in the shower.*

Ward looked at his wife and saw all the things that he'd loved about her from the beginning. *I haven't sent her flowers in ages. I think I shall send her a dozen red roses tomorrow. I'm sure she'll be at home with Glenn and 'Gene.*

"Lydia?"

"Yes?"

"Thank you for not changing with age either."

"Do you think that it's because we didn't have children that we are so much like we were all those years ago?"

"I'm not sure," Ward answered. "But what I am sure of is that God was in charge of that in our lives, too."

"I guess you're right," Lydia conceded, "but isn't it strange that He was so in control of us when we didn't even recognize Him as being there?"

214 Mangum
Chapel Hill N.C.
July 10, 1929.

My dear Glenn,

A short note to you this morning promised you I would write tonight. I had been planning to write you — even before I received your two letters the other day — telling you that I'm at Summer School here in Chapel Hill. Wonder if you're surprised? Well, I am, for I really had never planned to come here, but I'm so glad I came now for I've learned oh! so much and the place is just ideal. Doesn't this Carolina emblem "sorta thrill you?

You see I've been out of college five years and my certificate expires this year so I thought I'd better try and renew it since I want to keep in good standing. I'm renewing my certificate and taking graduate courses also. I'm enjoying my work immensely. I'm taking two sociology courses under Meyer and Groves — they're splendid — and a course in high school music methods under Mrs. Woodman. She has been music supervisor in the Jacksonville, Florida, schools for the past ten years. It's a wonderful course in conducting, directing and organizations of glee club, chorus, band, and orchestra in high schools. I've wanted this type of thing for a long time and I'm thoroughly enjoying it. I'm visiting a class in music appreciation given by Mr. Weaver. He's a trump, isn't he? I remember he was a

27

The impressive Carolina emblem immediately directed Lydia's eyes to the prestigious stationery. There was a flair about the design done in the famous shade of blue, "Carolina blue," that dominated the page. She remembered that Phillip had earlier mentioned his grandfather had graduated from the University of North Carolina, so she was shocked to see that this letter was from 'Gene, who had graduated from Duke.

I wonder if the two schools were such strong rivals back then, she reflected, thinking of the competition between the basketball teams of the two well-respected schools.

As she began to read the words, written over seventy-five years prior, she understood why it had been so long since Glenn had heard anything from his fair lady.

214 Mangum
Chapel Hill, N.C,
July 10, 1929

My dear Glenn,

A short note to you this morning promised you I would write tonight. I had been planning to write you – even before I received your two letters the other day – telling you that I'm at Summer School here in Chapel Hill. Wonder if you're surprised? Well, I am, for I really had never planned to come here, but I'm so glad I came now for I've learned oh! so much and the place is just ideal. Doesn't this Carolina emblem "sorta" thrill you?

You see I've been out of college five years and my certificate expires this year so I thought I'd better try and renew it since I want to keep in good standing. I'm renewing my certificate and taking graduate courses also. I'm enjoying my work immensely. I'm taking two Sociology courses – they're splendid – and a course in high school music methods. The professor has been music supervisor for the past ten years. It's a wonderful course in conducting, directing and organizations of glee clubs, band, and orchestras in high schools. I've wanted this type of thing for a long time and I'm thoroughly enjoying it. I'm visiting a class in Music Appreciation by Mr. Weaver. He's a trump, isn't he? I remember he was a friend of yours. My father's sister is my roommate in Snow Hill and is here with me and we're just having a glorious time. I've met lots of mighty cute boys and girls here and have made lovely friends. They're just wonderful to us. What would we do without our friends?

We swim often, ride much, but seldom go to the movies. We've had lovely trips to Pittsboro, Hillsboro, Durham and Raleigh several times. Chapel Hill has an airport now and many of the students are "going up" for a ride. I've threatened to several times but don't quite have the nerve - I guess I just _love_ _to_ _live_ too well!

We're boarding at Swain and our room is in Mangum - as you see - right near Emerson Field. It's very convenient though since we have the car with us. I'll declare I know I am the most fortunate girl in all the world! I wonder if I will ever own a car? I doubt it, since I've lived this long without it, but have always had access to one. Maye (my roommate) is precious - about my age. I wish you knew her too! She'd just give anything to know you _better_ since she's heard a tiny bit about you!

We go to our church here, of course, but have been over to Durham to Duke Memorial and Trinity on several occasions. Mr. Rozzelle (from Charlotte) is pastor here. Mr. James G. Phillips, whom you probably knew, is still Student Pastor. This week he's just back from his honeymoon. Married a girl he knew here in Summer School last summer - just because she went to the League meetings, you see what she got! He jokingly advised me to go to the League too - I guess I'd better try her plan. They're a mighty cute couple.

July 4th, our biggest National holiday now, has just come and gone with very little excitement around here. We did have a lengthy address by Josiah Bailey of Raleigh and a "big fireworks party" following that. In the afternoon we went over to Durham and went swimming in the new pool of the Duke gym. My sister, Prissy, is in school over there now. By the way, the plans for new Duke University are materializing and rapidly becoming realized and by the time you get home there will really be enough work complete for you to have a general idea of what it's like. Far be it from me to try and describe. I believe I sent a sketch (clipping) to you some time ago, didn't I?

We have had a splendid program of attractions here this season. Salvi, the famous harpist, presented a most impressive program, The Hampton Quartette, the South Sea Islanders, and Wallace, the Magician are all good. There are to be several others still. The Playmakers are presenting "The Dover Road" Friday and Saturday nights of this week and later a gang of players will present one of the Greek tragedies in the forest theatre.

So you were a member of the famous "Playmaker" group too! How did I know? Well, I've just been reading about you since finding your picture in the 1922 annual the other day. Your picture was splendid and the write-up was mighty nice. I guess the "bird" who gave you such a "flattering" write-up was quite surprised to know that your plans took you across the sea instead of allowing you to follow the lumber business here, don't you? You must have made a wonderful record here along musical lines! The more I know about you the more I appreciate your real value and the worth of your *friendship.*

Your letters are always such masterpieces. I dare not try and answer them. However, I will write soon and answer to your most interesting and acceptable letters I received recently.

This letter is as general and extremely unbalanced and I must apologize, for I've had constant interruptions tonight.

With all good wishes always, I am

Sincerely,
'Gene

Drama, huh? I knew these letters were full of drama.

So now we've learned that not only were our two stars great musical talents, who both loved religious education and had hearts for missions, but they've both written and directed their own plays.

Lydia wondered how many of the other female students, also doing graduate coursework and renewing teaching certificates, had seen the photo of Glenn with the list of his honors and heard all about his African journey and "the real value and worth" of his friendship.

I also wonder if they've heard that there may be something more than "friendship" lurking in the air, waiting for that special time for Glenn to tell his fair lady in person all those thoughts that have been refusing to surface during the past three years.

214 Mangum Building
Chapel Hill, North Carolina
July 18, 1929

My dear Glenn,

Your letters are perfect both in thought and phrasing and the more I read them the more I wonder just what I could have said to bring such a response. What can it be that I have expressed, it remains a mystery? That's the trouble with my letters, they're just entirely too much like me, <u>purely</u> <u>conversational</u>, and even though I am writing, I feel as if I am sitting talking to the one addressed. But really if I were talking to you I might not speak as I'm writing!

I am glad that you have known me better through my letters, but really I hate for anyone to judge me entirely from my writings. I wish I might tell you something interesting about myself, for I feel that we are still quite unknown to each other - in a way. No, I don't mean that we're strangers.

Yes, I am planning to return to Snow Hill this fall and teach in the High School there again. I enjoy teaching

Latin but I just <u>love</u> English, especially English literature. There are so many different phases of that wonderful subject. That was my major in college with Education and Religious Education minors.

You are just the most energetic person I know. I am sure the Lord gives you the strength to do the things that you are willing to do, but do be careful and take good care of yourself. Of course, good health is essential to effective work and I'm glad to know that so far you continue to keep well and happy in your work. It just seems that conditions there are most unfavorable to many of our workers, and I am certainly distressed to know that your assistant has had to be relieved of her duties there. I feel sure that her place may soon be filled and the work carried on. You are doing such a wonderful work out there, especially with the young people and Oh! how they need you <u>the</u> <u>whole</u> <u>world</u> <u>over</u>.

I 'most forgot to tell you how much joy your letters brought to me. They just made me feel so incapable and unworthy. I do want to <u>be</u> and <u>do</u> better all the time – and I just believe if I should hear from you often enough I might eventually be a "good girl." I know you are thrilled to think of coming back home. I still think you are the bravest and most courageous young man I ever knew to be willing to go <u>so far</u> <u>away</u> from home and stay <u>so</u> <u>long</u> a <u>time</u>. And don't you forget that we are all looking forward to your coming home, too.

I can't picture anything more vividly than you and the dear little lap organ. My! but it must be such a powerful consolation since you have such a musical soul and music means so much in your life. Did you not take your Victrola with you too? <u>Well</u> do I remember the night at Beulah's. 'Tis true I spent many hours at her house after church hours with the crowd, but surely I remember the night you came. I remember many of the songs you sang, too. And don't you remember one stormy Sunday night we had to keep ridin'? And another time, Glenn, I shall never forget that impressive little play you gave at Smith's Chapel at one of the Union meetings. Oh! well, there are lots o'things I remember.

Your little "namesakes" at Saint Paul are growing and doing fine work. They meet monthly at the church. Mrs. Harley Thompson (Virginia Kendall as you probably knew her) is their leader and she is just fine. They just love her and I'm sure she is thoroughly consecrated to the task. I forgot to tell you about the new Sunday School building at Saint Paul. It's perfectly marvelous and meets every modern demand. It seems that Sunday School teachers are extra hard to get at present, but I guess most of them have gone away for the summer. Mr. Underbill, a 1927 graduate of Elon College, has recently been employed as Director of Religious Education.

I still must mention "Bobbie" Brown since both of us admire him so greatly. He's just the finest young preacher in the Conference, I'm sure. Uncle William thinks he's a gem! Bobbie has gone to take his mother and sister who had <u>never seen an ocean</u>. They have recently come over from Texas for a prolonged visit. Young Mrs. Brown – I mean his wife – has been quite ill but is now greatly improved since she got her new teeth et cetera! His children are adorable and have grown the most to be sure.

I never see or hear anything of Mr. Daniel except he is still wooing most ardently. Who? Well, just anybody. Poor thing, I wish he could get married again. I hope you have heard from the new pastor at Saint Paul. Mr. McRae is splendid and I am sure all the Goldsboro folk like him very much. They're wonderful people – just the finest I ever knew. I still miss them more than I can ever tell. Please forgive me for gossiping a bit for really I didn't mean to.

This has been a rather full week since I am trying to keep up with my work, getting ready for my examinations, and trying to attend all meetings and things going on. I just must bring this letter to a close, for really I didn't mean to take so much of your time. I'll promise not to write so much next time.

With all good wishes and the constant prayer that you may be directed and kept safely each day, I am

Most sincerely,
'Gene

"I hope you don't have anything special planned for this evening," Ward said when Lydia answered the phone. "There's a

Greek tragedy being given by some of the drama students and I thought you might enjoy getting out of the house. It's been a while since we've taken in a play."

"I'd love nothing better," was Lydia's response."That would be a great way to start our weekend. And I have a letter from 'Gene that I think you'll especially enjoy reading afterwards."

"Sounds good. And I have something I found on the Web today that I think you'll be interested in reading about Red Bird Mission in Kentucky."

"Oh, I can't wait."

"I think you'll be as intrigued as I was, but I'm not going to tell you. I'm going to be like Glenn and wait until I see you in person. Oh, and don't fix dinner. We're going to have a night on the town."

"Are you sure we can stay awake that long?" Lydia laughed.

"Only because tomorrow is Saturday and I don't have classes. Why don't you be ready at five? That should be early enough that we can get a table somewhere before the show. We'll grab some dessert afterwards," Ward instructed.

"That's an easy enough request to fill."

Lydia hung up the phone feeling almost as eager for five o'clock to arrive as she had on that Saturday of the prom on their first date.

28

Wembo Nyama
July 24, 1929

My dear 'Gene,

Your letter of April 22ⁿᵈ (marked May 19ᵗʰ on the envelope) came in the mail last week and I was so happy to hear from you. The mail reached Wembo Nyama just before breakfast Thursday A.M. and I read your letter at breakfast. I am sure the others would have noticed how excited I got had they not been busy reading also.

This has been such a lovely day I hope it will aid me in expressing those thoughts which I desire to try to convey to you. There are so many lovely things of nature out here that it seems one should be able to express anything he may feel, but 'tis not always so.

I am so glad that you wrote to me as you did. I have

re-read your letter each day since its arrival and each time it's filled me with joy. 'Gene, I am so happy to find you such a friend. Perhaps in my letter which you referred to I may have been a bit vague but I am so glad to know that you reacted in the way you have. I appreciate so deeply the many things which you expressed to me. It is true that I have known you only such a short while but so many times as I read I thought – "How like 'Gene it is to have put it in that way."

'Gene, please don't think I am lonely here because I am just as happy as can be. I never think of being lonely. That may sound a bit strange but it is true. I don't mean to say that my soul has reached perfection nor that I never desire to see anyone else. What I mean is this. If I desire to talk with any of my friends I go to the door of my heart, call that one, and sit and chat awhile. This is nothing new that I have learned to do since coming to Africa but my life in the past has been conducive to such a growth.

Yes, I think I realize fully just what I wrote to you and if I had it to do over again I think I should perhaps do it again. Had you reacted in a different way your attitude would have been incompatible with my conception of your personality.

- - - - -

Sunday night

Just at this point I was interrupted by a message from Miss Armstrong asking me to assist her in redressing a man who was brought in late yesterday afternoon with a second-degree burn. This doctor who is stationed here is away at one of the other stations and last night Mr. Anker and I had helped her dress the burns.

Lydia stopped reading. *This tells about the man from Glenn's report in the first batch of letters.* She began flipping the pages and turned back to the date at the beginning of the letter. *July 24, 1929.* She read the year over and over, unsure why this letter was out of order, until finally she noticed a line that had been marked through the last "9", making it into a "7."

Oh, that I could turn back the hands of time for two years. What I wouldn't give to have two more precious years with Ward.

She skimmed over the remainder of the words, pausing to again read when she saw the sentence that began with, "Since you referred to it I am sure you will not mind if . . .

. . . I interject a comment here. Miss Armstrong is a very, very fine young lady indeed and a splendid nurse, as well. Her influence on the young life of our village has been truly great. I am glad to have the opportunity of knowing her and working on the same station with her. But 'Gene there is no possibility at all of my falling in love with her. I just couldn't that's all. She is a splendid young woman as I have said but I never could fall in love with her with that most consuming love which I must be filled with for the woman I shall marry.

I deeply appreciate your confidence in me and I hope and trust that I shall always be able to live up to that which you expect of me.

I know I am a very peculiar kind of a person who likes at times to be different from others, and no one knows my limitations so well as I do. I realize that I possess in only a small degree those qualities which are attractive to the fairer sex and for which they seem to always search for. But yet I am sure that I am capable of loving my companion and mate with as great a love as any man ever possessed.

No, I am not going to reveal to you the innermost depths of my heart at this time. Perhaps, if it be the will of the Father, you may come to know me better than you do at present. Perhaps, if the day should ever present itself, we may be able to talk even more intimately about the problems of life. Even if fate should decree that our paths should diverge rather than converge, I sincerely hope that nothing will cause you to regret that our paths met at one time. I am sure that I shall always be glad that I have known you and my hope is that we shall know each other better.

I have seen many summers, and will you permit me to say it?, I have seen only a few girls with whom I should have cared to face life. God has seen fit to direct my path away from each one of them and I am trusting His leadership now. Thousands of young ladies it has been my privilege to know and so many have helped to make my life more abundant. The one who is willing to face life with me has not yet been wholly revealed to me. But I do know that if there be such a one that in time God shall make her a blessing to me. And oh! such a wonderful blessing that will be.

Perhaps I have been too frank but if I have I ask your forgiveness because when time and space are so great it seems I must increasingly be so. I know that I need not ask you to keep in confidence what I have said or may say to you. You must trust your heart for that.

It will take at least two months for my letter to reach you and for an answer to get back to me. Since you have expressed your friendship so clearly I shall in the future write to you wherever "the spirit moves me" in that direction. If you have not yet discovered it I am sure that you will come to know that I, too, am a bit "old fashioned."

I always welcome your letters and when they come the only regret I have is that you did not write more, and more often. Don't force yourself to write, but won't you just let yourself write a little more frequently? I fear that I should get lonesome were it not for the letters I receive.

May you continue to be a blessing to the people of St. Paul is my prayer.

Your sincere friend,
Glenn.

Lydia felt compelled to sit down and write a letter of her own to Glenn.

"Dear Glenn," she said aloud as if dictating the words to him, "I don't believe that you've left anything to be revealed to 'Gene after this letter. If she cannot see through your words and come to her own wise conclusion of what few things you've left unsaid, then I don't understand how she earned a degree from Duke and she certainly wouldn't be intellectually compatible - as you had feared Sonny wouldn't be for her - with you, which therefore means that you wouldn't want her anyway."

She could hardly wait to see how the rest of the letters played themselves out, but she knew there was no more time for reading for this day. Besides, now that Glenn had 'Gene's attention with these words, there was cause for a celebration.

The real party will come when one of them dares to admit their heart's love for the other. I wonder how much longer that will be.

29

My dear 'Gene,

How is the summer heat serving you these days? Pretty bad? I wish that I could seal up some of the cool breezes which blow here so constantly during the day and send them to you. Really, in spite of the fact that I am in the tropics (and I must confess there was a time in my life when I thought that would be a terrible place to be) I have never suffered from the heat as I have during the summer months in the United States.

'Gene, why have you been silent so long? Many moons and many mails have passed since your last dear letter and I have looked forward so eagerly to the arrival of each mail with the hope that it would bring me a message from you.

The intervening months are passing rapidly but in a way I wish they could pass more rapidly yet. And then other times I wish that they did not go so speedily. We human beings are hard to please anyway, aren't we? It is so hard sometimes to just determine what we do want and hardest of all to make a choice after we have made a decision.

School has been going on now almost three weeks and it seems to me that the boys only came back last week. I suppose one reason that it seemed such a short time is that I had to go to Minga last week on the big motorcycle to finish some work that I started there during school vacation. It was my longest non-stop motorcycle trip since I have been in Congo, eighty-six miles each way. I was glad that it went without mishap or bad results because it demonstrated that my back has fully recovered from the sprain it underwent last November.

While there, I stayed with Elmo Tabb, Mary Tyler Mayer's husband. Mary was not at home as she is at Tunda, another of our stations where she is waiting the arrival of the stork. There is no doctor at Minga or Wembo Nyama now and that is why she had to go to our other station.

We are expecting our new doctor at Wembo Nyama next week. He has made the trip more quickly than any of us anticipated but he will not reach here a day too soon. We surely have needed one and the burden has been entirely too great on Miss Farrier, our nurse. She has done the best she could but it is too much for any nurse to be left alone with a big hospital.

Now don't wait so long to write because you know that I am wanting to hear from you.

Most sincerely,
Glenn

Lydia opened the windows to allow the cool, spring-fresh breeze of the North Carolina mountain air into the house. *Luckily, winter wasn't too unbearable and the snowfall was light for the area.* She stepped out into the side yard, where she noticed the fresh mint trying to see its first daylight next to the water spigot beside the basement doors.

Ah, before long I can cut a sprig for my iced tea. One of the simple pleasures of life, she sighed.

She debated on whether to plant a few vegetables so that they could enjoy them during Ward's shorter summer school hours. Lydia couldn't help but wonder if the time spent reaping what they'd sown would be as thrilling as the time spent with the letters - both the ones they'd read and the ones they'd sent.

Ward's comments about the beautifully remote area of Red Bird Mission ran through her mind as she decided to approach him about trying to go and work there for a week during his upcoming spring break.

In addition to Claudia in Cambodia, they had received a

cordial reply from Ruth Wiertzema, the Programming Director of the Red Bird Missionary Conference to whom they had sent a card, who had spent over thirty years of her life in the back hills of Kentucky serving others.

It's only three weeks before the final exams start and then there will only be a few days in between the summer sessions.

It was hard for Lydia to believe that they had owned their own home for nearly a year. She had gotten so involved with the UMW and a couple of volunteer projects that she was unable to spend time with the letters from the desk as she had during those first days.

This had been a refreshing afternoon of trying to tie up loose ends, one of which was getting through the second stack of letters. As she sat back down at the desk, she found herself also praying that Glenn would soon hear from his dearest. There was only one letter left in this stack with the blue ribbon and then she would be ready to begin a third stack, this one tied with a bright green ribbon.

I wonder if there's any significance to the different colors of the ribbons.

Wembo Nyama
September 6, 1929

My dearest 'Gene,

I wonder if I dare call you that and yet it seems perfectly natural that I should do so. I think that invariably "Thoughts have wings" as I know that many have been those which I have dispatched on silvery pinions and have received arriving on wings spangled with stardust. Great is distance but great as it is it can be annihilated by one simple thought which hath wings.

Your deeply appreciated letter and card arrived recently and I was so glad to hear from you. Your letter came in the last mail and I am so grateful for it. And to think that you spent the summer at Carolina! Dear old Carolina; she was the scene of many struggles and many joys in my life. It was while I was within her walls that I heard and answered the call to give my life to missionary service.

Many have been the times that I have wandered beneath the pergola near Davie Hall shown in the picture on the card from you. I have walked there late in the afternoon of a day in spring when the air was heavy with the enchanting aroma of the wisteria. I have plucked the petals from the wild roses which entwined themselves in impenetrable confusion but forming dense towers of beauty. I have at times been the first to break the spell of snows in the arboretum on a winter's morning, seeking to find the most beautiful and fantastic decorations of the snow elves who strove so hard to finish their work before morning so that the sun might stud them with diamonds. On late Sunday afternoons I have been there, many times alone, and sensed the presence of God there in His beautiful garden and sanctuary. In many ways it is a sanctuary to me and I want to go back there to enjoy it all again sometime.

When I reach home it will probably be near commencement time at Carolina. Wouldn't you like to drop everything and run away up there with me for a few days? I am sure that since you have been there, too, it would be much more enjoyable for me if you were there with me.

I intended to write to you just as soon as your card came but I was so busy rushing around getting ready to go over to Tunda to attend the Mission Meeting that I did not do so. While over there they kept me so busy with committee meetings when I was not in sessions that I had no time for anything. And then to make it worse, I had to act as secretary of the meeting.

It is over sixty miles from Wembo Nyama to Tunda, perhaps about sixty-five, and we had to make the trip on bicycles because the swamps make it impractical to use a motorcycle. I enjoyed the path trip very much.

The afternoon that we left here we were caught in a storm. It was a terrible one but we were fortunate enough to reach shelter before it broke. It was much fiercer at the mission than it was where we were. The first word we received stated that the wind blew down a big tree, demolishing the dining room of the Boys' Boarding School. Fortunately, all

the boys had gone home that day as it almost wrecked some
of the dwellings. It was one of the fiercest wind storms we
have had since I've been out here and there was plenty of
lightning and rain mixed in with it.

Now, when I should be getting down to real work
again, I've got to "bounce up" again and "chase off" to Minga
with a committee to search for a new site for that station.
(Please pardon the slang expressions.) The present site is not
suitably located and we have instructions from the Bishop
to look for a new place. I had very much rather stay here
with my work than to go.

And to think that you were interested in ancient history while you were at Carolina! It has been such a long time
since I have had a look in my '22 annual that I had just about
forgotten about what it contained. I am glad that you like
the picture even though it is so much better looking than I
have ever been. I would have a hard time convincing some
of my friends who have known me only in the last few years
that it is really the way I was once supposed to look.

Really, 'Gene, you must keep on writing me letters like
this last one. I have been so happy since it came that I've
scarcely known what to do with myself. I have read it and
re-read it and each time it seems to bring greater happiness
than it did with the previous reading.

Now don't forget that I shall be wishing and waiting
for the next one.

Your sincere friend,
Glenn

"Well, well, how did I know that I'd find you here?" Ward inquired, turning the doorknob and arriving two hours early.

"What happened?" Lydia responded, glancing at the clock. "Did all of your students cut class today?"

"Hardly. They had a test which always means they get out earlier. It was the last one before final exams." He sat his brief-case down on the sofa and dashed for the refrigerator. "That sun's a hot one out there today. You're lucky that you're on top of this hill with the windows open."

Ward sat down on the arm of the chair and put his arm around Lydia. "So, my dearest, what have we learned today?" he grinned, nodding toward the letters.

"That green means go."

"Huh?"

"This is a new bundle of letters and it's tied with a green ribbon. The pink and blue ones got bogged down, I think. At the end of the blue stack, 'Gene had stopped writing, but it must have been because she was in classes at Carolina. Thus the blue ribbon. The letters in the pink-tied bundle were more like what I'd call an introduction. The two of them were getting used to each other and feeling their ways toward common ground. And this bundle, I've decided, means go."

"What do you mean, 'go?'"

"Glenn's entire writing style has changed. He's lost that

straightforward – excuse me, dear – but he's lost that college professor tone and has begun to write a most poetic prose in some parts in talking about nature. He's becoming more aggressive with the tone of his letters, giving 'Gene a verbal taste of how tender and romantic he can be. I think he's giving old Sonny, who I hope is out of the picture, a run for his money."

Lydia laughed. "I'm sure if this were a Tour de France fight-to-the-finish for the girl, Glenn would win." She saw the puzzlement in Ward's eyes. "Here, read this," she instructed as she handed him the letter she'd just read.

She picked up the next letter and found that she was right in her "green means go" assumption.

Wembo Nyama
September 7, 1929

My dearest 'Gene,

Again I address you thus and this time it is not with wondering because now I know that this is what you are to me. I have tried at times to discourage such a feeling but you yourself know that where such is real that it is an impossibility to discourage it.

When the mail arrived tonight there was to my great joy a letter from you containing the two "snaps" of you. 'Gene, dear, I am so glad that you sent them. Have you ever longed for something and then when you were least expecting it have it come to you? Your pictures were like this.

As I sit here with them on the desk before me I wonder how I shall ever be able to wait until the first of next March to start home and to you, 'Gene, dear. I know now that all I have felt during the past few months is genuine and that it is true and that it can never end. I wish I could tell you tonight what my heart and very being are crying out to express but there is no pen which is a true enough medium for me to do so.

I should not say these things even now were it not that you feel them too. How do I know? That I can't tell you precisely, but this I am sure of, and that is I do know and you do know, too. Much is conveyed by the messages which your pictures bring.

And you are wondering what changes have taken place in me since I have been out here. I am sorry that I don't have any snapshots at this time but I promise that I shall have some made the very first opportunity I have and if they are good you shall have one. I have not said one word of thanks for yours but you know that I appreciate them with all my heart.

'Gene, dear, the evening is far spent and tomorrow is the Sabbath. Would that I might spend it with you! I have not yet prepared my talk for my Junior Church tomorrow A.M. and I shall have to close, go to bed, get a good rest and rise early to prepare my message.

Good-night, dearest, may God's guardian angels keep
watch over you each and every day.

Most sincerely,
Glenn

"Bingo!" yelled Lydia.

"What is it?" Ward asked, afraid something was wrong.

"I was right," she informed him. "Sonny Boy is out of the picture and Glenn is in. I mean 'Gene's in the picture and Glenn's about to be, and well . . ."

"Hold it!" Ward ordered. "Start over and tell me what's going on." Even he had become anxious to find the outcome of the letters and how the story ended.

"Did you see in that letter where 'Gene had looked up Glenn's picture in his senior yearbook from Carolina?"

"Yes."

"Well, in this letter, she sends him two pictures and he's going to have a new one made for her. I guess when she saw his face, that was all it took." Lydia walked over to the desk. "He put them on this very desk in his room in Congo." She ran her fingers across the wood grain of the desk. "It's hard to imagine that this desk was in Africa and now it's in our own 'museum.' And these letters are telling me everything that happened there. Glenn and

'Gene live on through these letters. To think that he placed her pictures right here," she said, pointing to a spot where they would lean up so that they could be seen. "This is the most beautiful love story I've ever read."

"Even more beautiful than ours?" Ward winked.

"You must admit the love between us has grown since we've moved in this house."

"You're right, I must," he conceded. "That statement you made a few days ago about moving from mediocre to terrific was right. I don't know how to explain it, but I, too, believe it has something to do with the love that was grown in this house before we got here."

"Do you still have any of the letters that I wrote to you while you were away at college?" Lydia asked.

Ward hated to admit that he wasn't sure. "There are probably some in one of my old textbooks that are stored away in those boxes downstairs. "What about you?"

Lydia laughed lightheartedly. "Do you remember how you wrote to me every single day?"

"I'm afraid I'd forgotten that, too."

"I sure didn't, and yes, I have every one of those letters in a box downstairs."

"You mean I didn't even rate upstairs?"

"Let's go find them right now," she coaxed, grabbing his hand, "and see when green became go."

"You're kidding, right?"

"Absolutely not! One of us has obviously forgotten how much in love we were. I want to relive those years again and those letters are exactly the key for doing it."

Ward had no choice but to walk hand-in-hand behind Lydia to the stack of boxes that had been pushed into a dark corner of the basement. "How are we ever going to find them in all of this mess?"

"They're right here," she pointed.

"You remember that?"

"I sure do. I may have misplaced some things in this move, but those letters were not one of them."

"They were really that valuable to you?" he asked, in a tone that said her sentimentality truly touched him.

A hug gave him her answer as she leaned into him and held tightly, not letting him see her suddenly induced tears.

Ward was glad that Lydia leaned into him, for he did not want her to see the dampness trying to fill his eyes.

30

September 22, 1929

As I mentioned in my last letter, I went to Minga station one week ago yesterday and came home two days ago. Each day we went out and made a search for a new site for the stations and when we reached our places of abode at night we were surely fatigued. Finally we located a beautiful spot and although we did not find everything we were looking for we were pleased with what we did find.

While at Minga I stayed with Elmo Tabb, the boy who married Mary Taylor Meyers whom you knew at Trinity. Mary Taylor was not there as she has not yet returned from Tunda . . .

"I will be so glad to see Wembo Nyama," Glenn stated.

"We've only been gone four days, but it seems more like home here to me now than any place on earth. I'm sure that it will always be home to me."

"I feel the same way about Minga. I wonder how Mary Taylor will feel when she returns from Tunda with the little one. It can't be easy for a woman to give birth here without any of the comforts of home. Sometimes I feel that those at home feel I shouldn't have brought us here, especially when they are concerned for her health, but God's call was so strong that there was no doubt that He'd take care of us."

"I'm glad to hear you say that, friend," Glenn replied. "I'll be going home on my first furlough in a few months. Sometimes it seems the days fly on leaden wings, but then there are times that I feel I have so much left to do before traveling back to the fair shores of America. I'm sure I miss my family, especially Papa, but I think I would stay here if it weren't for . . . ,"

"That's alright, dear boy. You don't have to finish that sentence. I see it in your eyes."

"The strange thing is, it's actually someone who was in school with Mary Taylor at Trinity."

"Really?" Elmo nodded. "It is strange that you sail all the way to the other side of the world to be connected with someone from home."

"I can't wait to see her and talk to her. Her letters are marvelously funny – just like she's sitting there with me. In fact, she always says that when she writes to me it's, "as if I am sitting talking to the one addressed."

"It would appear she feels just as strongly for you."

"I wasn't so sure for all these months prior, but now I know that her heart beats as mine."

"I take it you are hopeful that she will also feel the call into the mission field?" inquired Elmo.

"I don't want to be presumptuous, but her letters of late seem to indicate that she is also anxious to see me. Her last note included two pictures. When I get a letter from her, I'm so happy I hardly know what to do with myself."

"Glenn, you've stayed well and healthy the entire time you've been here, a feat that very few can boast about, but I'll be if you haven't been bitten, and bitten hard, by the love bug."

Oh 'Gene! I am so glad that I had the opportunity to know you even for the short while before I left for Africa and to know you better through your letters. I wish that I dared pour out to you tonight all that is welling up within me and demanding expression. Oh, why could I not have known what I know now before I departed from America's fair shores! Perhaps it has taken all these months to teach me, building on the foundations which were laid during those few hours when we were together.

Not only do you remember those occasions but I, too, recall them as if they were only last week - the Sunday night at Beulah's, the Sunday night we kept riding in the rain, the

League Union meeting at Smith's Chapel (and I recall those words you sang to me afterwards). Then there were others that I recall: one Sunday evening when you played the chimes and organ before the service started (I don't think you knew I was there until after the service), a morning in Mr. Daniel's office when we talked about the work out here, and then that last Sunday night I was home and the very last night as the train bore me away when you were away. 'Gene, dear, there are these and many more! Sweet are the memories of them all but sweeter will be those moments when I may be with you again. God has been good to us and may He grant that we may see each other again and may He teach us many, many things during the weeks and months just ahead. May He reveal His will to us for each of our lives.

'Gene, dear, I know you are busy with your classes in school but take a little time now and then to let me know how you are. Just remember how your letters always bring sunshine and happiness to me.

Your sincere friend,
Glenn

Ah, sweet mysteries of life, sighed Lydia as she leaned back in 'Gene's chair, closed her eyes and reflected on all the moments of sweet memories that had occurred during her lifetime with Ward.

31

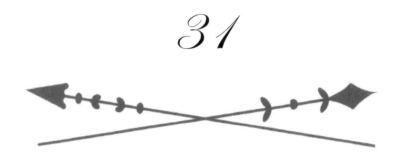

Wembo Nyama
October 28th, 1929

Dearest One,

How constantly you have been in my thoughts these days! How many have been the times that you seemed so near to me! How oft I have longed to be with you, to look into the depths of your soul and hear you speak to me! It seems that the time will never come when I may start to you.

This is the last week of vacation before the boys will return to school. It is hard for me to imagine that at the close of the next school term my fourth Christmas in Congo will be approaching. It has been in a way a very short time since that first one. When I begin to think of the many things which have transpired since then I begin to realize that "a great deal of water has run under the bridge."

It was a great relief last week to be able to relax a little when the evening arrived. I spent the time in reading. I had never read "The Three Musketeers" by Alexander Dumas (would you believe it?) and I indulged in that. I thoroughly enjoyed it and can readily understand why it has occupied and maintained its position in the realm of French literature.

Recently I have re-read "A Tale of Two Cities." It is a great book. There are so many good things about it. Dickens was surely a great understander of human life and the best thing about it was that he always tried to see the best in the life of people instead of the worst. It is so much more worthy of a writer to do that.

Just three years ago last Friday night I reached Wembo Nyama. I recall the great joy with which I reached my journey's end. Five months before I had left home and I can now visualize the crowd of faces which I left at the station as the train bore me away. You were at a district meeting that night with Sonny and Mrs. Beulah and little did we know or think what the years would bring forth. I wonder where the others are tonight and if they will still be there when I return. But, oh 'Gene, you'll be there, and what will it matter where the others are!

Good-night, dear, and God bless you.

Love,
Glenn

How intriguing! Lydia mused as she noted the beginning and ending of the letter. *"Dearest One" and "Love, Glenn" is a far cry from those first stately salutations and complimentary closings.* She could hardly wait to see the next one.

Wembo Nyama, Congo Belge
November 14, 1929

My darling 'Gene,

    I have been away form the station during the afternoon trying to find food for my boarding school. It is a time of great hunger here I am finding it quite hard to get enough food to feed my boys. When I returned about nightfall I found my mail which had arrived while I was away.

    It was time for supper and I could hardly wait to open your letter. But the joy of knowing that they were in my possession helped me to wait until I returned from supper and then such a good time I did have reading them.

    'Gene, dear, I get more anxious each day for the time to pass rapidly. It is now just a little more than three months

before I can start homeward. Oh, it will seem so good to see you again! And it will be all the more so for having been separated from you for all these years.

All those kind and noble things which you said of me I appreciate so very much but I feel so unworthy of them. I fear that you are relying on your imagination just a bit where you think I have been doing wonderful things because I have not. I have worked hard and there is a joy that comes from seeing a few of the fruits of one's labors.

But 'Gene, dear, it has not been easy. It has been hard, hard, hard trying to forge ahead and make a little progress. Traditions and prejudices have had to be contended with and not always overcome. It has been and still is a task of building from the ground up. Equipment of every kind is lacking and there are no helpers which have been efficiently trained and no time in which to train them. But I feel somehow that I have at least laid a foundation upon which I can later build if that foundation is not disrupted while I am home on furlough. At times we wish we could be two or three persons at a time. When I return I shall have many advantages over this term and I can go at my work again with renewed energy. I so often wish that I had several lives to give to this work instead of one.

I knew that you would get the graduate credit at summer school. It means much to one not only to study books but at the same time to have the opportunity to mingle with and study people. I am sure also that your courses at summer school will be of great value to you in your teaching next year.

It would be lots of fun to suddenly appear on the scene and pay an impromptu call at your apartment. It must be very lovely, for you and your roommate, and I also imagine it must be very conducive to your happiness. How do you think you'd like to have an apartment for two permanently? It is probably very conducive to rest to know that you do not always have to be so careful about not disturbing others as in a dorm.

'Gene, dear, after you receive this letter, perhaps you had better not address any other letters to me out here. If you do, I fear that I shall not receive them before I depart. But mail them to me at the following address:

> Methodist Mission Belgium
> 5 Rue du Champ-de-Mars
> Brussels, Belgium

I am writing to Dr. Twynham who is in charge of the mission there and asking him to hold my mail for me. I may not go to Belgium but in case I should not it can be easily forwarded to me in England. I can't have it sent to me there as I do not know any address.

I shall be looking forward to your letters each week. God bless you and keep you.

> Lovingly,
> Glenn

Yes! If he's telling her not to write to the old address, he'll be coming home soon and I can find out what happens.

"Lydia, dear, I'm home."

"I'm in here."

"How'd I ever guess? Mind if we have a bite of lunch together?"

"I thought you'd never ask." She stood and walked toward the kitchen.

"Nope, that's not what I had in mind." Ward gave Lydia an endearing kiss. "I saw that the Daniel Boone Inn is open for lunch now for the summer. I hope you're hungry."

"Do you know how long it's been since I've been there?"

"I know exactly how long it's been — sixteen years and three months, on our anniversary the year we snuck away and came here. We sat at the table next to where the tree comes through the building."

"I hope they have a table near it again."

"They do. I stopped and made sure before we get back there."

"Oh, Ward. I never thought of you being the romantic or sentimental type."

"Hey, who says that old dogs can't learn new tricks? Having our own home here is good for me, too. There's a peaceful calm that seems to bring out the best in both of us."

"You were always good to me."

"And you were always good to me, too, but I'm making sure you don't feel that we spent our entire lives being 'mediocre.' I don't want to go to my grave feeling like I gave my wife less than she deserved."

"Ward," she spoke as they walked down the hill from their home to the restaurant, "you've always been a good provider and treated me with great respect."

He took her hand and stopped her on the sidewalk, turning her so that she faced him. "That wasn't enough. Look at those letters. There was that guy on the other side of the world and he made his lady feel like a princess."

"Yes, but he was head over heels in love. Besides, they weren't married at that point in time."

"The love doesn't stop just because two people get married. I'm learning that more and more. Love is a gift, and God set the example of it through His Son. I do love you. I've loved you ever since the first time I saw you in high school when I had to dissect the frog in ninth grade while you held your hands over your eyes. I wanted to wrap my arms around you and tell you that it was okay."

His words stopped. "Well, I guess that told it all. 'That it was okay.'"

Lydia kissed Ward causing a passing teenage couple to snicker. "Don't laugh," she chuckled back. "It just gets better."

With that, Ward kissed her firmly on the lips. "C'mon, we'd better get going. They might give our table away."

"But you see what I mean," he concluded as he opened the

front door of the restaurant, "I'm tired of it just being 'okay' —
just like you."

When they got back to the house, Lydia noticed a book
on the top of Ward's briefcase.

"What are you reading?" she asked.

"*The Three Musketeers*," came his reply. "I haven't read that
since high school. I haven't the foggiest what possessed me to
pick that up again. When I passed the library this morning, I felt
the urge to pick up a book to read during the final exams. This
one looked interesting as I passed the aisles. I'd forgotten what a
great work of French literature it is."

"Here, I picked up something for you, too," he added.

"Don't tell me. Let me guess. *The Tale of Two Cities.*"

"It is your favorite book, isn't it? I've heard you mention
before how you loved the way Dickens saw and portrayed his
characters. I thought that we might curl up in front of the fire this
evening on the sofa and read together. We haven't done that in a
while and the evening air's still brisk enough to warrant a cozy
fire."

"If you keep this up, I'm going to wonder who you are
and what you did with my husband," Lydia laughed as Ward took
off to give his last exam for the second semester.

Wembo Nyama C. Belge
November 24, 1929

My dearest 'Gene,

I wonder what you are doing this Sunday night. I know it is not quite night there yet but I shall "play like it is." I wonder if you are sitting before a big, open, friendly fire dreaming or if you are curled up in a big chair before it reading a good book. Of course you went to church but church is already over.

Why could I not have been there to take you home and to help you enjoy that fire for a while afterwards!

Lydia pinched herself. *Am I dreaming? Did Ward really come home and take me to lunch and then talk about a fire this evening?* She could not believe the command that Glenn's letters seemed to have on this house and its inhabitants. Suddenly, she couldn't help but wonder whether another couple would have had the same experiences.

Ah, yes, but this house had our name on it. There is definitely a reason for all of this, she convinced herself as she kept reading.

    I sometimes wonder why these days pass so slowly and I know I should not wonder about it. It is easy during the day when I am busy with the host of things commanding my attention. But following the day, the evening always comes. There is still plenty to do but when I sit down at my desk for work my thoughts fly to you.

    "'Gene where are you tonight" they ask me and I have to reply that I do not know but if I did I'd be there too. They then try to tell me that it's no use to wonder because they'll find you for me, and off they rush on swift pinions. Out in the great space somewhere they find tidings of you and back they come again to me.

    I would that I could go to you this night! Paper and pens are useful things for certain circumstances but one feels like casting them from him forever when they so feebly express his feelings. But since they are the only means at hand one cannot be too disdainful of them, and will use them as best he can.

- - - - -

    Thanksgiving Day
'Gene, dearest, perhaps you may think that this let-

ter is being written on the installment plan but I was unable to finish it on Sunday night. It has seemed so good all day not to <u>need</u> to do anything except just what I wanted to do. This is one of the very few holidays we have out here and I have thoroughly appreciated it. I spent the larger portion of the morning getting rid of some of the junk which had accumulated in my house. After dinner I took a nap for about two hours and from which I have just awakened. It seemed good indeed not to be aroused by the bell at two o'clock as on the school days.

In a letter from my sister last week she enclosed two clippings of the death and internment of Mr. Daniel. It was a great shock to me and seemed to be to everybody at home as he had not been sick at all. He surely did have a peaceful and easy death. I hope when I die that it may be like that.

I looked for a letter from you in the mail on Tuesday but I suppose it missed the mail boat in Europe and that it will be here next Tuesday. I hope so as I shall be looking forward to its arrival each hour until it has been placed in my hands.

All the boys in the boarding school are home except a few. I gave them a grand surprise this morning by telling them that they could go home and come back on Saturday. At first they thought it too good to be true but then their happiness gave vent to itself and they began to jump about and run. They soon were on their way and an hour later all were gone except a few who are going to stay.

It is just three weeks now until Christmas, my fourth

in Congo. After Christmas the school will have a vacation of a month. During that time I shall be helping Mr. Tabb become familiar with all the duties of the office. He will arrive here next week but I cannot show him so very much while school is in progress. The remainder of the time I intend to use in packing my "duds" so that everything will be in readiness to go when the time rolls around in February.

I suppose that I shall just about freeze when I get to Europe and start across the North Atlantic. I left all my winter clothes in America and to keep comfortable I suppose I shall have to stay inside and go out on deck very little. However, that will be no matter at all as I know you'll be waiting.

God bless you and keep you.

Lovingly,
Glenn.

Lydia noticed that Glenn had gone to putting a period after his name. She couldn't help but think how that reflected the end. *I wonder if it signifies that there will be no others for 'Gene after him.*

32

Wembo Nyama
December 31, 1929

My dearest 'Gene,

This is the last night of the old year and although I do not feel very much like writing, on account of a cold, it is my last chance before the arrival of the new one.

It has been such a long, long time since I have heard from you. I would think that something terrible had happened were it not that your Greetings for my birthday and Christmas arrived just at the right time. You have been so good about remembering me each year on these two occasions and your thoughtfulness has brought me much happiness. This year you must have been thinking far ahead in order to have your thoughts reach me just at the time I am sure you wanted them to.

I almost had a holiday on my birthday and would have had one surely if I had been thinking. It was Friday and all the morning it rained. We had no school, but it stopped raining during the noon hour. I had school in the afternoon and work also in spite of the chilliness of the atmosphere. I did not think about it being my birthday until that night. But I am so happy to know that you remembered.

On Christmas Eve we had . . .

"Mr. Edgerton, what a fine idea this was to do the Christmas program in three parts. This way all the students were able to participate in a way that they shall long remember," congratulated Mr. Tabb.

"Yes, indeed," remarked Miss Ina C. Brown, a guest who along with her friend and colleague Miss Elizabeth Cols, was visiting the mission fields of the Methodist church around the world. "This is a most ingenious way to instruct the natives of Jesus and how his love affects their lives."

"Oh, I'm so happy we could be here at Christmas," agreed Miss Cols. "This is just such a lovely event. We could have never imagined seeing them do the various plays and then to have a band to also play. My goodness, we were awed at the very idea of doing a simple pageant."

"Mr. Edgerton has quite a way with the boys. It was his idea to make this change from our yearly pageant. By having his boys do the three-act play of *Joseph and His Brothers*, followed by the two selections by the band gave the Bible School time to set the 'stage' for the play, *Barabas*, given by the Bible School."

"A very fine job on the part of your boys, Mr. Edgerton," reiterated Mr. Tabb. "Do be sure to tell them how splendidly we thought they did."

"Yes, by all means," said Miss Brown.

"Why don't you tell them yourselves?" asked Glenn.

"Oh, however shall we do that?" inquired Miss Cols.

"Very simply," stated Glenn. "Otetela is a very simple language. He taught the two women how to express their thanks and say, "fine job."

"Your words will mean much more to them than mine," he instructed. "The fact that you took the time to learn those few words will mean worlds to them. It is a way to break the barrier between our two countries."

"Shan't we be ever so enchanting when we return home and speak these words to our sister Leaguers?" laughed Miss Brown. "We shall have to teach them to our entire group."

"Absolutely!" seconded Miss Cols. "If only we don't forget them during the course of the rest of our voyage."

"I'll write them down for you," offered Glenn. "But for now, we'd better let you greet the students before they take off for their holiday vacation."

"You mean they'll take off now?" asked Miss Cols.

"This late?" came Miss Brown's startled response.

"You must understand that home is sacred to these people. They, like we in America, want to be with our families at special times. These students will take off the second I dismiss them, which will not be until after everything from this evening is put away, and travel non-stop until they arrive at their homes."

"Dear me!" exclaimed Miss Brown. "I'd never thought of it this way, but the girls in our sorority were the same way when we finished our final exams in college. But then, Father had the means to pay for us to get there. I guess we truly would have done the same even if we'd had to 'hot-foot' it home."

"Traveling around the world to these missions is such an enlightening experience," stated Miss Cols. "We read of the stories from the foreign lands and hear about them in our Epworth Leagues back home, but to actually see and be a part of it. There is not a price we could put on this education."

"You're exactly correct in your observation," noted Glenn. "By your firsthand stories, you can do wonders for the mission stations by sharing your findings and stories with not only your unit of Leaguers, but through your conference bulletins to make them aware of both our needs and the work that is being done here."

"That's correct," nodded Mr. Tabb. "I think that people must know what their hard-earned dollars are going for in these places where they can't see. It's much easier to support a mission or a cause when you know that there is truly a reward coming from their endeavors."

"Well, rest assured, gentlemen," voiced Miss Brown, "I am a member of our National Board of the Women's Society of

Christian Service and I shall do everything I can to make sure our Methodist women hear of the fine work you are doing here in Wembo Nyama, as well as in the rest of the missions."

"How fortunate we were to be here for Christmas," said Miss Cols. "Do all of the missions offer this kind of program with their schools?"

"I feel quite certain that all of the missions of every church around the world try to manage a pageant of some sort," volunteered Mr. Tabb. "Whether they all have someone with the creative skills of our Mr. Edgerton is another question," he concluded as he slapped Glenn on the back.

"I'm sure that any teacher who's heard the call and given their life to go to a foreign land loves to teach as much as I," spoke Glenn in a most humble voice. "God gives us all the gifts that we need for our particular circumstances, I'm sure. That's a part of His promise."

"What a wonderful statement indeed," smiled Miss Brown. "I shall use that quote in my report when I return to the states."

"It is a most exciting honor to have visitors here for Christmas," said Mr. Tabb. "It's hard to imagine that you two lovely women have not only paid your own expenses for this worldwide venture, but that in the process, you are losing no opportunities to see everything and learn both the work and the problems that are involved with our missions around the globe."

"My dear Mr. Tabb," Miss Cols replied, "what better way to understand what we need to be doing in our churches back home to support you out here than to see it for ourselves?"

"Besides," added Miss Brown, "anyone can tour the world

and see the breathtaking scenery and the high spots of various cultures, but this way, we actually get to see the *real* world as we travel. We have surely been in a few hotels in our travels that we might get a glimpse of both worlds."

"How very blessed you are to have that financial capability at your disposal," said Mr. Tabb.

"Our fathers have been most successful in the last few years with their industries," offered Miss Brown. "Otherwise this adventure would be an impossibility for us."

"It would be a rare pleasure and treat if you would allow us to help with all the things that must be done after this glorious program," interjected Miss Cols. "Do you think we might help?"

"Customarily, we would not be very gentlemanly if we allowed that, but seeing that we are in Congo, where there is much work to do, I think your request is most fitting," accepted Glenn. "What better way for you to explain to your groups our work than to be involved in it?"

"So right, Mr. Edgerton, so right," agreed Mr. Tabb.

"And just think, Ina," reminded Miss Cols, "we will still be able to see the work in India, China, Korea and Japan before returning to America. I hope those places reap a reward as exciting as this one has been."

"Ladies, I'm sure that when you go home, you'll see things in a totally different light," nodded Glenn.

Lydia stopped to think about the visit of the two women for a moment. She glanced back at the date on the letter. *December 31, 1929. That's two months after Black Tuesday. I wonder if their fathers' successful businesses suffered the same demise as most other industries during the stock market's crash of 1929.*

I must make a note to ask Phillip if his grandfather ever heard from those two women again. She grabbed a piece of paper and pen and jotted herself a quick note before delving into the crevices of the letters of Glenn Edgerton. *I highly suspect that Miss Brown and Miss Cols came back to American soil to see their home in a much different light, indeed!*

"I trust that you ladies had a restful evening, even though it was after eleven when we finished putting away everything from the program, and that you awoke to a most Merry Christmas," greeted Mr. Tabb.

"This is a most memorable way to spend Christmas. I can't wait to tell everyone at home about everything that we've seen and done." Miss Brown reached into the bag that she'd brought with her to the dining table. "Miss Cols and I have brought you a few gifts to hopefully brighten your holiday. Friends from home made many of the items when they found out that we were traveling to the missions. The items are quite small, you see, for we had to pack them all in our trunks."

We have had a week of rest since Christmas and I surely have made good use of it. When I have not been sleeping I have been spending the time in packing. My house looks as though a cyclone struck it and I have been picking up the pieces. I started this chore early so that I would be sure to finish in time to catch the train the last week in February.

It is about impossible to believe that one could collect as much junk as I have in the past three years. Books, magazines, and almost everything have found a place somehow. I had to begin by throwing about half of everything away. But it will soon be all over.

'Gene I don't understand why I have not been hearing from you. You said you'd be writing each week but weeks have passed since I have had a letter. I do hope that they have not been lost en route, which might be possible as we have had no foreign mail for two weeks.

But anyway the time will not be long until I shall be on my way to America and you.

Lovingly,
Glenn

As Lydia folded the letter and placed it carefully back in the aged envelope, a sickening pang wormed its way through her body. *Perhaps the mail also suffered with the crash of 1929.*

I wonder how long it will be before dear Glenn finds out what has happened to the economy of his beloved homeland. She picked up the next letter. *And I wonder what has happened to his "dearest 'Gene."*

Lydia tidily stacked the envelopes back in order and tied the ribbon around them. This had become a gesture that she did daily . . . *with love.*

Enough for today. Tomorrow's a new day and also a New Year.

33

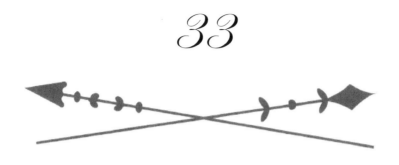

Wembo Nyama
February 11, 1930

My dear 'Gene,

The moon has again begun to grow and tonight it would be flooding everything with its beauty were it not for a filmy curtain of haze through which it shyly slips and then mystifies everything with its presence. Its dimmed radiance and the coolness of the evening call to one to go out and become a partaker in the beauties of the night. This would be a great pleasure to indulge in were you here with me.

This will perhaps be the last moon that I shall see grow in Africa for a while. Where the next one will sail above me I cannot tell. But wherever I may be I wish that you could be there, too.

Your dear little card of Dec. 8, so demure yet so sweet and filled with your own dear sweet self reached me on Friday of last week. I was indeed happy over its arrival but admit a little disappointed that it was so short. But I suppose I shall have to be content with thinking that the richest gifts always come in small packages. I am hoping that in the very near future there will be a real long letter from you.

I am so glad that your card was not in the mail which came the week before. If it had been it would never have reached me as that mail was burned. One of the mission cars was returning from Lusambo, caught fire and burned. It was the Dodge which Dr. Moore brought out with him. I just could not believe it when I heard about it. It had gotten stuck in a hole and had to be unloaded. Somehow in the process of getting out of the hole a connection on the tank broke and the gas ran out all over the ground. Someone went back with a lantern to see about reloading the things, not knowing that the gas had spilled out. The gas caught fire from the lantern and the conflagration followed. I am very worried about the mail which was burned. My new passport is over due and I fear that it was burned. If so, I don't know when I can leave Congo. At least not until I get another. That could be several weeks.

I shall be delayed a week or so anyway on account of the arrival of the bishop. Bishop Cannon is due here just about the time I was planning to start for home. Of course I shall wait until after his visit. It might be that he will want me to accompany him on the return trip. I don't know whether I should like traveling all the way with a bishop or not.

We are expecting the arrival of a party of missionaries. One is returning from furlough and will stop at Minga. The other two ladies will come on to Wembo Nyama and they will be located here. Miss Reas, who is to take over my schoolwork while I am home, is one of them. I am glad that I shall have the opportunity to work with her these next two weeks. I hope that she is going to have lots of new ideas which will greatly enrich our curriculum. I have never met either her or the new nurse and am wondering how I shall like them.

I wish I could seal myself within this message and surprise you when you open it. But as I cannot I shall fill it with all the best wishes that I have and lots of something else too. God bless you, dear.

Most sincerely,
Glenn

This definitely calls for a celebration.

Lydia looked through her favorite magazines to find a new recipe for something she thought Ward would enjoy. *Pork. He loves pork.* It wasn't long before she found a recipe for pork with a marinade that included ingredients of which she either had on the shelf or in the fridge.

She also found a recipe for a turtle cheesecake. *I haven't used my sponge cake pan in years. This should be loads of fun,* she laughed to herself as she tore off to the basement on a hunt for the pan.

I haven't gone to this much trouble since the first Valentine's Day after our wedding.

Lydia spent the entire rest of the day decorating the table with a lace cloth and a bouquet of fresh flowers, then polishing the silver and pulling out the china and crystal that was only used for special events.

Tonight is going to be a memorable event for both of us. I can just feel it!

It was all Lydia could do not to pick up the phone and call Ward to tell him how excited she was, but she decided rather to let him see for himself firsthand when he got home. She happened to remember that this was the last day that he had to report to ASU for a few days.

So there really is *call for a celebration. Our celebration!* She was nearly beside herself.

Then she remembered that they were hoping to take a trip to the Red Bird Mission and see if there was anything they could do to help for the few days that Ward had off before the summer sessions began.

A triple celebration.

"Yum!" Ward exclaimed as he came through the door. "What smells so good?"

"We're having a celebration," she proudly informed him.

"A celebration? For what?"

"Several different reasons, all of which I'll share with you at dinner, but mainly because as of right this minute, you're all mine for the next few days."

Ward noticed the festive table on his way upstairs to change clothes. "Do I need to rent a tux for the evening?"

Lydia shook her head at him, enjoying his playful antics. *Yes, it's going to be a memorable evening all right.*

She checked on the cheesecake which had turned out beautifully, and sneaked a peek at the roast.

"Call me fifteen minutes before you're ready. That will give me time to freshen up before your gala event. I want to mow the grass so that we can have the day to relax tomorrow. Then we can head to Kentucky whenever we feel like it."

"That sounds like a great plan."

Lydia recalled that there was only one more letter left in the third stack. As Ward headed toward the garage and the mower, she decided that she had just enough time to read it before taking the pork roast out of the oven.

She paid close attention to its words, knowing this letter had to hold some great significance since it was the final installment on one of the chapters in the life of Glenn and 'Gene.

Sunday A.M. March 30th

My dearest Jean,
I have been
on my homeward way now
almost a month, having left
Mombo Nyasa on March 6th,
and 15 tomorrow morning I
am due to arrive in
Southampton. From there I
shall go immediately to London where I am expecting
mail from home which will
determine my immediate return to—

we could not have asked
for more ideal weather. It
was quite hot at the time
we were crossing this equator.
But a day or so afterwards it
began to turn colder and now
it is quite cold to me. It
is so strange for it to be
so cold and I shall look for
some heavy clothing the first
chance I have after landing.
Every now and then I have
a feeling that I am really
going home but then I am
sure that it is all a dream
and that I shall soon be getting back to Mombo Nyasa.
But really I shall soon be
home and sooner than I shall—

Union-Castle Line
RMS Edinburgh Castle
Sunday a.m. March 30th, 1930

My dearest 'Gene,

I have been on my homeward journey way now almost a month, having left Wembo Nyama on March 6th and tomorrow I am due to arrive in Southampton. From there I shall go immediately to London where I am expecting mail from home which will determine my immediate activities.

During the last week in February I received a wire that my father was very ill. I was in a dilemma as my passport had been burned two weeks before in the Dodge on the way back from Lusambo. Bishop Cannon was due to arrive on February 28th and I had hoped to be able to return with him when he came as he had sprained his ankle in December. He needed someone to travel with him and had planned for me to return with him.

I told him about my father and my passport and he said if I wanted to go he would use all his influence to try to get me to Cape Town where I could get a passport. So I started with him and everything has opened up beautifully for me. I am so glad that I could come with him, as he has needed someone to be with him and help him.

When I reached Cape Town I received a reply, to a cable which I had sent, stating that Papa was improved and the danger passed. It was good news to me and I am hoping that he has continued to improve and will have completely recovered before I shall have reached home.

The voyage has been a most pleasant one and we could not have asked for more ideal weather. I was quite hot at the time we were crossing the equator. But a day of so afterwards it began to turn cooler and now it is quite cold to me. It seems strange for it to be so cold and I shall look for some heavy clothing the first chance I have after landing.

Every now and then I have a feeling that I am really going home but then I am sure that it is all a dream and that I shall soon be getting back to Wembo Nyama. But really I shall soon be home and sooner than I shall realize it.

I can't imagine what it will be like to see you again. So many things have happened since that Sunday night that we rode around in the rain. Do you remember it? I recall it as vividly as if it were yesterday. But to see you and talk with you again is something that I can scarcely realize will soon be. Oh, 'Gene, I do want to see you so much! One of the first things I shall do after reaching home is to run down to see you. There are so many things I want to tell you and to hear you tell me. How can I wait for the time to arrive!

I do so badly want to see the Passion Play at Oberammergau before going to America if I can. But all of my plans will be dependent upon the news of Papa which is awaiting me at London. It might be that I should never be in Europe at the time the play is being given.

I have had a good time on board. I was elected Secretary of the Sports Committee and the work connected with it took a lot of my time. However, I won three prizes and felt *myself very fortunate. I was contemplating a time of rest, sleeping and eating. It has been a little different. In fact I have had very little time for writing personal letters. I wanted to write to you more often but I did not have the opportunity.*

I am hoping there will be several letters from you waiting for me at Brussels. I shall be so happy if there are.

The best of wishes in everything and love,
Glenn

Lydia carefully placed the last letter of the third stack back in its place and tied the green ribbon around the bundle before hiding it in the far reaches of the desk drawer.

Perfect timing! she thought as the oven's timer went off to let her know that dinner was ready. As she reached for her mitt and opened the oven's door, she glanced out the window to see how much more of the yard Ward had to mow.

The pan, roast, gravy and all fell to the floor as she ran toward the front door.

34

Lydia sat in the waiting room of the coronary care unit staring at the wall on the other side of the room. She had tried to read the magazines or sip the coffee but was unable to do either for she felt as though she were trapped inside a bubble that was sucking all of the air and life out of her.

You must be strong for Ward! she kept reminding herself.

She had only been in a situation anywhere similar to this once before and then Ward had been seated beside her, enduring much of the same pain that she was now experiencing.

"Would you like for us to call someone for you so that you're not alone?" the lady in admitting had asked while Ward was whisked away straight to the emergency coronary unit.

Lydia had never considered this day in her mind. Not once had she thought ahead to the fact that one of them would be left to face the struggle of being alone one day.

Her mind was running a race of excuses of why things

hadn't been different and they weren't at home eating the meal she'd spent most of the day preparing. Nothing mattered now - not the kitchen floor, nor the mess that had been left on it, nor the cheesecake in the fridge, nor the fact that she hadn't eaten since mid-morning - nothing.

Nothing except Ward. Oh please God . . . She dropped her face into her hands and searched for the right words to express how much she wanted to hold onto this man who had been her entire life, her very existence, for the past twenty-seven years.

Lydia reached into her purse for a tissue but her hand came back instead with a small bundle of letters tied with a dainty white lace ribbon.

When did I put these in my purse?

So much happened so quickly once she discovered Ward's body in the yard that she didn't recollect much afterwards. Now, looking at the letters in her hand, Lydia still didn't recall opening the desk drawer to retrieve them. She wasn't sure if it had been a natural impulse, or if God knew that she needed not be alone at the hospital.

Vaguely, she remembered that the last letter she had read - *the one that I must have been reading while Ward needed me,* she blamed herself – was the one before Glenn was leaving for home. She looked down at the top of the stack she was holding to see that the envelope revealed that it was written on stationary of a cruise liner.

Glenn must be on his way home. She opened the envelope as hastily as she could to see where he was.

Norddeutscher Lloyd Bremen
D. "Bremen"
April 5, 1930

My dear 'Gene,

 Perhaps before this letter reaches you, you will have received the one I wrote to you on the "Edinburgh Castle."

 I was so disappointed when I received my mail from Brussels to discover that there was nothing from you. I was sure that there would be and all the way from Cape Town I had thought about how happy I'd be when I read your letter which was waiting for me in Europe. But since there was none in Europe, and it may be that I reached there earlier than you expected me to. I am looking forward to there being one in New York City when I arrive there next Tuesday.

 I have completely changed my plans since I last wrote. You know I wanted to see the Passion Play at Oberammergau but much to my sorrow I learned that they have decided not to open earlier but to retain the original date of May 11th. I could not afford to travel about in Europe until that time even though I should have liked to do so very, very much.

 Before I left Cape Town I received a wire that Papa was out of danger but I had no ultimatum of the nature of his illness until I received my sister's letters in Europe. She gave me a detailed account of how he was taken ill, carried to Johns Hopkins Hospital in Baltimore and operated on. He was there six weeks but I was so happy when she told me that he had returned home so much improved and on the road to recovery. I am so thankful to our Heavenly Father that Papa's life has been spared. Even though I know that he is getting stronger I am so anxious to get home to see him. God has been so good to me during these years. I have trusted everything into His hands. I am hoping that there will be other letters awaiting me in New York City.

One of the first things I shall do when I reach New York is to go to Prince George Hotel and inquire for my mail. If you only knew how anxious I am to hear from you you'd have a host of them waiting for me.

From where I am sitting I can look out on the stormy sea. The weather has been rough all the way from Southampton but last night shortly after midnight we ran into a heavy storm. The sea rolled and beat against the ship that was trying to go ahead. It grew so rough that the Captain had to slacken the speed. The remainder of the night and this morning we have been running at reduced speed. This means that we shall be late in getting to New York. But as I look out I think of that other storm years ago when the Master stilled the waves on the Sea of Galilee and I know that He is present here now and that we are in His care. 'Tis Sunday and except for the waves all is quiet! (I started this Sat. P.M. but did not finish).

'Gene, you may have already made your plans for

Easter and if you have don't hesitate to tell me. I have just realized that I am going to be home for Easter. But if you have not made other plans I should like very much to be with you that day. I don't yet know what arrangements I shall have to make when I reach home but you can let me know. In all probability I shall have seen you before that time. Write to me right away so that there'll be a letter for me at home when I arrive.

God bless and keep you, 'Gene.

Lovingly,
Glenn

Even though what she was holding were only pieces of paper, through them Lydia sensed that the same Master who had calmed the sea for Glenn's return - who was also the same Master that calmed the Sea of Galilee - was in this very room with her. She knew that the Master was present with her even without the letters, but there was something unexplainably peaceful about being here with the letters. Maybe it was simply the act of having something to hold in her hands or to read to keep her mind off what was going on down the hall.

Like anything could help with that! She knew that although her body and the letters were in the waiting room, her mind was in the surgical suite.

The paper in front of her had a large hotel pictured on it. Its words had been written while Glenn was in Greensboro, North Carolina at The O. Henry Hotel. Lydia didn't notice the date on the letter for it was turned to the second page, something that seemed immediately odd for all of the other letters had been stacked in an orderly fashion with all of the them perfectly intact in the envelopes. This one was out of the envelope and the words on the back of the page seemed to scream at her.

But then, how good life is! Just think how drab, how simply life would be for me were it not for you, dear. You are my sunshine and my stars to say nothing of my moon. Although you are absent you are ever present and I know you are always near just as the moon is when night has drawn a cloudy film across her brow and veiled her face.

Be good, dear. Pray daily that the time may pass rapidly and I may soon be with you again.

Lovingly,
Glenn

Once she read the words, the incident of the letter being opened to the second page no longer seemed a rarity. *These words were not from Glenn, but rather from God to me,* she noted. *As have been all three stacks of these letters,* she decisively reconciled with her inner being.

An unusual happening, yes; an impossible happening, no!

"Mrs. Mason," called the volunteer stationed at the phone in the waiting room.

Lydia rushed to the desk, the letter still clutched in her hand. "Yes?" she asked expectantly.

"The doctor is on his way to speak to you."

"Did he say how my husband is?"

"I'm sorry, no, he simply said that he would be right out to speak to you."

Lydia's mind began to imagine the worst. *The other doctors sent messages that the patients were out of danger or were going to be all right. Why didn't this doctor make any comment?*

She looked down at her hand and saw where her thumb rested on the paper. *"You are my sunshine and my star to say nothing of my moon,"* Lydia read to herself. *Oh, Ward . . . please God, spare him.*

The sound of footsteps coming down the hall caused her to look up in their direction.

"Mrs. Mason, your husband is out of surgery" came the words she had been waiting to hear. Rather than shaking her hand, the cardiac surgeon led her down the hall. "Why don't we go down here so that we can talk?"

"Is he okay? Is he going to be all right?"

"There are several things I want to tell you and I felt we would have more space and privacy in one of these family rooms," he indicated as he turned a corner that opened into several small private consultation rooms.

"Please, sit down," he offered, opening the door for her.

She followed his advice, looking almost robotic in her actions, as her every movement hinged on his next words.

"Mrs. Mason, as I said, your husband is out of surgery. I'm afraid that his condition warranted a quadruple bypass. We are hoping that the outcome is going to be fine following recovery, but he did suffer a major heart attack and several of the valves have suffered extensive damage. We've tried to repair them, but at this point, we have to sit back and see if his system will accept the repairs. He has lost a lot of blood as a result of the heart attack, so we're having to monitor that closely, too."

"So what you're saying is that he . . . ," Lydia's faint and trembling voice broke off.

The surgeon waited patiently for her words.

"You're saying that he . . . that he . . . he still might not make it?"

"I don't want to say that, Mrs. Mason, but there are still some dangerous curves ahead in his road to recovery. We have an excellent cardiac wing and they are all both highly trained and equipped in these matters."

"But sometimes it is out of your control," she managed to

throw out in slow individual syllables.

"Yes," the surgeon replied, wishing he could have offered anything else.

Lydia bowed her head and fought back the tears.

The surgeon sat there for a moment and let her emotions follow their own natural course, a course he had seen on other occasions, but one that never got any easier to watch loved ones endure.

"Will I be able to see him anytime soon?" she asked faintly, after the tears became controllable.

"I'll have one of the nurses in recovery to call you periodically as they monitor his progress. For now, they are working to make sure that Ward is stable and stays that way. Recovery could take a good while. Would you like to go home and rest and then come back tomorrow when, if things remain the same, he will go to a room in the intensive coronary care unit and you will have visiting privileges at certain times during the day?"

Lydia tried to smile. "Thank you, but I would really like to stay here if it's okay. I don't want to leave him just yet."

"I understand," the doctor said in a consoling manner, remembering exactly how he'd felt when he'd been in her shoes at the time of his father's heart attack. He prayed that the outcome would be the same.

The grieving wife looked again at the paper in her hand, having forgotten all about it. "Although you are absent you are ever present and I know you are always near just as the moon is when night has drawn a cloudy film across her brow and veiled her face," she read.

"Is that something Mr. Mason wrote to you?" he asked, seeing the letter in Lydia's hand.

"No," she feebly smiled. "No, it's actually from a letter, that was written in Africa back in 1930, to a woman here who is about to become engaged, from the man who is her true love. Somehow its words seem to speak to me right at this moment."

"Love knows no time or space barriers," acknowledged the surgeon. "I have to get back to another patient. Would you like to go back to the waiting room or would you prefer a few more minutes here? I can have the volunteer call the chaplain to be with you, if you'd like."

"Thank you, but I think I'll stay here for a moment longer, then go back to the waiting room until I can see Ward."

"Very well, I'll make sure the nurses call you as soon as they have him settled in the recovery unit."

Lydia could not even manage a verbal "Thank you," so she gave the surgeon an appreciative nod and an attempt at a smile as he walked out the door. She collapsed onto the sofa, bursting into tears as she hit the leather of the plush piece of furniture. *Oh God, are You here. I know You are. Please let me feel Your presence.*

A light knock on the door signaled her that one of the volunteers must have come to check on her. She peeked out the small narrow glass to see two familiar faces.

"Oh, God, You are here!" she cried as she opened the door and fell into the arms of Phillip and Francie.

Neither of them said a word, but allowed Lydia a fresh flow of tears as an escape for a part of the hurt and uncertainty that Lydia was feeling at the moment. They led her to the sofa, where they sat on either side of her.

"I didn't expect you to come . . . I only called you because . . . well . . . you told me to call you if I ever needed anything and I needed to tell someone . . . to have someone to pray with me. You were the first . . . the only ones to come to mind."

"As we hope it will always be," replied Phillip. "And my entire family is praying for you. They have all sent their well wishes with me and they are all in prayer for Ward."

"And for you," smiled Francie. "You need strength through this, too. We are concerned for Ward, but he has an entire hospital staff to care for him right now. We are here for you."

"Thank you," sniffed Lydia, "oh, thank you. I can't tell you how much it means that you're here. And I'd just asked God to let me know He was here with me. That very instant, you knocked on the door."

Phillip and Francie both gave her a hug.

"Why don't we go back to the waiting room so that you'll be near in case anyone calls for you?" Francie suggested.

"Yes," Lydia nodded. "Since you're the ministers, can you say a prayer for him with me?"

"I'll be glad to pray for you and with you, Lydia, but you know that your words are just as powerful as ours, and God knows the words of your heart already," Phillip responded as he bowed his head.

Following a few dwindling tears after the prayer, the trio walked the short distance to the surgical waiting area where the volunteer was announcing for Mrs. Mason.

"The recovery room nurses told me to let you know that Mr. Mason is a bit more stable now. If you'd like, the doctor has informed them to let you walk back and see that he's resting for a couple of minutes."

Phillip, who realized that was - as a rule - strictly against hospital orders, walked as far as he was permitted with Lydia until they reached the recovery unit. A former parishioner of his, who was one of the cardiac nurses, recognized him.

"You're allowed to come back with her," the nurse invited. "Do you have your clergy badge?"

"Yes, I have it, but I think Mrs. Mason needs to be alone with her husband right now." He turned to Lydia. "So that you will know, Francie and I both have clergy badges, and should you need us, we'll be right here waiting for you. But you go back there now for Ward. He probably won't know that you're there, but if he does, let him know that he has many concerned friends."

"Thank you," she said going through the door. Then she paused and grabbed his arm. "Thank you for everything. Will you be here for a while?"

"We're here just as long as you need us," he assured. "We'll be right out in the surgical waiting area should you need us. Just have one of the nurses call for us and we'll be right there."

She nodded. "I feel much better now that you're here."

"That's why we're here," Phillip acknowledged. "We were hoping that would be the case."

She disappeared through the wide doors as the ministers began to pray silently for both of their well-beings - Ward's and Lydia's.

35

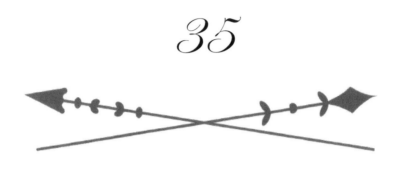

The few hours rest that Lydia caught were enough to get her up and rolling the next morning. Phillip and Francie had finally convinced her that Ward would need her more once he was awake and moved to the less critical coronary care unit. They had agreed to spend the night with her, in the same bedroom where Phillip had stayed as a child during the summers when he visited his grandparents, but only if they were allowed to clean up the mess in the kitchen.

Always the gracious host, Lydia insisted that they take the cheesecake to the hospital. "There's no sense in it going to waste. It took me too long to find that pan and make it. Talk about a hunt - it was like having my own safari in the basement!"

The couple was glad to see that both her senses of humor and responsibility were back in tow.

Knowing how anxious Lydia was to get to the hospital, Phillip dropped her off, with Francie, and ran down the street to pick up coffee and breakfast sandwiches. "You've got to keep up your strength," he insisted. "You'll be of no use to Ward or any of the rest of us if you don't eat and rest."

Lydia knew his was the voice of experience, just as had been his grandfather's voice - both of which she trusted. It was difficult to follow his advice, but she forced herself to do so.

Apologizing to Francie for seeming aloof, she sat quietly in the waiting area with the letters, which were neatly packed in a tote bag. Lydia reached slowly and decisively into the bag and pulled out the stack of letters, running her fingers over the top of the note she'd read earlier, the one that had been opened to the middle of the message. She looked long and hard at the envelope that bore a sketch of the grandiose O. Henry Hotel from whence the reflective words of Glenn had been written. Her fingers slowly untied the white lace ribbon and Lydia's eyes purposefully read the words again, wanting to see if the words again spoke to her in the same way.

But then, how good life is! Just think how drab, how simply life would be for me were it now for you, dear. You are my sunshine and my stars to say nothing of my moon. Although you are absent you are ever present and I know you are always near just as the moon is when night has drawn a cloudy film across her brow and veiled her face.

Be good, dear. Pray daily that the time may pass rapidly and I may soon be with you again.
Lovingly,
Glenn

Even in the midst of the emotional pain running throughout her body, the hurting wife felt that she had been blessed by the words that God had chosen for her to read. Tears that had threatened to make an appearance had been traded for a serene composure that was a result of God's presence in the room with her.

Lydia flipped the pages back to the first one of the letter and read the words that Glenn had inscribed to his "dearest" once he was back on his native North Carolina soil.

My Dear 'Gene,
I am in Greensboro for a few hours between trains and I must drop you a note and let you know that I am still alive. I have started to write to you several times since I was

with you but have destroyed everything that I have written

'Gene, dear, have I really been with you or it is all a happy dream. I have thought of you every minute and wondered what you are doing and where you are. How I wish I could be with you instead of going further and further from you! Will the time never come when I can be with you for a while without having to rush madly away somewhere else?

Wasn't yesterday a glorious Easter? I am sure that it was one of the most lovely Easter Days I have ever experienced. Wasn't it great to be alive and to know that God loves us? But throughout the whole day I longed to be with you. I thought of you and wanted to go but I could not. But perhaps the next Easter we may be together.

Did you see the announcement in yesterday's "News and Disturber" of the engagement of Miss Lear to Mr. G.M. "Sonny" Ledford? Do you think now that anyone would have anything to say about my having gone to see you so soon? I don't think so. I am hoping that they are going to be supremely happy and I know you do too.

Be good until I come back about two weeks from now and remember that my thoughts are continually of you.

God bless you and keep you.

Lovingly,

Glenn.

Without speaking a word, Lydia handed the note to Francie and waited for her to read it.

"Isn't it bizarre how the words of each of the letters could have just as easily been written from Ward in the coronary care unit as from Glenn in Africa and then North Carolina? It isn't only now that this is the case. It's been that way from Day One. I can't tell you how many parallels I've noticed between their lives and the events and words of these letters."

Francie, who had felt, as Phillip, that this couple had been divinely selected for The Rhododendron now conceived that The Rhododendron had been divinely selected for this couple. It was hard for her not to burst into tears as she read the words of one man coming to his sweetheart and another in danger of leaving his.

"Mrs. Mason?" The voice of the volunteer receptionist unexpectantly startled both women. "Your husband is awake and you may see him now if you'd like."

Phillip walked up just in time to hear the announcement. "Here, take a couple of bites before you go back there."

Lydia nearly swallowed the breakfast croissant whole as she washed it down with the coffee, not even bothering to add her usual ratio of cream.

"You may all move to the other waiting area now that Mr. Ward is out of the intensive unit. It will be closer for you and there are designated visiting hours for the patient."

Lydia looked like a new person when she came back to the waiting area.

"I'd say from the glow on your face that Ward is much better than when you checked in on him last night."

She nodded. "I know how he felt that day in Charlotte with his brother now. If you're still here when the next visitation period starts, he'd like to see you if you don't mind."

"We don't mind at all." Phillip was actually glad for the invitation. Francie and he had never met Ward and he wanted to see the man who had so many shared qualities of his grandfather. "But until then, you need some lunch, young lady. It's not every day that I get the pleasure of two women for lunch."

Lydia smiled. The lines of stress that had been evident the night before and during the morning had faded and her color was back to its normal state.

As they were walking toward the hospital's cafeteria, Phillip heard his name being called from down the hall. He turned to see Dr. Thomas George, the Charlotte District Superintendent of The United Methodist Church. "Dr. George, I'm not used to seeing you in this neck of the woods. At least not anymore. What brings you to Boone?"

"A former parishioner who was very close to us during my ministry here. Her family called to tell me of her condition yesterday afternoon and I felt the urge to visit her."

"Lydia, allow me to introduce one of our superior officers. This is Dr. Thomas George. He was the minister here at Boone United Methodist Church when my grandparents were still alive. In fact, he did Grandfather's memorial service. His position is now much like that of the Presiding Elder, Uncle William, of Grandfather's letters. He serves over the Charlotte District."

"Dr. George, this is Lydia Mason. She and her husband, Ward, moved here last year. They bought Grandfather's old house, they are members at Boone Methodist, and Ward is a professor of education at ASU."

"How well I remember The Rhododendron!" Dr. George exclaimed. "I've had numerous visits there. Dr. and Mrs. Edgerton were an extraordinary couple. I've never met another quite like them."

"We were just going to get some lunch," stated Phillip. "Can you join us? I think Lydia would love hearing some of your stories. Her husband had a quadruple bypass last night following a heart attack and we want to get back before the next period of visitation."

"I'm so sorry," Dr. George extended to Lydia. "I hope things are going well for him."

She nodded. "Yes, thank you. Much better than last night."

Dr. George looked at his watch. "I've got to catch a bite somewhere before returning to Charlotte. Sure, if I wouldn't be imposing, I'd love to have lunch with all of you."

The group was soon seated around a table in the cafeteria with Phillip and Dr. George rattling off remembrances of the elder Edgerton's one after another. Their conversation, mixed with

Lydia's stories of the letters, wound up taking the foursome back to the waiting area."

"Grandfather was famous for singing the *Doxology* or *Blest Be the Tie that Binds* at the table," Phillip recounted. "He always had us to sing the blessing. But my favorite time of doing that was one Christmas when Grandfather stood at his place at the head of the table, silver carving knife and fork in hand, ready to carve the turkey when he calmly," he looked around at Lydia to explain, "everything he ever did was done calmly," and then turned back to face the entire group. "He calmly said, 'Let us stand and sing the third stanza of *O Little Town of Bethlehem.'* We all sat speechless for a second, then my brother turned to me and asked, 'He is kidding, right?'

"But Grandfather wasn't kidding. He began to belt out all the words as if they were as familiar as *Old McDonald Had a Farm.* No one dared laugh, but the minute we got outside, it was hard to keep from rolling on the ground.

"Boy, was that *the* Christmas. There are a ton of stories from that year. So many that we'll have to wait until another time," he directed at Lydia. "Besides, I don't want to spoil your surprise with all the other letters."

Phillip turned back to Dr. George. "We wanted to sing *Blest Be the Tie* at Grandfather's service, remember? But we weren't sure how Grandmother would take it."

"I do remember it," Dr. George admitted.

"But we did sing it at her service," Phillip shared.

"I remember how, in that typical eastern North Carolina ladylike drawl, she'd yell out, 'Honey.' Then she'd wait a couple of seconds and if Dr. Edgerton didn't answer, she'd try it again, the second time much louder."

"Ah, yes!" seconded Phillip.

"Do you know what my very favorite story of them is?" Dr. George asked. "I'm sure you've heard me tell it before. I told it at his service." He suddenly paused and looked at Lydia, hoping the sharing of it wouldn't be too much for her with the present situation with her husband. Deciding she looked incredibly strong spirited, he continued.

"It was one day when I went to The Rhododendron to visit. Dr. Edgerton had been in the hospital and we weren't sure he'd make it home. Then when he did get home, Mrs. Edgerton wound up here with something even worse. We were sure we'd never see her again. However, God had another plan.

"I had been to the house already a couple of times that month due to their health issues, and as always, had left feeling the outpouring of their love. Not only for me as a minister, but that devoted commitment they had for each other. In all my years in the ministry, I've never witnessed anything like the love they shared."

He glanced at Lydia. "Those must have been some awfully powerful letters."

She beamed. "They were . . . and still are." Her eyes twinkled as she looked at Phillip.

"On that particular day," continued Dr. George, "Dr. Edgerton went to the kitchen to get something for her. While he was out of the room, Mrs. Edgerton looked at me with that huge mischievous grin she'd get, and revealed that they had spent the entire afternoon recalling all the experiences they had shared, even back to those first Congo days, and how wonderful they had all been." He took a deep breath and shook his head. It was apparent to all three listeners that the story still held great meaning for him.

"When he returned to the bedroom and took his seat right beside her at the bed - now keep in mind that he's just come home from the hospital himself and wasn't doing well - I asked, 'Dr. Edgerton, when was the best time, the very best time?'

"He looked at me with those deeply sincere, but gentle, eyes and without so much as a pause answered, 'Right now. It's always this minute. Right now.'"

Lydia, as well as Phillip and Francie, heard the catch in his voice as he uttered those last couple of phrases.

Dr. George lowered his head for just a second and then proceeded. "Most people would have been complaining about all they had been through for the past month, but not them. They had a love for each other that surpassed anything I've ever seen. It wasn't just love or devotion. It was a covenant in the truest sense of the word."

Lydia not only heard, but felt every word of what Dr. George had just described for it was exactly what had gone on between she and Ward from the day they had moved into The Rhododendron.

"Dr. George, would it be too much of a bother for you to share that same story with Ward? I know that as a minister you're allowed to visit him and I think it would be most healing for him to hear that account. You see, since we've moved into that house, our marriage, which was always good, has undergone the most amazing transformation. We've had several conversations there, much like the one you just described. I really want him to hear you tell it."

Dr. George gave Lydia a most congenial smile. "It would be my pleasure."

"If you're ever in the area, please come and visit us," Lydia invited.

"Thank you," replied Dr. George. "I'd love to. That old house holds many wonderful memories for me. I'm glad it is doing the same for you." He shook hands with Lydia to say good-bye. "I'll be praying for Ward and his continued improvement," he offered as he exited the waiting room. "See you back in Charlotte," he called to Phillip and Francie.

He barely got out the door before the surgeon came to the door and called for "Mrs. Mason."

"We are having a bit of a problem with Mr. Mason," explained the doctor. "His blood pressure has dropped significantly and there are a few other signs that all point to a bleed. I'm afraid that we're going to have to take him back in for surgery."

Lydia's heart sank.

"This is not altogether uncommon," he assured her, but Lydia read the lines around his eyes. He'd seen this before and she could gather that Ward's chances weren't good.

"May I see him?"

"Yes, you may, but he will be taken to surgery very soon. Please not for long."

"I understand." This time it was she who felt she had been in his shoes.

Phillip grabbed her arm. "Do you need us?"

She heaved a huge sigh and shook her head. "No," she smiled confidently. "I think this is one I've got to do on my own."

"Glenn was right, you know?" Ward managed to say. "Right now is the best time for it's when I'm with you."

Lydia reached down, careful not to hit any tubes, and kissed him. "Oh, Ward, it has been a lifetime of right now's."

"And it's going to be another lifetime of many more," he spit out with as much stamina as he could muster, which was relatively none.

Lydia refused to let him see the hurt ravaging inside her body.

"You are my sun and my moon and my stars," Ward said, his voice dying away into a whisper. "I love you, darling," he slowly stated as a man came and rolled him out of the room and back to surgery.

"I love you, too," Lydia called behind him, waiting for

him to disappear down the hall before she unhurriedly retraced her steps to the waiting area.

"Perhaps we'd better move back to the surgical suite's waiting area," suggested Francie.

Lydia nodded and began to walk in that direction. She did not catch the glance that Phillip shot to his wife as they followed her down the long hall.

She reached into her tote bag, took out the letters and began to read snipets of Glenn's writings to his life's partner, all of which spoke to her of the love wafting between the waiting room and the surgical suite. Not a word was spoken to either of the members of her newly claimed family.

Phillip found it odd that his grandfather, through letters that had been written seventy-five years prior, could minister to this woman in a way that he couldn't. *If they have this effect on this woman, how many more lives could they touch.* It was then that he decided that the letters should be used for the UMW programs that she had mentioned.

As she took the words and drew strength and God's peace from them, his mind was busy thinking of all the memorabilia that his grandparents had left behind for a legacy of teaching that she could use with the letters.

Lydia began to read aloud, softly but loud enough that Phillip and Francie could share in the words. "O, My Sweet Evening Star, I wonder where you are shining tonight and what you have done with all your spangles. Won't you tell me and won't you send me a few to make these days and nights pass more rapidly?

"It seems ages since the night I drove with you. But the

softness of your dear hand still lingers and reminds me that you were near, oh, so near, but yet how far away now. Would that I could be with you tonight! Outside the trees are all swaying in the softness of the new moon's beams to the rhythm of the sighing zephyrs as they gently caress them. It would all be so much more beautiful if you were here. Perhaps some day . . ."

She made no comment, but picked up the next letter and again read. "My darling Sweetheart, You have been in my thoughts and in my heart constantly all day. I have gone about on the pinions of song wafted gently by your love. As I rode along this morning and enjoyed the glories of the early morning I could not keep the joy of my heart from expressing itself. Dearest, it's heavenly to love you but it is divine to be loved by you. Last night as I left you I could still feel you near me. I still held you in my arms and your kisses still burned in love on my lips. You were with me as you are always near me no matter where I am. In the darkness and in the light you are always near, very near, very close to me. I want you to be always and forever."

Francie wondered if the similarity of the letters to Lydia's current situation were not too painful, but she watched quietly as the woman read another.

"Dearest Darling Sweetheart, I miss you more and more as each moment wings its flight in gleeful ecstasy to join its fellows in the revelry of the beyond. I long for you and my heart cries out for you and pleads with me to hasten the time when it may beat again pillowed against you. Oh Darling! How I want to be with you just now!

"But in the midst of all my longing I find joy in knowing

that you love me. Your kisses still burn on my lips and I know that you miss me too. I know that you are mine and mine alone and no matter where I am or may go I still hear those soft words from your sweet lips, "Darling, you know I love you." I know that you are thinking of me now as I am of you and somewhere "out where the blue begins" our souls are communing with each other in blissful harmony."

"Mrs. Mason?"

It was at that moment that both Phillip and Francie realized that the letters had merely been there to cushion the blow.

Lydia looked up to see a woman calling her name. "The doctor will be out in a minute to speak to you. Why don't you go to Room 5 of the family rooms? Do you know where they are?"

"Yes, he took me there earlier."

Phillip took her elbow and stood with her. Francie stood close behind.

When the doctor entered the room, Lydia calmly stood and took his hand. "Thank you, Doctor. I know you did all you could do. Thank you for keeping Ward as relaxed and peaceful as you could."

He looked extremely puzzled.

"Do you remember the letters and how you said that love has no barriers of time and space? You were right. I knew exactly what was going on through the letters." She held the last one out for him to see.

As his eyes read, Phillip and Francie both fought with all their might to hold their composure.

"Mrs. Mason, you are indeed a blessed child of God. In all

my years of practice, I have never seen anything exactly like this. You and your husband must have had one wonderful marriage full of love."

She smiled gently, the tears beginning to appear in her eyes. "Yes, we did. And a home full of love, too."

The doctor closed the door behind him as Lydia fell into Phillip's arms.

36

"Thank you for volunteering to housesit for me for a few days," Lydia struggled to smile. "I think you were right that I need a few days away by myself."

"We understand and we're glad to do it," Phillip said, giving her a hug.

"Yeah," added David. "You've left me plenty of Moravian cookies and I'm going on a hunting expedition to see what other cool things I can find in the desk besides the teeth."

"David!" shouted Phillip and Francie at the same time.

"We're sorry," apologized Francie, embarrassment written all over her face.

"Not to worry," laughed Lydia. "I needed a good chuckle." She moved over to David and gave him a big hug. "You help yourself," she invited. "But beware, there is a beating of a drum here that will take you to mystic and foreign places if you're not careful," she winked smugly.

"Isn't it odd how you heard the beating of that drum from

the first day you moved here?" Phillip pondered aloud.

"I think that drum was something much deeper than the call of those letters," she admitted. "I think it was a signal that drew me to what it was that would make the union between Ward and me stronger. Now after what has happened, I keenly recall laying my head on his chest one afternoon while he sat in Glenn's old chair and I heard its irregular beat. I didn't think anything of it at the time. I guess I just figured that as we age, our bodies behave differently. It didn't keep the same steady pulse as the drum I'd been hearing, but it somehow didn't register."

A distraught expression spread over Lydia's face. "Perhaps if I'd been more attentive. Perhaps that was a signal for me to have him go to the doctor."

"Lydia, dear, you can't blame yourself for any of this," consoled Francie.

"Besides, you said that he had a complete physical upon his arrival here for the insurance and everything was fine."

Lydia nodded. "Yes, but I've wondered so many times since then if it really was and he just didn't tell me."

"Ward and you became very close these past few months," Phillip observed. "I believe he'd have told you if he felt the slightest thing were wrong with him."

"I really do believe you're right. We shared everything, especially these past few months. " A look of realization came into her eyes. "God knew when we moved here, didn't He?" Lydia looked at Phillip and then Francie for an answer.

"Lydia," Phillip said, his voice full of solace, "I believe that God did know. I also believe that's why you heard the beat of the drum." He glanced at his wife, who showed her support. "Francie and I have had this conversation several times. We both believe that you were meant to have this house, and more than that, that you were to find the letters. They were of a pure and true love, one that you already possessed, but that perhaps had not been expressed. Through those letters and these past few months, the love that you and Ward shared since the day of that frog dissection came to know perfection. It was a perfect love that only comes when Christ is at the center of it."

Tears streaked Lydia's face as she nodded. Phillip and Francie moved to hug her, with David moving in between them to show that he, too, was a part of her "new" family.

"Do you know what he said to me at the end?" she asked. "I've wanted to tell you this, but I couldn't bring myself to say it. Now I not only feel that I have the courage, but I feel that I must." Lydia wiped her eyes. "Ward said, 'Glenn was right when he said that every day's the best day, wasn't he?'"

She swallowed hard. "Even when we both knew that it was over, he looked up at me and whispered, 'And today's the best day.'"

Lydia dropped her head against Phillip's shoulder and let the tears that she'd been hiding have a blessed release.

The four of them stood quietly for the next few minutes as the woman who'd both gained and lost everything in this house, it seemed for the moment, felt the full support of friends she'd met, also as a result of the house and the letters. After a few minutes, the wave of emotion began to clear from the air as she held her head up. A new sense of strength seemed to have taken control of her.

She sat in 'Gene's chair. "Phillip, tell me about them. Tell me about the wedding of Glenn and 'Gene."

He smiled graciously and sat on the same sofa where he'd once eaten his own grandmother's Moravian cookies. "They were married on September 9th of 1930. The wedding was at Stantonsburg Methodist Church, the first wedding that was held in that sanctuary. It was where 'Gene was living at the time with her aunt.

"It was a very formal wedding. In fact, Grandmother's dress was designed by a New York designer and just the silk to make the dress cost over four hundred dollars. I still have both the dress and the bill."

Lydia gasped. "And in the heart of the depression."

"Yes. Luckily the two families owned all their homes and land so they were not hit as hard as the people who had all their belongings tied up in stocks and investments. They were married fifty-six years when Grandfather died, which happened two weeks after the story Dr. George shared with you."

"You know, when he retold that story in Ward's room, I knew that our meeting at the hospital played a part in all of this. I knew he was to tell that story at Ward's memorial service and that Ward would be laid to rest in Boone's Mountlawn Cemetery near the mausoleum where your grandparents are." She sighed. "I think Ward knew it, too."

Suddenly, both her eyes and ears perked. "Listen," she whispered. "It's there . . . the beating of the drum. I hadn't noticed it for the past . . . ," Lydia swallowed hard one last time. "It was here all the time, wasn't it? I simply became so addled that I didn't hear it."

No one commented, but allowed her emotions to again come in contact and find rhythm with her mental and physical being.

"Every time I hear the beat of the drum, I will hear the beat of Ward's heart — and it will be always and ever here with me," Lydia said, tapping lightly over her heart. "Here, inside me."

This time it was Francie who swallowed hard. "That is the most beautiful thing I've ever heard. What a rewarding way to think of your relationship with Ward."

Lydia smiled. "If you think that's beautiful, you should read some of the letters from Glenn to 'Gene. They are what's beautiful." Again composed, she walked over to the coffee table and picked up a small paper bag as she headed toward the door.

"Did you get yourself a present?" David asked.

"Yes," she smiled half-heartedly. "Yes, I did." She looked down at the paper bag in her hand. "I bought myself a present the week we moved here. It's a book, a historical romance that I picked up down at Skyland Books in Blowing Rock." The smile turned into a full-size grin. "I picked it up the morning that I sawed into the lock on the desk. Once I began reading those letters that day after lunch, I realized that Glenn and 'Gene had written their own story."

Lydia gave David a wink. "Your story." She looked at Phillip. "Your father's story and your grandfather's story.." Her gaze fell back on the boy. "And my story. It's a story of love that never changes, David. Not any place in the world. For it's also a love story of Jesus. That belief is what allowed your great-grandfather to accept his call as a missionary. It is what allowed him to patiently wait for his beloved to become his bride and work with him. It is what allowed him to so greatly influence a wonderful family."

She looked at the three faces in front of her. "And it's what allowed him to spread the Gospel everywhere he went every day of his life."

Lydia handed the bag to Francie. "Here, you might enjoy this. It has somehow lost its appeal. I don't think there could be a better story than the one Grandfather Edgerton told."

The three Edgerton's followed her to the front door, where she turned around and looked long and hard at each of them before gazing squarely into Phillip's eyes.

The words came out in a lyrical and rhythmical manner as she faintly whispered, "'Tis so sweet to trust in Jesus."

'Tis So Sweet to Trust in Jesus

'Tis so sweet to trust in Jesus, And to take him at his word;
Just to rest upon his promise, And to know, "Thus saith the Lord."
Jesus, Jesus, how I trust him! How I've proved him o'er and o'er!
Jesus, Jesus, precious Jesus! O for grace to trust him more!

O how sweet to trust in Jesus, Just to trust his cleansing blood;
And in simple faith to plunge me neath the healing, cleansing flood!
Jesus, Jesus, how I trust him! How I've proved him o'er and o'er!
Jesus, Jesus, precious Jesus! O for grace to trust him more!

Yes, 'tis sweet to trust in Jesus, Just from sin and self to cease;
Just from Jesus simply taking life and rest, and joy and peace.
Jesus, Jesus, how I trust him! How I've proved him o'er and o'er!
Jesus, Jesus, precious Jesus! O for grace to trust him more!

I'm so glad I learned to trust thee, Precious Jesus, Savior, friend;
And I know that thou art with me, Wilt be with me to the end.
Jesus, Jesus, how I trust him! How I've proved him o'er and o'er!
Jesus, Jesus, precious Jesus! O for grace to trust him more!

- Louisa M.R. Stead -